D0175575

Also by James Alan McPherson
Published by Fawcett Books:

HUE AND CRY

ELBOW ROOM

Stories by

James Alan McPherson

C.2

FAWCETT CREST • NEW YORK

A Fawcett Crest Book
Published by Ballantine Books
Copyright © 1972, 1973, 1974, 1975 by James Alan
McPherson

ISBN 0-449-21357-9

This edition published by arrangement with Little, Brown
and Company in association with The Atlantic Monthly
Press.

"The Silver Bullet" originally appeared in *Playboy;*
"Problems of Art" in *The Iowa Review;* "Why I Like Country
Music" in *The Harvard Advocate;* "The Faithful" and "The
Story of a Scar" in *The Atlantic Monthly;* "A Sense of Story"
in the *Massachusetts Review;* "I Am an American" in
Ploughshares.

Printed in Canada

First Fawcett Crest Edition: September 1979
First Ballantine Books Edition: December 1983
Eighth Printing: July 1993

Cover Art: George Tooker
          Window I, 1955
          Walker Art Center,
          Minneapolis
          Gift of the T. B.
          Walker Foundation, 1955

To the memory of my father,
James A. McPherson, Sr.
And to my wife, Sarah, and the residents
of both our houses

I don't know which way I'm travelin'—
  Far or near,
All I knows fo' certain is
  I *cain't* stay *here*.

  —*"Long Gone"*
    STERLING A. BROWN

Contents

Why I Like
Country Music

No one will believe that I like country music. Even my wife scoffs when told such a possibility exists. "Go on!" Gloria tells me. "I can see blues, bebop, maybe even a little buckdancing. But not bluegrass." Gloria says, "Hillbilly stuff is not just music. It's like the New York Stock Exchange. The minute you see a sharp rise in it, you better watch out."

I tend to argue the point, but quietly, and mostly to myself. Gloria was born and raised in New York; she has come to believe in the stock exchange as the only index of economic health. My perceptions were shaped in South Carolina; and long ago I learned there, as a waiter in private clubs, to gauge economic flux by the tips people gave. We tend to disagree on other matters too, but the thing that gives me most frustration is trying to make her understand why I like country music. Perhaps it is because she hates the South and has capitulated emotionally to the horror stories told by refugees from down home. Perhaps it is because Gloria is third generation Northern-born. I do not know. What I do know is that, while the two of us are black, the distance between us is sometimes as great as that between Ibo and Yoruba. And I do know that, despite her protestations, I like country music.

"You are crazy," Gloria tells me.

I tend to argue the point, but quietly, and mostly to myself.

Of course I do not like all country stuff; just pieces that make the right connections. I like banjo because sometimes I hear ancestors in the strumming. I like the fiddle-like refrain in "Dixie" for the very same reason. But most of all I like square dancing—the interplay between fiddle and caller, the stomping, the swishing of dresses, the strutting, the proud turnings, the laughter. Most of all I like the laughter. In recent months I have wondered why I like this music and this dance. I have drawn no general conclusions, but from time to time I suspect it is because the square dance is the only dance form I ever mastered.

"I wouldn't say that in public," Gloria warns me.

I agree with her, but still affirm the truth of it, although quietly, and mostly to myself.

Dear Gloria: This is the truth of how it was:

In my youth in that distant country, while others learned to strut, I grew stiff as a winter cornstalk. When my playmates harmonized their rhythms, I stood on the sidelines in atonic detachment. While they shimmied, I merely jerked in lackluster imitation. I relate these facts here, not in remorse or self-castigation, but as a true confession of my circumstances. In those days, down in our small corner of South Carolina, proficiency in dance was a form of storytelling. A boy could say, "I traveled here and there, saw this and fought that, conquered him and made love to her, lied to them, told a few others the truth, just so I could come back here and let you know what things out there are really like." He could communicate all this with smooth, graceful jiggles of his round bottom, synchronized with intricately coordinated sweeps of his arms and small, unexcited movements of his legs. Little girls could communicate much more.

But sadly, I could do none of it. Development of these skills depended on the ministrations of family and neighbors. My family did not dance; our closest neighbor was a true-believing Seventh Day Adventist. Moreover, most new dances came from up North, brought to town usually by people returning to riff on the good life said to exist in those far Northern places. They prowled our dirt streets in rented Cadillacs; paraded our brick sidewalks exhibiting styles abstracted from the fullness of life in Harlem, South Philadelphia, Roxbury, Baltimore and the South Side of Chicago. They confronted our provincial clothes merchants with the arrogant reminder, "But people ain't wearin' this in New Yo*kkk!*" Each of their movements, as well as their world-weary smoothness, told us locals meaningful tales of what was missing in our lives. Unfortunately, those of us under strict parental supervision, or those of us without Northern connections, could only stand at a distance and worship these envoys of culture. We stood on the sidelines—styleless, gestureless, danceless, doing nothing more than an improvised one-butt shuffle—hoping for one of them to touch our lives. It was my good fortune, during my tenth year on the sidelines, to have one of these Northerners introduce me to the square dance.

My dear, dear Gloria, her name was Gweneth Lawson:

She was a pretty, chocolate-brown little girl with dark brown eyes and two long black braids. After all these

years, the image of these two braids evokes in me all
there is to remember about Gweneth Lawson. They were
plaited across the top of her head and hung to a point just
above the back of her Peter Pan collar. Sometimes she
wore two bows, one red and one blue, and these tended to
sway lazily near the place on her neck where the smooth
brown of her skin and the white of her collar met the
ink-bottle black of her hair. Even when I cannot remember her face, I remember the rainbow of deep, rich colors
in which she lived. This is so because I watched them, every weekday, from my desk directly behind hers in our
fourth-grade class. And she wore the most magical perfume, or lotion, smelling just slightly of fresh-cut lemons,
that wafted back to me whenever she made the slightest
movement at her desk. Now I must tell you this much
more, dear Gloria: whenever I smell fresh lemons,
whether in the market or at home, I look around me—not
for Gweneth Lawson, but for some quiet corner where I
can revive in private certain memories of her. And in pursuing these memories across such lemony bridges, I redis-
cover that I loved her.

Gweneth was from the South Carolina section of
Brooklyn. Her parents had sent her south to live with her
uncle, Mr. Richard Lawson, the brick mason, for an un-
specified period of time. Just why they did this I do not
know, unless it was their plan to have her absorb more of
South Carolina folkways than conditions in Brooklyn
would allow. She was a gentle, soft-spoken girl; I recall
no condescension in her manner. This was all the more
admirable because our unrestrained awe of a Northern-
born black person usually induced in him some grand
sense of his own importance. You must know that in
those days older folks would point to someone and say,

"He's from the North," and the statement would be sufficient in itself. Mothers made their children behave by advising that, if they led exemplary lives and attended church
regularly, when they died they would go to New York.
Only someone who understands what London meant to
Dick Whittington, or how California and the suburbs function in the national mind, could appreciate the mythical
dimensions of this Northlore.

But Gweneth Lawson was above regional idealization.
Though I might have loved her partly because she was a
Northerner, I loved her more because of the world of
colors that seemed to be suspended above her head. I
loved her glowing forehead and I loved her bright, dark
brown eyes; I loved the black braids, the red and blue and
sometimes yellow and pink ribbons; I loved the way the
deep, rich brown of her neck melted into the pink or white
cloth of her Peter Pan collar; I loved the lemony vapor on
which she floated and from which, on occasion, she
seemed to be inviting me to be buoyed up, up, up into her
happy world; I loved the way she caused my heart to tum-
ble whenever, during a restless moment, she seemed about
to turn her head in my direction; I loved her more, though
torturously, on the many occasions when she did not turn.
Because I was a shy boy, I loved the way I could love her
silently, at least six hours a day, without ever having to
disclose my love.

My platonic state of mind might have stretched onward
into a blissful infinity had not Mrs. Esther Clay Boswell,
our teacher, made it her business to pry into the affair.
Although she prided herself on being a strict disci-
plinarian, Mrs. Boswell was not without a sense of humor.
A round, full-breasted woman in her early forties, she
liked to amuse herself, and sometimes the class as well,

by calling the attention of all eyes to whomever of us violated the structure she imposed on classroom activities.
She was particularly hard on people like me who could
not contain an impulse to daydream, or those who allowed
their eyes to wander too far away from lessons printed
on the blackboard. A black and white sign posted under the electric clock next to the door summed up her
attitude toward this kind of truancy: NOTICE TO ALL CLOCK-
WATCHERS, it read, TIME PASSES, WILL YOU? Nor did
she abide timidity in her students. Her voice booming,
"Speak up, boy!" was more than enough to cause the
more emotional among us, including me, to break into
convenient flows of warm tears. But by doing this we
violated yet another rule, one on which depended our
very survival in Mrs. Esther Clay Boswell's class. She
would spell out this rule for us as she paced before her
desk, slapping a thick, homemade ruler against the flat
of her brown palm. "There ain't no *babies* in here,"
she would recite. *Thaap!* "Anybody thinks he's still a
baby..." *Thaap!* "...should crawl back home to his
mama's *titty*." *Thaap!* "You little bunnies shed your *last
water*..." *Thaap!* "...the minute you left home to come
in here." *Thaap!* "From now on, you g'on do all your
cryin'..." *Thaap!* "...in *church!*" *Thaap!* Whenever one
of us compelled her to make this speech it would seem
to me that her eyes paused overlong on my face. She
would seem to be daring me, as if suspicious that, in addition to my secret passion for Gweneth Lawson, which she
might excuse, I was also in the habit of throwing fits of
temper.

She had read me right. I was the product of too much
attention from my father. He favored me, paraded me
around on his shoulder, inflated my ego constantly with

what, among us at least, was a high compliment: "You my nigger if you don't get no bigger." This statement, along with my father's generous attentions, made me selfish and used to having my own way. I *expected* to have my own way in most things, and when I could not, I tended to throw tantrums calculated to break through any barrier raised against me.

Mrs. Boswell was also perceptive in assessing the extent of my infatuation with Gweneth Lawson. Despite my stealth in telegraphing emissions of affection into the back part of Gweneth's brain, I could not help but observe, occasionally, Mrs. Boswell's cool glance pausing on the two of us. But she never said a word. Instead, she would settle her eyes momentarily on Gweneth's face and then pass quickly to mine. But in that instant she seemed to be saying, "Don't look back now, girl, but I *know* that bald-headed boy behind you has you on his mind." She seemed to watch me daily, with a combination of amusement and absolute detachment in her brown eyes. And when she stared, it was not at me but at the normal focus of my attention: the end of Gweneth Lawson's black braids. Whenever I sensed Mrs. Boswell watching I would look away quickly, either down at my brown desk top or across the room to the blackboard. But her eyes could not be eluded this easily. Without looking at anyone in particular, she could make a specific point to one person in a manner so general that only long afterward did the real object of her attention realize it had been intended for him.

"Now you little brown bunnies," she might say, "and you black buck rabbits and you few cottontails mixed in, some of you starting to smell yourselves under the arms

without knowing what it's all about." And here, it sometimes seemed to me, she allowed her eyes to pause casually on me before resuming their sweep of the entire
room. "Now I know your mamas already made you think
life is a bed of roses, but in *my* classroom you got to
know the footpaths through the *sticky* parts of the rose-
bed." It was her custom during this ritual to prod and
goad those of us who were developing reputations for
meekness and indecision; yet her method was Socratic
in that she compelled us, indirectly, to supply our own
answers by exploiting one person as the walking symbol
of the error she intended to correct. Clarence Buford,
for example, an oversized but good-natured boy from a
very poor family, served often as the helpmeet in this
exercise.

"Buford," she might begin, slapping the ruler against
her palm, "how does a tongue-tied country boy like you
expect to get a wife?"

"I don't want no wife," Buford might grumble softly.

Of course the class would laugh.

"Oh yes you do," Mrs. Boswell would respond. "All
you buck rabbits want wives." *Thaap!* "So how do you let
a girl know you're not just a bump on a log?"

"I know! I know!" a high voice might call from a seat
across from mine. This, of course, would be Leon Pugh.
A peanut-brown boy with curly hair, he seemed to know
everything. Moreover, he seemed to take pride in being
the only one who knew answers to life questions and
would wave his arms excitedly whenever our attentions
were focused on such matters. It seemed to me his voice
would be extra loud and his arms waved more strenuously
whenever he was certain that Gweneth Lawson, seated
across from him, was interested in an answer to Mrs. Es-

ther Clay Boswell's question. His eager arms, it seemed to me, would be reaching out to grasp Gweneth instead of the question asked.

"Buford, you twisted-tongue, bunion-toed country boy," Mrs. Boswell might say, ignoring Leon Pugh's hysterical arm waving, "you gonna let a cottontail like Leon get a girlfriend before you?"

"I don't want no girlfriend," Clarence Buford would almost sob. "I don't like no girls."

The class would laugh again while Leon Pugh manipulated his arms like a flight navigator under battle conditions. "I know! I know! I swear to *God* I know!"

When at last Mrs. Boswell would turn in his direction, I might sense that she was tempted momentarily to ask me for an answer. But as in most such exercises, it was the worldly-wise Leon Pugh who supplied this. "What do *you* think, Leon?" she would ask inevitably, but with a rather lifeless slap of the ruler against her palm.

"My daddy told me..." Leon would shout, turning slyly to beam at Gweneth, "...my daddy and my big brother from the Bronx New York told me that to git *anythin'* in this world you gotta learn how to blow your own horn."

"Why, Leon?" Mrs. Boswell might ask in a bored voice.

"Because," the little boy would recite, puffing out his chest, "because if you don't blow your own horn ain't nobody else g'on blow it for you. That's what my daddy said."

"What do you think about that, Buford?" Mrs. Boswell would ask.

"I don't want no girlfriend anyhow," the puzzled Clarence Buford might say.

And then the cryptic lesson would suddenly be dropped.

This was Mrs. Esther Clay Boswell's method of teaching. More than anything written on the blackboard, her questions were calculated to make us turn around in our chairs and inquire in guarded whispers of each other, and especially of the wise and confident Leon Pugh, "What does she mean?" But none of us, besides Pugh, seemed able to comprehend what it was we ought to know but did not know. And Mrs. Boswell, plump brown fox that she was, never volunteered any more in the way of confirmation than was necessary to keep us interested. Instead, she paraded around us, methodically slapping the homemade ruler against her palm, suggesting by her silence more depth to her question, indeed, more implications in Leon's answer, than we were then able to perceive. And during such moments, whether inspired by selfishness or by the peculiar way Mrs. Boswell looked at me, I felt that finding answers to such questions was a task she had set for me, of all the members of the class.

Of course Leon Pugh, among other lesser lights, was my chief rival for the affections of Gweneth Lawson. All during the school year, from September through the winter rains, he bested me in my attempts to look directly into her eyes and say a simple, heartfelt "hey." This was my ambition, but I never seemed able to get close enough to get her attention. At Thanksgiving I helped draw a bounteous yellow cornucopia on the blackboard, with fruits and flowers matching the colors that floated around Gweneth's head; Leon Pugh made one by himself, a masterwork of silver paper and multicolored crepe, which he hung on the door. Its silver tail curled upward to a point just below the face of Mrs. Boswell's clock. At Christmas, when we

drew names out of a hat for the exchange of gifts, I drew
the name of Queen Rose Phipps, a fairly unattractive
squash-yellow girl of absolutely no interest to me. Pugh,
whether through collusion with the boy who handled the
lottery or through pure luck, pulled forth from the hat the
magic name of Gweneth Lawson. He gave her a set of
deep purple bows for her braids and a basket of pecans
from his father's tree. Uninterested now in the spirit of
the occasion, I delivered to Queen Rose Phipps a pair of
white socks. Each time Gweneth wore the purple bows
she would glance over at Leon and smile. Each time
Queen Rose wore my white socks I would turn away in
embarrassment, lest I should see them pulling down into
her shoes and exposing her skinny ankles.

After class, on wet winter days, I would trail along behind Gweneth to the bus stop, pause near the steps while
she entered, and follow her down the aisle until she chose
a seat. Usually, however, in clear violation of the code of
conduct to which all gentlemen were expected to adhere,
Leon Pugh would already be on the bus and shouting to
passersby, "Move off! Get away! This here seat by me is
reserved for the girl from Brooklyn New York." Discour-
aged but not defeated, I would swing into the seat next
nearest her and cast calf-eyed glances of wounded affection at the back of her head or at the brown, rainbow
profile of her face. And at her stop, some eight or nine
blocks from mine, I would disembark behind her along
with a crowd of other love-struck boys. There would then
follow a well-rehearsed scene in which all of us, save
Leon Pugh, pretended to have gotten off the bus either
too late or too soon to wend our proper paths homeward.
And at slight cost to ourselves we enjoyed the advantage
of being able to walk close by her as she glided toward

her uncle's green-frame house. There, after pausing on the wooden steps and smiling radiantly around the crowd like a spring sun in that cold winter rain, she would sing, "Bye, y'all," and disappear into the structure with the mystery of a goddess. Afterward I would walk away, but slowly, much slower than the other boys, warmed by the music and light in her voice against the sharp, wet winds of the February afternoon.

I loved her, dear Gloria, and I danced with her and smelled the lemony youth of her and told her that I loved her, all this in a way you would never believe:

You would not know or remember, as I do, that in those days, in our area of the country, we enjoyed a pleasingly ironic mixture of Yankee and Confederate folkways. Our meals and manners, our speech, our attitudes toward certain ambiguous areas of history, even our acceptance of tragedy as the normal course of life—these things and more defined us as Southern. Yet the stern morality of our parents, their toughness and penny-pinching and attitudes toward work, their covert allegiance toward certain ideals, even the directions toward which they turned our faces, made us more Yankee than Cavalier. Moreover, some of our schools were named for Confederate men of distinction, but others were named for the stern-faced believers who had swept down from the North to save a people back, back long ago, in those long-forgotten days of once upon a time. Still, our schoolbooks, our required classroom songs, our flags, our very relation to the statues and monuments in public parks, negated the story that these dreamers from the North had ever come. We sang the state song, memorized the verses of homegrown poets, honored in our books the names and dates of historical events both before and after that Historical Event which, in our region, supplanted even the division of the millennia introduced by the followers of Jesus Christ. Given the silent circumstances of our cultural environment, it was ironic, and perhaps just, that we maintained a synthesis of two traditions no longer supportive of each other. Thus it became traditional at our school to celebrate the arrival of spring on May first by both the ritual plaiting of the Maypole and square dancing.

On that day, as on a few others, the Superintendent of Schools and several officials were likely to visit our schoolyard and stand next to the rusty metal swings, watching the fourth, fifth, and sixth graders bob up and down and behind and before each other, around the gaily painted Maypoles. These happy children would pull and twist long runs of billowy crepe paper into wondrous, multicolored plaits. Afterward, on the edges of thunderous applause from teachers, parents and visiting dignitaries, a wave of elaborately costumed children would rush out onto the grounds in groups of eight and proceed with the square dance. "Doggone!" the Superintendent of Schools was heard to exclaim on one occasion. "Y'all do it so good it just makes your *bones* set up and take notice."

Such was the schedule two weeks prior to May first, when Mrs. Boswell announced to our class that as fourth graders we were now eligible to participate in the festivities. The class was divided into two general sections of sixteen each, one group preparing to plait the pole and a second group, containing an equal number of boys and girls, practicing turns for our part in the square dance. I was chosen to square dance; so was Leon Pugh. Gweneth Lawson was placed with the pole plaiters. I was depressed until I remembered, happily, that I could not dance a lick.

I reported this fact to Mrs. Boswell just after drawing, during recess, saying that my lack of skill would only result in our class making a poor showing. I asked to be reassigned to the group of Maypole plaiters. Mrs. B. looked me over with considerable amusement tugging at the corners of her mouth. "Oh, you don't have to *dance* to do the square dance," she said. "That's a dance that was made up to mock folks that couldn't dance." She paused a second before adding thoughtfully: "The worse you are at dancing, the better you can square dance. It's just about the best dance in the world for a stiff little bunny like you."

"I want to plait the Maypole," I said.

"You'll square dance or I'll grease your little butt," Mrs. Esther Clay Boswell said.

"I ain't gonna do *nothin'!*" I muttered. But I said this quietly, and mostly to myself, while walking away from her desk. For the rest of the day she watched me closely, as if she knew what I was thinking.

The next morning I brought a note from my father. "Dear Mrs. Boswell:" I had watched him write earlier that morning, "My boy does not square dance. Please excuse him as I am afraid he will break down and cry and mess up the show. Yours truly . . ."

Mrs. Boswell said nothing after she had read the note. She merely waved me to my seat. But in the early afternoon, when she read aloud the lists of those assigned to dancing and Maypole plaiting, she paused as my name rolled off her tongue. "You don't have to stay on the square dance team," she called to me. "You go on out in the yard with the Maypole team."

I was ecstatic. I hurried to my place in line some three

warm bodies behind Gweneth Lawson. We prepared to march out.

"Wait a minute," Mrs. Boswell called. "Now it looks like we got seventeen bunnies on the Maypole team and fifteen on the square dance. We have to even things up." She made a thorough examination of both lists, scratching her head. Then she looked carefully up and down the line of stomping Maypoleites. "Miss Gweneth Lawson, you cute little cottontail you, it looks like you gonna have to go over to the square dance team. That'll give us eight sets of partners for the square dance . . . but now we have another problem." She made a great display of counting the members of the two squads of square dancers. "Now there's sixteen square dancers all right, but when we pair them off we got a problem of higher mathematics. With nine girls and only seven *boys*, looks like we gotta switch a girl from square dancing to Maypole and a boy from Maypole to square dancing."

I waited hopefully for Gweneth Lawson to volunteer. But just at that moment the clever Leon Pugh grabbed her hand and began jitterbugging as though he could hardly wait for the record player to be turned on and the dancing to begin.

"What a cute couple," Mrs. Boswell observed absently. "Now which one of you other girls wants to join up with the Maypole team?"

Following Pugh's example, the seven remaining boys grabbed the girls they wanted as partners. Only skinny Queen Rose Phipps and shy Beverly Hankins remained unclaimed. Queen Rose giggled nervously.

"Queen Rose," Mrs. B. called, "I know you don't mind plaiting the Maypole." She waved her ruler in a gesture of casual dismissal. Queen Rose raced across the room and squeezed into line.

"*Now*," Mrs. Boswell said, "I need a boy to come across to the square dancers."

I was not unmindful of the free interchange of partners involved in square dancing, even though Leon Pugh had beat me in claiming the partner of my choice. All I really wanted was one moment swinging Gweneth Lawson in my arms. I raised my hand slowly.

"Oh, not *you*, little bunny," Mrs. Boswell said. "You and your daddy claim you don't like to square dance." She slapped her ruler against her palm. *Thaap! Thaap!* Then she said, "Clarence Buford, I *know* a big-footed country boy like you can square dance better than anybody. Come on over here and kiss cute little Miss Beverly Hankins."

"I don't like no girls *noway*," Buford mumbled. But he went over and stood next to the giggling Beverly Hankins.

"Now!" said Mrs. B. "March on out in that yard and give that pole a good plaiting!"

We started to march out. Over my shoulder, as I reached the door, I glimpsed the overjoyed Leon Pugh whirling lightly on his toes. He sang in a confident tone:

> *"I saw the Lord give Moses a pocketful of roses.*
> *I skid Ezekiel's wheel on a ripe banana peel.*
> *I rowed the Nile, flew over a stile,*
> *Saw Jack Johnson pick his teeth*
> *With toenails from Jim Jeffries' feets . . ."*

"Grab your partners!" Mrs. Esther Clay Boswell was saying as the oak door slammed behind us.

I had been undone. For almost two weeks I was

obliged to stand on the sidelines and watch Leon Pugh allemande left and do-si-do my beloved Gweneth. Worse,
she seemed to be enjoying it. But I must give Leon proper
credit: he was a dancing fool. In a matter of days he had
mastered, and then improved on, the various turns and
bows and gestures of the square dance. He leaped while
the others plodded, whirled each girl through his arms
with lightness and finesse, chattered playfully at the other
boys when they tumbled over their own feet. Mrs. Boswell
stood by the record player calling, "Put some *strut* in it,
Buford, you big potato sack. Watch Leon and see how *he*
does it." I leaned against the classroom wall and watched
the dancers, my own group having already exhausted the
limited variations possible in matters of Maypole plaiting.

At home each night I begged my father to send another
note to Mrs. Boswell, this time stating that I had no interest in the Maypole. But he resisted my entreaties and
even threatened me with a whipping if I did not participate and make him proud of me. The real cause of his irritation was the considerable investment he had already
made in purchasing an outfit for me. Mrs. Boswell had required all her students, square dancers and Maypole
plaiters alike, to report on May first in outfits suitable for
square dancing. My father had bought a new pair of dungarees, a blue shirt, a red and white polka-dot bandanna
and a cowboy hat. He was in no mood to bend under the
emotional weight of my new demands. As a matter of
fact, early in the morning of May first he stood beside my
bed with the bandanna in his left hand and his leather
belt in his right hand, just in case I developed a sudden
fever.

I dragged myself heavily through the warm, blue spring
morning toward school, dressed like a carnival cowboy.

When I entered the classroom I sulked against the wall, being content to watch the other children. And what happy buzzings and jumping and excitement they made as they compared costumes. Clarence Buford wore a Tom Mix hat and a brown vest over a green shirt with red six-shooter patterns embossed on its collar. Another boy, Paul Carter, was dressed entirely in black, with a fluffy white handkerchief puffing from his neck. But Leon Pugh caught the attention of all our eyes. He wore a red and white checkered shirt, a loose green bandanna clasped at his throat by a shining silver buffalo head, brown chaps sewed onto his dungarees, and shiny brown cowboy boots with silver spurs that clanked each time he moved. In his hand he carried a carefully creased brown cowboy hat. He announced his fear that it would lose its shape and planned to put it on only when the dancing started. He would allow no one to touch it. Instead, he stood around clanking his feet and smoothing the crease in his fabulous hat and saying loudly, "My daddy says it pays to look good no matter what you put on."

The girls seemed prettier and much older than their ages. Even Queen Rose Phipps wore rouge on her cheeks that complemented her pale color. Shy Beverly Hankins had come dressed in a blue and white checkered bonnet and a crisp blue apron; she looked like a frontier mother. But Gweneth Lawson, my Gweneth Lawson, dominated the group of girls. She wore a long red dress with sheaves and sheaves of sparkling white crinoline belling it outward so it seemed she was floating. On her honey-brown wrists golden bracelets sparkled. A deep blue bandanna enclosed her head with the wonder of a summer sky. Black patent leather shoes glistened like half-hidden stars beneath the red and white of her hemline. She stood smiling before us and we marveled. At that moment I would have given the world to have been able to lead her about on my arm.

Mrs. Boswell watched us approvingly from behind her desk. Finally, at noon, she called, "Let's go on out!" Thirty-two living rainbows cascaded toward the door. Pole plaiters formed one line. Square dancers formed another. Mrs. Boswell strolled officiously past us in review. It seemed to me she almost paused while passing the spot where I stood on line. But she brushed past me, straightening an apron here, applying spittle and a rub to a rouged cheek there, waving a wary finger at an overanxious boy. Then she whacked her ruler against her palm and led us out into the yard. The fifth and sixth graders had already assembled. On one end of the playground were a dozen or so tall painted poles with long, thin wisps of green and blue and yellow and rust-brown crepe floating lazily on the sweet spring breezes.

"Maypole teams *up!*" called Mr. Henry Lucas, our principal, from his platform by the swings. Beside him stood the white Superintendent of Schools (who said later of the square dance, it was reported to all the classes, "Lord y'all square dance so *good* it makes me plumb *ashamed* us white folks ain't takin' better care of our art stuff."). "Maypole teams up!" Mr. Henry Lucas shouted again. Some fifty of us, screaming shrilly, rushed to grasp our favorite color crepe. Then, to the music of "Sing Praise for All the Brightness and the Joy of Spring," we pulled and plaited in teams of six or seven until every pole was twisted as tight and as colorfully as the braids on Gweneth Lawson's head. Then, to the applause of proud teachers and parents and the whistles of the Superintendent of Schools, we scattered happily back under the wings of our respective teachers. I stood next to Mrs.

Boswell, winded and trembling but confident I had done my best. She glanced down at me and said in a quiet voice, "I do believe you are learning the rhythm of the thing."

I did not respond.

"Let's *go!*" Leon Pugh shouted to the other kids, grabbing Gweneth Lawson's arm and taking a few clanking steps forward.

"Wait a minute, Leon," Mrs. Boswell hissed. "Mr. Lucas has to change the record."

Leon sighed. "But if we don't git out there first, all them other teams will take the best spots."

"Wait!" Mrs. Boswell ordered.

Leon sulked. He inched closer to Gweneth. I watched him swing her hand impatiently. He stamped his feet and his silver spurs jangled.

Mrs. Boswell looked down at his feet. "Why, Leon," she said, "you can't go out there with razors on your shoes."

"These ain't razors," Leon muttered. "These here are spurs my brother in Bronx New York sent me just for this here dance."

"You have to take them off," Mrs. Boswell said.

Leon growled. But he reached down quickly and attempted to jerk the silver spurs from the heels of his boots. They did not come off. "No time!" he called, standing suddenly. "Mr. Lucas done put the record on."

"Leon, you might *cut* somebody with those things," Mrs. Boswell said. "Miss Gweneth Lawson's pretty red dress could get caught in those things and then she'll fall as surely as I'm standin' here."

"I'll just go out with my boots off," Leon replied.

But Mrs. Boswell shook her head firmly. "You just run

on to the lunchroom and ask Cook for some butter or mayo. That'll help 'em slip off." She paused, looking out over the black dirt playground. "And if you miss the first dance, why, there'll be a second and maybe even a third. We'll get a Maypole plaiter to sub for you."

My heart leaped. Leon sensed it and stared at me. His hand tightened on Gweneth's as she stood radiant and smiling in the loving spring sunlight. Leon let her hand drop and bent quickly, pulling at the spurs with the fury of a Samson.

"Square dancers *up!*" Mr. Henry Lucas called.

"Sonofa*bitch!*" Leon grunted.

"Square dancers *up!*" called Mr. Lucas.

The fifth and sixth graders were screaming and rushing toward the center of the yard. Already the record was scratching out the high, slick voice of the caller. "*Sonofabitch!*" Leon moaned.

Mrs. Boswell looked directly at Gweneth, standing alone and abandoned next to Leon. "Miss Gweneth Lawson," Mrs. Boswell said in a cool voice, "it's a cryin' shame there ain't no prince to take you to that ball out there."

I do not remember moving, but I know I stood with Gweneth at the center of the yard. What I did there I do not know, but I remember watching the movements of others and doing what they did just after they had done it. Still, I cannot remember just when I looked into my partner's face or what I saw there. The scratchy voice of the caller bellowed directions and I obeyed:

> "*Allemande left with your left hand*
> *Right to your partner with a right and left grand . . .*"

Although I was told later that I made an allemande right instead of left, I have no memory of the mistake.

> *"When you get to your partner pass her by*
> *And pick up the next girl on the sly . . ."*

Nor can I remember picking up any other girl. I only remember that during many turns and do-si-dos I found myself looking into the warm brown eyes of Gweneth Lawson. I recall that she smiled at me. I recall that she laughed on another turn. I recall that I laughed with her an eternity later.

> *". . . promenade that dear old thing*
> *Throw your head right back and sing* be-*cause, just*
> *be-cause . . ."*

I do remember quite well that during the final promenade before the record ended, Gweneth stood beside me and I said to her in a voice much louder than that of the caller, "When I get up to Brooklyn I hope I see you." But I do not remember what she said in response. I want to remember that she smiled.

I know I smiled, dear Gloria. I smiled with the lemonness of her and the loving of her pressed deep into those saving places of my private self. It was my plan to savor these, and I did savor them. But when I reached New York, many years later, I did not think of Brooklyn. I followed the old, beaten, steady paths into uptown Manhattan. By then I had learned to dance to many other kinds of music. And I had forgotten the savory smell of lemon. But I think sometimes of Gweneth now when I hear country music. And although it is difficult to explain to you, I still maintain that I am no mere arithmetician in the art of the square dance. I am into the calculus of it.

"Go on!" you will tell me, backing into your Northern mythology. "I can see the hustle, the hump, maybe even the Ibo highlife. But no hillbilly."

These days I am firm about arguing the point, but, as always, quietly, and mostly to myself.

The Story
of a Dead Man

IT is not true that Billy Renfro was killed during that trouble in Houston. The man is an accomplished liar and likes to keep his enemies nervous. It was he who spread this madness. The truth of what happened, he told me in Chicago, was this: After tracking the debtor to a rented room, Billy Renfro's common sense was overwhelmed by the romantic aspects of the adventure. That was why he kicked open the door, charged boldly into the room, and shouted, "Monroe Ellis, give *up* Mr. Floyd's Cadillac that you done miss nine payments on!" Unhappily for Billy, neither Monroe Ellis nor the woman with him was in the giving-up mood. The woman fired first, aiming from underneath Ellis on the bed. Contrary to most reports, that bullet only wounded Billy's arm. It was one of the subsequent blasts from Monroe's .38 that entered Billy's side. But this wound did not slow Billy's retreat from the room, the rooming house, or the city of Houston. He was alive and fully recovered when I saw him in Chicago, on his way back from Harvey after reclaiming a defaulted Chevy.

Neither is it true, as certain of his enemies have maintained, that Billy's left eye was lost during a rumble with that red-neck storekeep outside Limehouse, South Carolina. That eye, I now have reason to believe, was lost during domestic troubles. That is quite another story. But I have this full account of the Limehouse difficulty: Billy had stopped off there en route to Charleston to repossess another defaulting car for this same Mr. Floyd Dillingham. He entered the general store with the sole intention of buying a big orange soda. However, the owner of the joint, a die-hard white supremacist, refused to execute the transaction. Being naturally suspicious of governmental intervention, Billy fell back on his own resources: He reached for the .22 he carried under his shirt for just such dalliances. But the storekeep was too swift. While Billy's right hand was still moving cloth, the red-neck was caressing the trigger of his Springfield and looking joyous. "Private club, *Mr.* Nigger!" the red-neck sang. Though he is a liar and a madman, my cousin Billy Renfro is no fool. He allowed himself to be two-stepped and back-backed out of the place, the storekeep, of course, making all the leading moves. As Billy sped off, the red-neck fired several rounds into the air and gave a hungry rebel yell. Billy did not respond.

On his return from Charleston, however, the defaulted car reclaimed, he experienced an overpowering thirst for a big orange soda. This thirst became obsessive as he neared Limehouse. It was a hot, sleepy day, nearing sunset, and his arrival at the general store went unnoticed. Billy was at the counter blowing gently on his .22 before the storekeep could resurface from the reveries he en-

joyed, dozing in his wicker rocking chair. "*Two* big
orange sodas and a dill pickle!" my cousin ordered. Liar
that he is, he told me in Chicago that he belched nonchalantly before departing from the store. I do not believe
this, but I believe him when he said he shot off five
rounds, and gave a swamp cry, when he was in his car
and pointed toward Atlanta. Ah, Billy! It is part of his
style to add such touches.

I bother to refute these rumors because the man is my
cousin, and I am honor-bound to love him as I know he
really is. He and I are one with the same ancestors, and
whatever fires rage in him I must look to find smolderings
of within myself. Recognizing this obligation, I here attempt to deflate mean rumors circulated by his enemies,
cut through the fat of Billy's own lies, and lay bare the
muscles of his life. From youth onward, he has possessed
a warm heart and a certain tolerance of misfortune; and
he is as likely, for a friend, to strip the shirt from his
back as he is to murder. That he contains such broad ex-
tremes speaks favorably of his eventual reform.

I myself have contributed considerable energy toward
this goal. In Chicago, when we drank together in that dive
on Halstead, I offered my best advice for whatever it was
worth to him. "We are no longer young men," I said.
"The foam has settled down into the beer. I, myself, no
longer chase women, speak hotly, challenge opinions too
far different from my own. I have learned it is to my advantage to get along. Chelseia, the woman I plan to
marry, you will meet in a few hours. She is steady and re-
fined, and will bear me sturdy children. In short, Billy, in
my manhood I have become aware of complexity. You
owe it to the family, and to the memory of your mother,
to do the same."

Billy swished his Scotch and drank it down, then rapped the glass on the table to alert the barmaid. When she looked, he pointed two fingers downward toward our glasses and kissed at her. Then, turning to focus his single, red-rimmed eye on my face, he said, "Bullshit!"

He was dressed in the black gabardine suit of an undertaker. Dried purple-black blood streaked his coat sleeves, his black string tie, and the collars of the dirty white shirt he wore.

"People change, Billy," I said.

"Bullshit!" Billy Renfro said.

I looked closely at him and saw a gangster. He was not the kind of man I wanted to meet my family. I glanced at my watch and sipped my drink. I listened to his stories.

Billy spun his usual lies.

This meeting in Chicago took place three years after he began work for this Mr. Dillingham, seven years after his mother's death, and thirteen years after Billy, at seventeen, went to prison for life. But I will speak here of his life before he went to prison, for insights into what he might have become. His mother was my father's sister, and both gave their first-born males the same treasured family name. Both my cousin and I were named "William" after our paternal grandfather, Willie Joe Warner, a jackleg Baptist preacher. But because her child was somewhat older, Billy's mother claimed for him the more affectionate nickname "Billy." I will not speak here of the grandfather in whose shadow we both lived, but I have heard it mentioned in the family that he favored, in his old age, the name "William" over the more secular "Billy." I would not swear to this, however, because my father winked when he told it to me. And Billy's mother, whom we nicknamed "Mama Love," laughed loudly when I asked her confirmation. I accepted my name. Billy gloried in his, draining from it as much territory as the world would concede.

He outgrew me from the start, perhaps because his father succumbed to alcohol before Billy was ten. And his mother, soon afterward made invalid by a stroke, let her son roam freely. Evenings at his house, playing in his room, Billy taught me the dozens, chanted bawdy songs, drilled me on how to eyeball a girl with maximum style. I followed as much of his advice, given the stricter circumstances of my home, as was discreet. I loved him, but I loved his mother more. Billy loved only the streets. And since Mama Love could not contain his wanderings, she gave up finally and developed a defensive sense of humor. While Billy gallivanted, I would go and sit with her and listen to her spin raucous anecdotes about her wayward son. She loved him deeply. This was witnessed in the contrast between her merry, mysterious eyes and her unhappy face whenever she shook her head and sighed, and said, "Ah, Billy! He just won't *do!*"

I suffered with Mama Love when Billy, at sixteen, threw away his youth. Here, as I recall, is how it happened: Always one to embrace completely any adventure, Billy ran wild with a crowd of older boys whose imagination lacked the brakes of self-restraint. Following their tottering lead, Billy was dared to test the first full wetness of his manhood in the arms of a much experienced girl. This girl, I have reason to believe, knew better than he how unerringly passion can boomerang, especially when heated by the trusting flame of innocence. I believe that Billy was unaware. At least this was his defense to the girl's father, and also to the female judge notorious in our city for curbing wayward boys, and protecting the coffers of the state, with one stiff dose of justice.

"You feed that baby," Judge Gladys Moon told him.

I was with him in court that day and heard Billy's plea. He said, "Judge, that baby don't even *look* like me."

Judge Moon sat stone-faced and sober. "You feed it anyway," she told Billy, "and it might look like you. Feed it for twenty-one years, and if it don't look like you after twenty-one years, you don't have to feed it no more."

While I completed school, he worked as the relay man on a garbage truck. While I attended church and learned social graces, he became more a loner, grew sullen, worked a tentative cynicism into his voice. The whites of his eyes reddened. He cultivated a process, dressed flashily, began socializing on a certain street corner sanctified by a tree that had once stood there. These developments cracked his mother's heart. She believed with Judge Gladys Moon that it was Billy's baby. He protested this violently, expressing bitterness that of all the boys who had known the girl, he alone had had to pay. And because Mama Love could not bear to fight him, she ordered him finally out of her home. Yet she still loved her son, and often sent messages and food to him by me. But during this time I began avoiding most social contacts with Billy, because I too believed that he was guilty. Besides, our vocabularies were growing rapidly apart. He moved into a rented room with his common-law wife and child, a room in a section of the city I dreaded to enter. The year I finished high school and won a church scholarship to college, Billy stabbed during a dice game a man who had questioned the honor of Billy's common-law wife. But to Billy's credit it must be said that he waited until the man, who was winning, had lost back to the others in the game

as much as they had lost to him. The code required such
graciousness, even before a deadly act. This man died,
and Billy's life was finished.

As a favor to his mother, who could not go herself, I
took off from college and went by bus to Harper's farm,
where, in those days, black men were stocked for the road
gangs. I waited for Billy in the moist, chicken-wired reception room. Around me sat weeping mothers, sportily
dressed sweethearts, somber wives. The pungent smells of
overripe peaches, sweat, potato salad, toilet water and
fried chicken assaulted my nose. Over in a corner, on a
wooden bench, a sun-whipped trustee, with his eyes
closed and his face turned upward toward the ceiling, was
singing:

> They 'cuse me of mur-der,
>   Never harm a man
>   Never harm a man.
> I say, "Wake up, old Dead Man
>   Help me ca'ry my load
>   Help me ca'ry my load! ..."

I did not want to be in such a place.

When Billy came out and took his seat, I studied him
through the chicken wire. This was long before he lost the
eye, and there was the beginning of a rough hand-
someness about his face. His hair, processed heavily now
in the style of Nat King Cole, was protected from the flies
and red dust by a blue and yellow cloth bandanna. He
wore prison-issue blues, the worn paleness of which contrasted favorably with his sun-glossed skin. He chewed
gum rapidly. Behind him, coming in the door from the
prison section, I could see gelded young men walking with
legs jangling loosely. Caged, they seemed bent on proving,

to watching wives and sweethearts, that their manhood was still intact.

"Billy," I said through the dirty wire, "why do you insist on breaking your mama's heart? She suffers because she cannot be here. Yet she would suffer even more if she could see you here in this death-infected place. Look around you at these wasted men," I urged him, "then look me in the eye and tell me you like the future you have set for yourself."

But he would not look me in the eye. Nor would he respond to my pleadings. Instead, he chewed arrogantly. Then he smiled. In that smile was a mysterious humor that I had not, before this meeting, observed in his manner. Billy looked past me, perhaps at the waiting women seated on the benches against the walls, perhaps at the humming trustee. He tossed his head and said, "Me, I'm a dead man."

I drew my chair up closer to the wire. "It does not have to end that way," I told him.

"What you doin' with your life?" he asked me.

"Making something of it," I answered.

"That's good," Billy said.

Over in the corner, the trustee stopped humming and sang:

> *Well, the load so* hea-vy
> *I can* hardly *go*
> *I can* hardly *go* . . .

I talked a while about college. Billy chewed in a relaxed way and listened. I tried my best to communicate to him some sense of the broader options available to the man in possession of salable knowledge. I mapped out my future in blocks of years, stepladders of subgoals, ending with an affirmation of my ultimate ambition to settle into the good life in Los Angeles.

Billy smiled and gave several agreeable nods. But when my conversation came to dwell on the wonders of Los Angeles, he interrupted suddenly. "Looka here," he said. "How 'bout runnin' cross the road and get me a hot sausage sandwich, heavy on the mustard, and a big orange soda."

I looked hard at him and wanted to weep. "Is that *all* you want?" I asked.

Billy chewed steadily. "No," he answered, looking out over the crowded room. "Bring me a side of fries, hold the salt."

Then he laughed, a strange, uncaring demon laughter. The sound bragged of his urge to self-destruct. Ah, Billy! He just would not *do!* He listened only to the beating of his own heart.

The last time I saw him, before we drank together in Chicago, was when he was furloughed from Harper's Farm to attend Mama Love's funeral. She died, I believe, from a broken heart and loneliness, although the doctor claimed it was the predictable second stroke. I returned home from college to gather with the family. And after the burial, while the others ate, Billy and I drank heavily together in the back room of his mother's rented house. All day he had smiled broadly at the grief and embarrassment of the family. Now he sat on his old bed, drinking with absolute detachment. I sat near him on a hard-back chair, talking aimlessly of college, of the admirable habits of girls met there, of my ambition to find, in a year or so, permanent employment in Los Angeles. Billy said nothing. But toward midnight, after the other members of the family had left and I grew tearful in recollecting the martyred life of Mama Love, Billy turned to face me. "What *you* cryin' for, *motherfucker?*" he said. "It's *my* mama!" Just then the prison guard, who had escorted him home, came in the room and touched Billy on the shoulder. My cousin rose slowly from the bed, and laughing with that same clucking sound in his chest, he sang:

> *I'm Wild Nigger Bill*
> *From Red Pepper Hill;*
> *I never did die, and I never will . . .*

He chanted his song with such complete absorption, and laughed so menacingly, that I shuddered, and covered my face, and knew with his mother that Billy was doomed.

Seven years later, following his parole, Billy Renfro began work for Mr. Floyd Dillingham of Atlanta's Dillingham Automotives, Inc. A liberal man, Mr. Dillingham had negotiated with the state for Billy's release. The job was to track down Negroes who had defaulted on their car payments. No white man would even consider such employment. I do believe that Dillingham wanted a Negro with a reputation for ruthlessness sufficient to strike fear into the hearts of the deadbeats. In the inevitable tug between desire and justice, some of Dillingham's clients had been known to kill. Paid agents do not grow old in such an enterprise. Had I seen Billy Renfro I would have advised him of this, but I did not see him after the funeral for almost ten years. However, word-of-mouth reports from members of the family, bits of gossip from home folk passing through, placed him now in New York, now in California, one month wounded in a Detroit hospital, another month married to a woman romanced during a repossession mission outside Baton Rouge.

In contrast to him, I moved weswtard, but only as far as Chicago, and settled in against this city's soul-killing winter winds. I purged from my speech all traces of the South and warmed myself by the fire of my thirty-year plan. Employment was available in the credit reference section of the Melrose Department Store, and there I established, though slowly, a reputation for efficiency and tact. Because I got along, I began moving up. In my second year in Chicago, I found and courted Chelseia Raymond, a family-backed, efficiency-minded girl. She was the kind of woman I needed to make my children safe. Her family loved me, and had the grace to overlook the fact that I had once been a poor migrant from the South. Third-generation Chicagoans, they nonetheless opened their hearts and home to me as if I had been native to their city. With their backing, I settled into this rough-and-tumble city and learned to dodge all events detracting attention from the direction in which I had determined to move. From time to time, trudging through the winter slush on Michigan, I would pause to explore a reflection of myself in a store window. By my fifth year in Chicago, I became satisfied that no one could have mistaken me for a refugee from the South.

This was my situation when Billy Renfro came to visit.

But it is certainly not true, as Billy has gossiped among the family, that when he arrived I refused to see him at my office. I do not call the man a liar, but I do say his imagination is sometimes a stranger to the truth. For the sake of accuracy, here is the truth of what happened: It was not my fault that Billy got only as far into our office as the receptionist's desk. It may be he was not dressed properly for the occasion. I know that I received his card from Mrs. Mohr only *after* he had left the building, when I was going out to lunch. She told me, with a nervousness I could not at first understand, "The gentleman said he's related to you." On my honor as a member of the family, I did not deny the bond. I accepted his card. Its face was embossed in elegant script:

RED PEPPER COLLECTION AGENCY
"We Bring Back the Goods"
B. J. Renfro, Pres.

On the back of the card Billy had scribbled: "Got me a turkee over in Harvey. Call soon. Yours truly, Billy Joe."

We met, as I have said, in the late afternoon of the following day at a bar over on Halstead. At first I did not recognize Billy. The years had treated him so unkindly. A single red eye inspected me as I approached the booth where he sat drinking. His left eye socket was hollow, no more than a shriveled piece of flesh pressed grimly against skull. His outfit—the black gabardine suit, the dirty white shirt, the black string tie—brought to my mind the image of an undertaker. Dried blood and dirt smeared the fabric of his sleeve, looking eerily green in the blue-smoked light. We shook hands awkwardly, and I slid into the booth across from him. I looked closely at his face and saw death walking.

Billy grinned foolishly.

"I have heard," I began with much politeness, "that at

the point of death your whole life passes in review before your eyes. Knowing this, I wonder about the agony you will suffer with only one eye in service. Won't it take twice as long, and prolong your pains, before your full life passes and goes away?"

Billy looked hurt. He insisted the eye had been lost during domestic troubles with a woman. I did not believe this, and he began embellishing the statement with extravagant lies. He drained his glass, leaned forward across the table, and said, "It was a hard-hearted woman down in Eufaula, Alabama, that done it, a widow-woman name of Miss Ruby Watson. I was laid up at her place, tired of runnin' the road for Mr. Floyd. She done root work, said she was gonna make me smart and set me up in business, if I done right by her. It didn't make no nevermind to me. I just laid on in the cut and took these white pills she give me. But I didn't feel no smarter. Mr. Floyd, he sent a telegram over there. He said, 'Billy Joe, *son*, come on *home*, these niggers just *a-stealin'* my cars!'" Billy laughed loudly, using the sound to catch the attention of the barmaid. When she looked, he held up two rough brown fingers. She brought the drinks over and Billy tried to feel her rump. The woman jostled playfully against his arm. He rinsed his mouth with the Scotch and continued.

"I said, '*Motherfuck a Mr. Floyd!* I'm livin' my life *right here!*' I kept takin' them pills, layin' steady in the cut, but I didn't feel no smarter. Then one day I seed her go out to the fields. I seed her pickin' up *jackrabbit* shit. I didn't say nothin'. I just snuck on back to the house and got in bed with my twenty-two. She come in and go to give me the stuff. I sit up and say, 'Miss Ruby, all this time I been wastin' round here, and all you been givin' me is jackrabbit shit!' She was a old widow-woman, Ruby, and I guess they just crafty that way. She just laugh at me and stood over the bed and say, 'Now you gettin' smart.' Well, that's when I whip my twenty-two under her nose. But she just keep laughin' and say, 'Them bullets dead by now. Don't you know them bullets dead?' She had me. She knowed it. I knowed it. She sat down on the bed and commence to stroke my chest. She say, 'Now ain't you a sight? Don't even know whichaway is up. But you my sweetmeat now, and there ain't a damn thing you can do about it.' "

Billy looked calmly around the barroom, like a priest about to say Mass. And yet beneath his cool exterior I thought I sensed, in the broad sweep of his red eye, the hint of a certain rough pride. "When she said that," he went on, "I knowed what I had to do. I gived the gun to her. I made her point it at my head. I told Miss Ruby, 'Me, I'm just dumb enough to believe it ain't even loaded. And if it is, it won't be the first time I been dead.' Then I ram my fist in her jaw."

I waited. The clink of glasses and the noisy blend of barroom voices teased my anticipating ear. Billy was a master of suspense. Finally, I said, "So you called her bluff, got your eye shot out, but proved you were a man."

Billy laughed, his demon thumping triumphantly in his chest. "Naw," he said. "She pulled the trigger and killed me. That's how come I'm back on the road for Mr. Floyd today."

Such were his lies that evening in that bar on Halstead.

While the purple and red jukebox belted accommodating rhythms, and while a couple slow-dragged, Billy spun yarns about his adventures. He told magnificent lies. He spoke of the chain gang, of buddies still anchored there, and hummed snatches of songs, remembered from that time, which still sustained him. He assessed his errors in the Houston incident, and as an aside contrasted the pungency of Mexican cuisine in joints as far apart as Brownsville, Oakland, Tempe, Arizona. Billy pantomimed, while standing, his one eye fixed on the barmaid, the body movements of black men in Savannah and San Francisco, and speculated how the spirit of a region informed the rhythms of a man's fucking. From this he moved to assessments of women in Buffalo, Cleveland, Hartford, Newark, and East Saint Louis, offering details about liaisons in these cities that convinced him, should he ever marry, that Southern women provide the safest, strongest havens. He spoke of Limehouse, South Carolina, but only in passing on his way to recollections of a Newark house-rent party, the highlights of a fish fry in Baltimore, the economics of picking beans in New Jersey if one is ever stranded there, in August, without cash. Billy recited his contributions to bus-depot graffiti inscribed on stalls in Memphis, Little Rock, Phoenix, and Los Angeles, and observed that practitioners of this art became more assertive, sexually and politically, the farther west one went. I heard his accounts of fights, poker games, epic bouts of wrestling, with recalcitrant claimers of defaulted cars. Billy conveyed the flow of his emotions while contracting an assignation, on a lonely highway driving southward from Denver, when he and the woman driver of a car licensed in Maine sped sexual brags for three hundred miles before ending, in silent completion, in a wet cornfield just west of Kansas City.

While he was still reciting, I went quickly to the telephone and called Chelseia.

It is certainly not true, though Billy maintains otherwise, that my in-laws and Chelseia ordered him out of their home. What happened that evening with the Raymonds is still fresh in my mind. They were civil to Billy, though a little bit wary about why he wore blue sunshades. I had advised him to take this precaution while at my apartment, where Billy had bathed and shaved and changed into one of my better suits. Before visiting the Raymonds he had been completely transformed. His muscles rippled in the close embrace of my gray pinstripe; his face, clean shaven now, was set off favorably by one of my sky blue shirts; my very best red and white polkadot tie swept deftly into the V of my chest-hugging vest. Even Billy's scuffed shoes had been spit-polished and shone like hot tar. This outfit, together with my blue sunshades shielding his eyesocket from inspection, gave Billy the appearance of a publicity-shy banker.

Mr. and Mrs. Raymond were enormously impressed.

"What business are you in, Mr. Renfro?" Mrs. Raymond asked, while her husband passed around the cheese board.

Conforming to my warnings, Billy spoke briefly. "Automotives," he answered.

Chelseia, seated next to me on the sofa, said nothing. But she watched Billy very closely.

"Selling?" Mrs. Raymond asked. She was a round, self-possessed woman who called me "darling" and winked reassuringly whenever we drank more than two glasses of sherry. She had already given me the understanding that Chelseia was mine. "You have a dealership, then?" she asked Billy.

He sat on a purple settee, his legs crossed elegantly, a

glass of sherry posed in his hand. He pretended he had not heard Mrs. Raymond.

I had not anticipated that Chelseia's parents would be at home. Usually on Thursday evenings they played canasta with a church group. But, being selfless people, they had canceled their engagement when they heard from Chelseia that my cousin was in town. Mr. Raymond himself had prepared the dinner. I wanted things to go smoothly. "Billy is more a traveling salesman," I answered for my cousin. "His business takes him around the country."

Mr. Raymond sighed and stroked the top of his head. He was completely bald. He said, "It does my heart good to see the younger generation getting a few breaks. Why, in my day, with two degrees, all I could get was being a redcap down at the Union Station."

"Of course you've been out to California?" Mrs. Raymond said quickly. Both she and her husband had worked very hard to achieve the good life, and she did not like to hear him reminisce.

"Yes, m'am," Billy answered.

"We've got relatives out in Culver City," Chelseia volunteered. She had sensed my tension, and had not asked why Billy was wearing a suit she had selected for me at Marshall Fields. But she stared long and hard at the blue-tinted sunshades, familiar to her from our long summer walks along the lakeshore.

"Is it true what they say about those movie stars?" Mr. Raymond asked Billy.

Such was the flow of conversation during dinner.

For well over an hour, Billy successfully maintained his cloud of mystery. And at such moments when it seemed about to break apart in the breeze of chitchat, I puffed it

back into place with a swift retort. We were relaxed until
after dinner, when Mr. Raymond, still rummaging in the
storehouses of his youth, lit up a cigar and became expansive. He loosened his tie and began telling anecdotes about
his escapades as a redcap. Chelseia, her eyes flitting nervously, kept saying, "Please, don't get naughty now,
Daddy." But her words were of no avail. Billy, puffing
fiercely on a cigar, laughed and egged him on. Mrs. Raymond smiled painfully. Several times Chelseia knocked her
knee against my leg beneath the table. Toward ten-thirty
Mr. Raymond brought out a bottle of bourbon. He said,
"How about a little snort, Mr. Renfro," and winked at
Billy. My cousin willfully ignored the suggestion in my
stare. "Call me Billy," he said to Mr. Raymond, draining
his water glass.

In less than half an hour, drunk now, Billy was offering
tales about his own exploits on the Coast. Mr. Raymond
kept laughing, shaking his head wistfully, and saying, "I
knew it was true what they say about them stars." And
while Billy dived for more details on this point, Mr. Raymond regaled us with anecdotes drawn from his days as a
bellhop at the Palmer House. When he mentioned the adventures of a hustling bellhop named "Swifty," Billy leaned
forward, pounded the table, and shouted, "Damn if I don't
know that nigger. He in *Dee*troit now, still *just as crazy as
a bedbug!*"

Mrs. Raymond coughed violently and left the room.

From this point onward the evening deteriorated.
Chelseia sat with a cold and distant expression on her
face. From time to time she kicked my foot beneath the
table. I flashed signals to Billy, tried to head off his
speech when I perceived where it was leading, suggested
many times that we should go. But none of it was of any

use. Billy seemed to have induced some unhealthy chemical reaction in Mr. Raymond. He and Billy seemed locked in some unholy union. He laughed, giggled, and hooted as he talked. Even when Mrs. Raymond returned to the room in a housecoat, her husband did not lower his voice. When Mr. Raymond, on his fourth bourbon, started to recite a salacious jingle, Billy jumped up and overruled it with a more earthy variant. But in the rush of excitement while reciting the punch line, he laughed lustily, screeched, and tore off his glasses. This one gesture destroyed all his mystery. His single eye, red-rimmed and watery, flashed horribly in the soft glow of the green and red Tiffany lamp.

Chelseia gasped.

"Why, Mr. Renfro," said Mrs. Raymond, the back of her hand drawn to her mouth, "whatever happened to your eye?"

"Nothing but a knife fight," Chelseia muttered.

"Let it go," called Mr. Raymond across the littered dining table. "It's not our business." He was drunk, but there was an extreme soberness in his voice. He said to all of us, "Let it go."

Mrs. Raymond acted on this cue. "When you get back South," she said to Billy, "tell the family that William is a very nice young man." She rounded the table with her right arm outstretched. She grasped and wagged Billy's limp right hand. "What did you say your business was?"

Billy looked confused. "Automotives, ma'am," he told her.

"Washing or pumping gas?" Chelseia said. It was not a question, and the tone of her voice I had heard before in the chill of the winter winds off Lake Michigan. When I looked at Chelseia I saw in her face a vengeful twist I had not before then, and have never since, seen in her store of expressions. Mrs. Raymond had this very same look.

Billy stiffened. He jerked his hand away from Mrs. Raymond. He looked enraged.

The rest of the evening has been clouded by his lies.

But it is certainly true that I tried hard to save the situation, although Billy has maintained that I turned on him. The man is a notorious liar, and likes to keep the family jumpy. Here is the truth of what happened: I moved quickly to Billy's side. I put my hand on his shoulder. I faced the Raymonds for the two of us. I said, "Thank you for a splendid evening." But all my tact was introduced too late. With a purposeful shrug, Billy separated his shoulder from my hand. All our eyes were on him. Only Mr. Raymond, sitting drooped and still in his chair, seemed distracted by thoughts of other matters.

Someone had to take control. I took it as best I could. "A red-neck down in South Carolina shot out Billy's eye," I said. "Billy is too proud to speak of it."

"*Bull*shit!" Billy said.

By this one word, and through his subsequent actions, Billy himself completely severed what was left of our family bond.

He stripped off my coat, my vest, my polka-dot tie. These he flung on the purple settee. My sky blue shirt he let fall to the floor. Billy stood broad-shouldered and brown in a ragged, yellowed undershirt. He directed all our eyes to weltlike scars on his arms and neck. "These here come from runnin' round the country," he grinned. "And I'm *keep* runnin' till the pork chops get thicker and they give me two dollars more."

"Please, Billy," I pleaded. "Please, Billy, tell the truth now."

He laughed wickedly, his teeth clamped tight. His eyes darted from me, to Chelseia, to Mrs. Raymond standing by the table with her right hand clutching her chest.

But Billy did not tell the truth. His story to me in the bar on Halstead vanished like a summer cloud. He pointed to his empty eye socket and said, "I lost this over in Harvey several years ago. Mr. Floyd Dillingham, my boss, was the one that sent me up here. He had this here turkey that flew the coop with a fistful of notes due on his Impala. Nigger's name was Wilfred 'Inner City' Jones, and he had balls enough to cruise pass Mr. Floyd's lot and honk when he was leavin' town. People on the corner saw him frontin' off Mr. Floyd. It looked bad. Mr. Floyd called me in and give me my runnin' orders. He say, '*Fuck* the *money*, Billy. What he done is bad for *business!* Now bring me back my *car* or that nigger's *ass!*'" He pounded the table twice, with great seriousness in his face, as if still hearing the beat of his boss's voice. Mrs. Raymond and Chelseia jumped each time he pounded. But Mr. Raymond remained seated in his chair, his head bowed, his eyes closed. Billy smiled slightly. "I put out word I was lookin' for Inner City. He put out word he was lookin' for me to come lookin' for him. Said I would find him waitin' for me over in Birmingham, if I came lookin' that far. But I knowed that Earline, his old lady, was up here in Harvey and he only felt safe with his head up under her dress. So I bought me a one-way bus ticket." Billy moved to the table, swished the last of the bourbon in his glass and drank it down. Then he set the glass on the white tablecloth and arranged soiled knives and forks around it, setting the scene. "He must have been layin' for me," he went on, "cause when I knock on the door people commence to scuffle round inside. Then

Earline sing out, 'What you want?' I holler back, 'Them keys to that Impala park outside or a piece of Inner City's ass, it don't matter to me which one!' They was quiet for a minute, then Inner City holler, 'Come on in, *motherfucker*, and take your choice!' I went on in."

His single eye, though red-rimmed and watery, sparkled dimly with pride. I sensed that he was enjoying himself, though Mrs. Raymond was almost in a swoon. She was dabbing excitely at her forehead with a dinner napkin. I saw Billy watching her. I saw him smile. I thought I saw him lick his lips. "Inner City was shootin' wild from behind the bed," he continued. "Though he is in bad with Mr. Floyd, I won't bad-talk his reputation by sayin' where them bullets hit. But I stood in the middle of the room and shout, 'Missed me, *sapsucker!*' Then I opened up with my thirty-eight, whistlin' whilst I worked. My habit is to aim high when ladies is present, cause a scared woman can talk quick sense to a hard-headed man. Pretty soon Inner City yell out, 'Hey Billy, let's be *gentlemens* and do this without no heat!' He slide his gun out from under the bed. I throwed mine on the sheets and wait. Then Earline yell, 'Hey Billy, what about that twenty-two you keeps strap to your spine?' They was quiet for a minute. Me, I didn't move. Then I heard Inner City pop Earline in the jaw. While she was still hollerin' he rise up from under the bed, limber as a bear. His eyes was steamin' and his jaws was tight. He wolf, 'I'ma *keep* that Impala, Billy, but first I'ma do me some business on your *ass!*' "

By now Billy had moved the gravy-stained knife closer to the glass. He leaned over the table like a magician about to pluck a pigeon from thin air. But suddenly his body relaxed. He straightened and reached one hand into his pocket. "Now I ain't sayin' it was *easy*," he said, look-ing directly at Chelseia, "but I *do* say I just ain't *use* to buyin' no bus ticket and ridin' with a sore ass and a bleedin' eye all the way home." He tossed a set of car keys onto the table. Tiny flecks of dried blood flew from the keys as they clinked against the glass. Then Billy laughed loud and confidently. It was an even, bass-filled laughter that sounded the image of a persistent demon pounding happily against a friendly door. "One of us knowed he had to die," he announced calmly. "Next time, it might be *me*."

"You common *street nigger!*" Chelseia shouted.

Billy held his naked arm toward me as if he were a ringmaster introducing an act. "And this here's my cousin William," he told Chelseia.

Mrs. Raymond shuddered and rushed from the room.

And then there came a burst of wild, almost hysterical laughter. But this was not Billy. I turned and saw Mr. Raymond. His bald head was bent almost into his empty plate. He seemed to be shedding tears.

"Billy!" I pleaded. "Tell the truth. Sometimes, Billy, please tell the *truth!*"

But he ignored me. Instead, he joined with Mr. Raymond in this wild, uncaring laughter.

"Gangster!" Chelseia shouted.

"God bless Mr. Floyd!" Billy yelled.

Someone had to keep order. I assumed that responsibil-ity. I was the one who asked Billy out.

But it is not true, contrary to rumors circulating in my family, that Billy Renfro is unwelcome in my home. His own lying stories spread this madness, and both he and I know the truth of where I stand. As far as I am con-

cerned, he is welcome here at any time. Chelseia is another matter, but even she has said she would not
interfere if Billy chose to come again. She would even let
me prepare dinner for him. Whenever I am confronted by
members of the family with one of his lies, I say this in
response. For whatever it is worth to them, or to Billy.
The man is, after all, my cousin. It is a point of family
pride. Chelseia agrees, and says our family unit will likely
be the place where Billy finds ultimate reconstruction,
once he has put aside his wanderings. I say it is just a
matter of time. We are, after all, the same age. Yet I have
already charted my course. I have settled into Chicago,
against the winter whippings of this city's winds. He can
do the same. But as things stand now, he is still someplace out there, with a single eye flickering over open
roadways, in his careless search for an exciting death. Ah,
Billy!

The Silver Bullet

WHEN Willis Davis tried to join up with the Henry Street guys, they told him that first he had to knock over Slick's Bar and Grill to show them what kind of stuff he had. Actually, they needed the money for the stocking of new equipment to be used in a pending reprisal against the Conchos over on the West Side. News of a Concho spring offensive was in the wind. But they did not tell Willis this. They told him they had heard he had no stuff. Willis protested, saying that he was ready to prove himself in any way but this one. He said that everyone knew Slick was in the rackets and that was why his bar had never been hit. As a matter of fact, he did not know this for certain, but he did not really want to do the job. Also, no one could remember having seen Slick around the neighborhood for the past three years.

"Slick ain't in no rackets!" Dewey Bivins had screamed at Willis. "You just tryin' to get outta it on a *humble!* Slick died of TB over in Jersey two years ago. And don't come tellin' me you don't know that." Dewey was recognized as the war lord of the group, and there were many stories circulating, some dating several years back, about the number of dedicated Concho assassins who were out to get him. Some said that at least two of the Concho membership had taken a blood oath and waited at night in the darker areas of Henry Street for Dewey to pass. Others maintained that the Concho leadership, fearing disproportionate retaliations, had given orders that Dewey, of all the Henry Street guys, should go unmolested. Dewey himself argued that at least four guys were looking for him, day and night, and liked it known that he walked the streets unarmed, all the time. In fact, each time he was seen walking, his reputation grew. People feared him, respected his dash, his temper, the way he cocked his purple beret to the side. The little fellows in the neighborhood imitated his swagger. He was a dangerous enemy, but a powerful associate. So Willis decided to give it a try.

But first he went around to see Curtis Carter, hoping to get him to go along. Carter wanted no part of it. "I know for a fact that Slick ain't dead," he pointed out. "You'd be a fool to mess with his establishment."

"Aah, *bull*shit!" Willis replied. "When was the last time you seen Slick? There's another guy runnin' the joint now." But his voice was not as convincing as he wanted it to be. And Carter was not moved, not even when Willis suggested that this job could lead to a closer association for both of them with the Henry Street guys.

Carter was not impressed. "If Slick takes after you," he said, "how can them guys help you run any faster than you'll have to run by yourself?" Willis did not like to think about that possibility, so he called Carter a ball-less son of a bitch and announced that he would do it alone.

But now that he was forced to do it alone, Willis began to really wonder about Slick's connections with the rackets. He remembered hearing stories about Slick in the old days. These stories frightened him. And even with Slick gone for good, the bar might still be covered. He wanted to ask around about it, but was afraid of calling attention to himself. Instead, he made several brief trips into the place to check out the lay of the land. The bar opened sometime between eleven and twelve o'clock, when Alphaeus Jones, the bartender, came in; but it did no real business, aside from the winos, until well after three. He figured that two o'clock would be the best time. By then the more excitable winos would have come and gone and the small trickle of people who went in for the advertised home-cooked lunch would have died away. Alphaeus Jones took his own lunch around one-thirty or two, sitting on the stool at the end of the counter, just in case any customer entered. And the cook, Bertha Roy, whom Willis recognized as a neighbor of his aunt's in the projects over on Gilman, left the place around that same time to carry bag lunches to the ladies at Martha's Beauty Salon down the block. This kept her out of the place for at least half an hour. He did not want Bertha to see him, so he decided the best time would be the minute she left with the lunches.

Again he went to Curtis Carter, begging for help. Curtis worked in an auto-parts warehouse about four blocks away from Slick's. Willis told him that the job would be much softer if they could pull it off together and then make a run back to the warehouse to hide out until after dark. But Curtis still did not want any part of the operation. He made a long speech in which he stressed the im-

portance of independent actions, offering several of his
own observations on the dependability of the Henry Street
guys; and then disclosed, by way of example, that he already had a nice steady income produced by ripping off,
from the stockroom, new accessories and mended parts,
which he sold to a garage over on the West Side. "There
ain't no fair percentage in group actions," he concluded,
the righteousness of a self-made man oiling his words.
Willis called him a mild-fed jive and said that he was after
bigger stuff. Curtis checked his temper and wished him
luck.

 The following afternoon, Willis waited across the street,
leaning against the window of a barbershop and smoking
a cigarette, until he saw Bertha Roy come out the door
with the lunch bags. When he was sure that she was not
going to turn around and go back, he threw the cigarette
into the gutter and crossed over, trying to work up a
casual amble. But his knees were much too close together.
He pushed through the door, sweeping with his eyes the
few tables against the wall on his left. The place was
empty. Alphaeus Jones, a balding, honey-colored man
with a shiny forehead, looked up from his lunch. A blob
of mustard from the fish sandwich he was eating clung to
the corner of his mouth. "What you want?" he asked,
chewing.

Willis moved closer to the end of the bar and licked his
lips. "What you got?" he asked.

Jones raised his left arm and motioned to where the
sunlight glittered through the green and brown and white
bottles on the shelves behind him. With his other hand, he
raised the fish sandwich and took another bite. Willis
licked his lips again. Then he shook his head, trying hard
to work the amble up into his voice. "Naw, man," he

said, his voice even but still a bit too high, "I mean what you got in the register?" And he made a fist with his right hand inside the pocket of his jacket.

Jones eyed him, sucking his teeth. Then he said, "A silver bullet." And looking up into the space above Willis's head, he lifted the sandwich again in his right hand. But just before it reached his mouth, he looked Willis directly in the face and asked, impatience hurrying his voice on, "You want it, Roscoe?"

"It ain't for *me*," Willis said very fast.

"Ain't for nobody else. You the first fool to come in here for years. You want it now, or later?"

Willis thought it over. Then ever so slowly, he took his right hand out of his jacket pocket and laid both hands, fingers spread on the bar.

Jones sucked his teeth again. "You done decided?" he asked.

"A beer," Willis said.

When he reported to the Henry Street boys what had happened, Dewey said: "You a silver-bullet lie!" The other guys crowded around him. They were in the storage basement at 1322 Henry. There was no door. "Chimney" Sutton, high on stuff, stood by the stairs leading up to the first floor, smashing his fist into his open palm. Besides needing the money for the coming offensive, they did not like to have an initiate seem so humble in his failures. "First you come with that mess about Slick," Dewey said. "Now you say old Jones bluffed you outta there on a bullshit tip." He paced the floor, making swift turns on his heels and jabbing an accusing brown finger at Willis, who slumped in a green metal chair with his head bowed. Sutton kept slamming his fist. The others—Harvey Gomez and Clyde Kelley—watched Willis with stone faces. "I know what your problem is," Dewey continued. "You just wanna get in the club without payin' no dues. You didn't never go in there in the first place."

"That ain't true," Willis protested, his hands spread out over his face. "I'll pay. You guys know how bad I wanna get in. But there wasn't no sense in takin' a chance like that. A guy would have to be crazy to call a bluff like that," he said, peering through his fingers at Dewey. "I tell you, his hands was under the counter."

"Aah, get off my case!" Dewey shouted. He jerked his head toward the stairs where Chimney Sutton was standing, still pounding his fist. Willis slid off the chair and eased across the room. Sutton was about to grab him when he saw Dewey wave his hand down in a gesture of disgust. Sutton moved a few inches away from the bottom step. Willis got out of the basement.

He hurried away from Henry Street, thinking it through. He still wanted to get into the organization. He felt that a man should belong to something representative. He was not against people going to work or joining churches or unions if these things represented them. But he wanted something more. And the Henry Street guys were not really bad, he thought. The papers just made them out to be that way. Several of them were family men. Dewey himself had been a family man at one time; that showed that they respected the family as an organization. But this by itself was not enough. There was not enough respect in it. And after a while you realized that something more was needed. Willis was not sure of what that thing was, but he knew that he had to try for it.

In the late afternoon, he went back around to the warehouse to see Curtis Carter. It was near closing time, but

Curtis was still sorting greasy valves and mufflers into separate piles on the floor. His blue overalls were dirty and rust-stained. When Curtis saw him come in, he motioned him over to the john in the rear of the shop, where McElrath, the manager, could not hear them. "You do it?" Curtis asked, his voice hollow with suppressed excitement.

"No."

Curtis grinned. He seemed relieved. His mouth was smeared with black grease from his hands. "Couldn't get up the balls by yourself, huh?"

Willis told him about the silver bullet.

Curtis laughed aloud and said, "That's some more jive. Jones wouldn't never shoot nobody in there. In the afternoon they wouldn't have no more than fifty dollars in the register, anyhow. You think he wanna get in the news for somethin' like that?"

Now Willis felt bad. He knew that, from all angles, Curtis was right. He could see that Curtis knew it, too. He began to feel cheated, tricked, a laughingstock. "What can I do now?" he asked. "The guys are gonna be hard on me 'cause I didn't deliver."

"I told you so in the first place," Curtis said. "Now you go'n get it, no matter whichaway you turn. Don't think that old Jones go'n keep his mouth shut about what happen today."

"What can I do?" Willis asked, his lowered voice begging support.

"Get yourself some protection," Curtis said. "Maybe try a new approach."

"Like what?"

Curtis, still with the air of an objective adviser, told him about some guys with a new approach. They were

over on the West Side. He offered no names but gave
Willis the address of an office that, he suggested, might be
friendly to Willis's situation.

On Wednesday morning, Willis took the bus over to
the office. Once he had located it, he began to suspect
that he might have been given the wrong address. This office had the suggestion of real business about it, with large
red lettering on the window that read: W. SMITH ENTER-
PRISES. When Willis entered, he saw two new hardwood
desks and tall gray file cabinets on each side of the small
room. On the floor was a thin, bright red, wall-to-wall
carpet; and behind one of the desks sat a man who wore
a full beard, with a matching red shirt and wide tie. The
man was watching him and looking very mad about something. Willis approached the desk, holding out his hand as
he introduced himself. The man ignored the hand and
continued to look very mad. The new hand-carved name-
plate on the desk said that his name was R. V. Felton. He
was the only person in the office, so Willis had to wait until Felton was through surveying him. Finally, still not
seeming to focus on the physical presence before him, the
man named Felton asked: "What you want?"

Willis said what he had been told to say: "I got a problem in community relations."

R. V. Felton looked even madder. His cheeks puffed
out. His nose widened as he sat erect in the brown leather
chair. Then, as if some switch had been clicked on, he began to speak. "Well, brother," he said, "that's our
concern here. This office is committed to problems vis-à-
vis the community. That's our only concern: an interest in
the mobility of the community." His voice as he talked
seemed tightly controlled and soft, but his hands suddenly

came alive, almost on their own, it seemed to Willis, and began to make grandiose patterns in the air. The index finger of his right hand pumped up and down, now striking the flat palm of his left hand, now jabbing out at Willis. The hands made spirals, sharp, quick cutting motions, limber pirouettes, even while the fingers maintained independent movements. "There are profound problems that relate to community structure that have to be challenged through the appropriate agency," he continued. "We have friends downtown and friends in the community who see the dynamics of our organization, vis-à-vis the community, as the only legitimate and viable group to operate in this sphere. They support us," he said, his eyes wandering, his hands working furiously now, "we support the community dynamic, and together we all know what's going down. That's our dynamic. Dig it?" And he fixed a superior eye on Willis's face.

"Yeah," Willis said.

Now R. V. Felton relaxed in the chair and lifted a pencil from the new brown holder at the edge of the desk. "Now, brother," he said, "suppose you articulate the specifics of your problem."

At one-thirty that same afternoon, Willis, with R. V. Felton behind him, walked into Slick's Bar and Grill. Bertha Roy was back in the kitchen, preparing the bag lunches; at the end table in the far-left corner of the room, a single customer was getting drunk. Jones was pulling his own lunch out of the kitchen window with his back to the door. When he turned and saw that it was Willis standing by the bar, he smiled and asked, "A born fool, hey?"

R. V., looking especially mean, came up to the bar and

stood beside Willis. Jones sighed, laid the plate on the
bar, and dropped both hands out of sight. "How much this
place earn in a week?" R. V. demanded. He had puffed
out his cheeks and chest, so that he now looked like a
bearded Buddha.

"We eat steady," Jones told him, still smiling.

Bertha Roy looked out at them from the kitchen, her
sweating face screwed up in puzzlement.

R. V. sighed, intimating ruffled patience. "A fat mouth
make a soft ass, brother," he said to Jones.

"What you boys want?" Bertha called from the kitchen.
Her voice sounded like a bark.

"Tend your pots, momma." R. V. called to her. Then
he said to Jones: "How much?"

"You better get on out," Jones told him.

Willis, standing beside R. V., tried to look as mad. But
his cheeks could not hold as much air, and without a
beard, he did not look as imposing.

"Now, listen here, brother," R. V. said to Jones. "As
of this minute, I declare this joint nationalized. Every dollar come in here, the community get back twenty-five
cents, less three cents for tax. Every plate of food pass
over that counter, the community get ten percent of the
profit, less two cents tax. Paying-up time is Friday mornings, before noon. You can play ball or close down now."

"Can I ask who go'n do the collecting for the community?" Jones asked, his voice humble.

R. V. snapped his fingers twice. Willis moved in closer
to the bar. "This here's our certified community collector
vis-à-vis this bar," R. V. announced. "Treat him nice.
And when he come in here on Friday mornings, you
smile."

"Why wait for Friday?" Jones asked. "I'll smile right

now." And he raised his hands from under the bar. He was holding a twelve-gauge shotgun. "See how wide my jaws are?" he asked. "I'm smiling so much my ass is tight. Now, what about yours?" And he lifted the gun and backed off for range.

"Let's go, man," Willis said to R. V. He was already moving toward the door.

But R. V. did not move. He held up one long finger and began to wave it at Jones. "A bad move, brother," he said.

"Why don't you boys go on home!" Bertha Roy called from behind Jones. "You oughta be *shame* of yourselfs!"

"Bertha, you don't have to tell them nothin'," Jones said over his shoulder. "They'll be goin' home soon enough."

Willis was already at the door. He did not mind being the first one out, but then, he did not want to leave without R. V. "Let's go, man," he called from the door.

"Tomorrow's Thursday," R. V. said to Jones, ignoring Willis. "We'll be in to inspect the books. And remember, if you get any ideas about disrupting the progress of our dynamic here, there'll be some action, vis-à-vis you." Then he turned sharply and walked toward Willis at the door.

The drunk over in the corner lifted his head from the table and peered after them.

"You boys need a good whippin'," Bertha Roy called. Jones just watched them go, smiling to himself.

That night, Willis went into Stanley's pool hall and told Dewey Bivins what had happened. He explained that since R. V. Felton and his organization had taken over, there would be a guaranteed cut of 12 percent for him,

Willis, every Friday. And since he had decided to join up with the Henry Street guys, rather than with R. V., this would mean a weekly income of from twenty to thirty dollars for the gang. He said that he envisioned new uniforms for the guys, better equipment and a growing slush fund for more speedy bail bonding. But Dewey did not seem to share his enthusiasm. He laid his cue on the table, frowned, and asked, "Who is these guys, anyhow? They don't live round here. This here's *our* territory."

Willis tried to explain, as concretely as possible, the purposes of the organization. And though he made a brave effort to repeat, word for word, the speech that R. V. had given him, he could tell that without the hand movements, it sounded uninspiring. In fact, Dewey said as much even before Willis had finished. "That's bullshit!" he said, his face going tight. "They ain't go'n pull that kind of shit round here. Any naturalizin' that's done, *we'll* be doin' it!"

"Nationalization," said Willis.

"And we'll be doin' it, not them phonies."

"But then I'll be in trouble," Willis explained. "These guys have already taken over the job. If I let you take it from them, they'll be after *me*."

"That's your problem," Dewey said, his eyes showing a single-mindedness. "You wanna be with them or us? Remember, we live round here. If you join up with them, the West Side ain't go'n be far enough away for you to move." He allowed a potent pause to intervene, then asked, "Know what I mean?"

Willis knew.

The following morning, he waited outside the barbershop across the street from Slick's. He smoked, walked up and down the block several times, then got into a throw-to-the-wall game with the boy who worked in the shop. He lost seventeen cents, and then quit. The boy went back into the shop, shaking the coins in his pocket. Willis waited some more. He had planned to go in with the group that arrived first; but as the wait became longer and longer, he began to consider going in alone and apologizing to Jones for the whole thing. He decided against this, however, when he saw Bertha Roy leaving to deliver the lunch bags. The place seemed unsafe with her gone.

Finally, a little after two, R. V. Felton and another fellow drove up in a dark blue Ford. R. V., behind the wheel, was wearing green sunshades. He double-parked and kept the motor running while his man got out and went into Slick's. Willis crossed over and leaned against the car. R. V. was looking especially mean. He looked at his reflection in the rearview mirror, and then looked at it in the side mirror. Willis waited patiently. Finally, R. V. said, "We talked it over. Six percent for you."

"You said twelve!" Willis protested.

"Six," R. V. said. "This here's a small dynamic. Besides, I had to cut Aubrey in on your share. You'll get twelve, maybe more, when you line up some more of these blights on the community."

"I don't wanna get involve no more," Willis said.

"I figured that. That's why it's six."

Willis was about to make further protests when Aubrey came back to the car. He opened the door on the curb side, leaned in, and said, "R. V., you better come on in, man. That dude done pull that heat again."

"Aah, fuck!" R. V. said. But he got out of the car, pushing Willis aside, and followed Aubrey into the bar. Willis entered behind them.

Jones was standing behind the bar, holding the shotgun.

"You want some trouble, brother?" R. V. asked.

"There ain't go'n be no trouble," Jones said.

"Then let's have them books."

"We don't keep no books," Jones said.

"A strange dynamic," R. V. said, pulling on his beard. "Most strange."

Jones cradled the gun butt against the bend of his right arm. "And here's somethin' stranger," he said. "If I was to blast your ass to kingdom come, there wouldn't be no cops come through that door for at least six hours. And when they come, they might take me down, but in the end, I'd get me a medal."

Now R. V.'s lips curled into a confident grin. He shook his head several times. "Let me run something down for you, brother," he said. "First of all, we are a nonprofit community-based grass-roots organization, totally responsive to the needs of the community. Second"—and here he again brought his fingers into play—"we think the community would be very interested in the articulation of the *total* proceeds of this joint vis-à-vis the *average* income level for this area. Third, you don't want to mess with us. We got the support of college students."

"Do tell," Jones said. "Well, I ain't never been to college myself, but I can count to ten. And if you punks ain't down the block when I finish, that street out there is gonna be full of hamburger meat." He braced his shoulder and lifted the gun. "And one last thing."

"You better say it quick, then," R. V. told him.

"I'm already way past five."

Willis, backing off during the exchange, had the door almost open when it suddenly rammed into his back. Before he could turn around, Dewey Bivins and Chimney Sutton pushed him aside and stepped into the room. As Sutton pushed the door shut again and leaned his back against it, Willis glimpsed Bertha Roy, her face a frightened blur, moving quickly past the window and away down the block. He turned around. Dewey, a tight fist pressed into each hip, stood surveying the room. Both he and Sutton were in full uniform, with purple berets and coffee-colored imitation-leather jackets. Dewey swung his gaze around to Willis, his eyes flashing back fire. Alphaeus Jones, still in the same spot behind the bar, held the gun a bit higher.

"Who are these dudes?" R. V. asked Willis.

Willis, trying to avoid Dewey's eyes, said nothing.

"Who the hell are *you?*" Dewey asked.

"Nine," Jones said.

Willis was still trying for the door. But Sutton moved up behind him, forcing Willis to edge almost to the center of the room.

Dewey walked closer to R. V. "Where's the money?" he demanded.

R. V. began to stroke his beard again. He looked more puzzled than mad. "Brother," he said, "there's some weird vibrations in here. What we need now is some unity. Think of the ramifications that would evolve from our working together. This here's a large community. The funds from this one joint is pure chicken shit compared to the total proceeds we could plow back into community organizations by combining our individual efforts into one dynamic and profound creative approach."

"Yeah?" asked Dewey, his head cocked to the side.

R. V. nodded, looking less puzzled. "Our organization, for example, is a legitimate relevant grass-roots community group," he said, making hyphens with his fingers. "We have been able to study the ramifications of these here bloodsucking community facilities. We have the dynamic. You have the manpower. Together we can begin a nationalization process—"

"You a naturalizin' lie!" Dewey screamed. "*We* the only group operate round here. You better take that bullshit over to the *Conchos*."

"Let's git 'em," Chimney hissed, moving forward and pounding his fist.

Jones grinned and raised the gun.

The room tensed. Chimney and Dewey stood close together, almost back to back. Similarly, Aubrey inched closer to R. V. and both stood facing Chimney and Dewey, their backs to Jones. Eyes narrowed, hands began to move toward pockets, fingers twitched. Dewey turned to Willis, standing near the door. "Which side *you* on?" he asked through his teeth. Without answering, Willis began to move toward the center of the room.

"Hey, Alphee!" someone said.

They all looked. A man was coming through the door. "Hey, Alphee," he began again, seemingly unaware of the fury he had temporarily aborted, "a cop out there writin' a ticket on that car that's double-parked. The owner in here?" He walked past the group and over to the bar, his face betraying no curiosity.

"Could be," Jones told him, now lowering the gun. "But you know how these big-time businessmen can fix tickets."

The man smiled, then, in the same loud voice, asked, "What you doin' with that gun, Alphee?"

"Fixin' to swat some flies," Jones answered.

Now the man turned and looked at the five in the

middle of the room. "Them?" he asked, nodding his head as he surveyed the faces.

Jones smiled. "That's right."

The man smiled, too. He was dressed in a deep green suit and starched white shirt open at the collar. "Which one's the big businessman, Alphee?" he asked, a suggestion of amusement tugging one corner of his mouth.

"You got me," Jones said.

"Is it you?" the man asked R. V. "You the only one in here don't look like a bum."

"Lemme take 'em, R. V.," Aubrey said.

But R. V. didn't answer. He was obviously in deep thought.

Dewey and Chimney began to look troubled. Willis's mind was racing. He looked out the window. The cop was standing with his left foot on the bumper of the car, writing. He began to wish that Bertha Roy would come back or that the cop would finish quickly and then go away.

"Now, a *real* businessman," the man was saying to no one in particular, "he would own him at least six cops, a city councilman, one and a half judges and a personal letter from the mayor. He wouldn't have to worry about one little old cop writin' a ticket." He paused and the smile left his face. "You own anything like that?" he asked R. V.

"Let's go, man," R. V. said to Aubrey in a low voice.

The man walked over and slapped R. V. across the face. "You own anything like that?" he asked again, his voice suddenly dropping the hint of amusement.

R. V. stiffened and drew back his fists. The man slapped him again. "What you wanna do that for?" R. V. whimpered.

"Floor the mother!" Dewey said. "He come in here tryin' to take over."

The man turned to Jones. "Who's that?" he asked.

"Some of them punks that hang out on Henry Street."

"Get out," the man said to Dewey.

"For what?" Dewey asked. "We on *your* side."

"No, you ain't," the man said. "Now, get out before I change my mind."

Dewey and Chimney headed for the door. Willis followed them.

"Not you," the man called after Willis. "You with these other businessmen, ain't you?"

Dewey turned at the door. "Yeah," he said, malice in his voice, "he ain't wearin' our uniform."

"I told you to get out," the man called.

"You go'n let him talk that way?" Chimney asked Dewey.

"Shut up!" Dewey hissed at him, an unfamiliar fear in his eyes.

Willis watched them go out the door. He felt trapped. Now there was only Bertha to hope for. Through the window, he could see that the cop had already left the car. Turning to the room, he saw R. V. and Aubrey standing unnaturally straight, like mechanical toys. R. V.'s lips were pushed out, but now the mean look was gone and R. V. was sulking like a little boy. The man stood at the bar, seemingly engaged in some private conversation with Jones. But after a few seconds, he turned to R. V. again. "Alphee, here, says I should just let you fellows go. He got a good heart and don't want to see you boys in any more trouble." Then he hit R. V. again, this time a quick, hard blow with his fist. R. V. screamed as the knuckles thudded into his face. "Waste him, Aubrey!" he moaned, his face turning deep brown.

But Aubrey did not move. He was looking past the man. Willis looked, too, and saw Jones holding the shotgun again and smiling. "Ten," Jones said.

R. V.'s head fell. He backed off, roughly pushing Aubrey aside. "You go'n be sorry you done that," he muttered, fighting to contain his rage. "We got—"

"Give the boys a beer before they go, Alphee," the man said.

"Let 'em pay," Jones said, following R. V. with the gun.

The man smiled. "Just a regular businessman, huh?"

"We don't want nothin' from here," Aubrey said. R. V. was standing behind him, nursing his face. He didn't say anything.

"Then take that dummy out of here," Jones ordered.

R. V. and Aubrey slowly moved toward the door. Again, Willis followed.

"Not him," Jones said. "He been in here three times already. I want to make sure he don't come back."

Willis stopped. The two others went on out, R. V. pausing only long enough at the door to say, "You ain't seen the last of our dynamic," and to shake his fist vengefully.

"Punks," Jones said.

Now Willis stood alone, frightened and frozen, eager to be going, too. He faced the men. "I didn't know," he said, his voice little more than a tremble.

"Know what?" the man asked in a softer tone.

"That this place was covered by the rackets."

The man laughed. He closed his eyes and kept the laugh suppressed in his throat. He laughed this way for almost a minute. "You hustlers kill me," he said at last. "All that big talk and you still think a black man can't have no balls without being in the rackets."

"I didn't know," Willis said again.

"Aah, *go on* and get out!" Jones said.

"Let him have a beer, Alphee," the man said, still containing his laughter.

"No," Jones said. "Go and get out. You give me a pain."

"They just young," the man told Jones.

"The hell with that," Jones said.

Willis moved toward the door. Any moment he expected them to call him back. But all he could hear as he moved was the jerking laughter coming up from deep inside the man as he made low comments to Jones. When he was going out the door, he heard Jones say, "Sure, I was young. But I ain't never been no *fool.*"

Willis ran down the block. As he passed Martha's Beauty Salon, Bertha Roy saw him and raced to the door. "You!" she called after him. Willis turned. Bertha's face was stern and her eyes flashed. "Your momma oughta give you a good whippin'," she said.

Willis pretended he had not heard and ran faster down the block.

The Faithful

THERE is John Butler, a barber, looking out his shop window on a slow Monday morning. Impeccable, as usual, in his starched white jacket, he stands and surveys the procession of colors blending into the avenue, a living advertisement for his profession. The colors are blurred because the window needs a cleaning; the red lettering has been allowed to fade, almost to a mere outline. Some of the passing faces he cannot recognize. But some recognize him behind the window and wave as they hurry past. Others, wanting to avoid all contact with the shop, pretend that he is not there. They ease out of view without acknowledging his nodding head. Still, he stands in his usual place between the edge of the window and the door; and when a familiar face moves by the window without glancing toward the shop, he shares the embarrassment and turns his own eyes away. In his mind he forgives the workers; but the shiftless, the workless, the timeless strollers up and down the avenue he does not spare.

"They still tryin' to starve us out," he says, turning to

the members of his shop. Today they consist of Ray Powell, the second barber; Mickey Norris, who has again played hooky from school in order to earn a few dollars shining shoes; and two loafers, who have come in for a game of checkers and a chance to enjoy it. All wince to hear him start again.

"Maybe I'll go on down the block a minute," Mickey says, moving toward the door.

"Maybe you better go on to school," Butler tells him. "There ain't go'n be no work in here today."

Mickey, a sly boy, does not stray far from the green metal chair.

Butler gives him a severe look. "Not tomorrow either," he adds.

Mickey slinks back to the chair and sits, his hands going into his pockets for coins to toss.

Ray, a fat brown man who likes to give the impression of habitual efficiency, runs the edge of a hand towel between the teeth of his own black comb and puckers his lips in an exaggeration of effort. "It's just the first of the week, Reverend," he says. "Things are bound to pick up."

One of the loafers, Norm Tyson from the Projects, knows better: he allows his opponent an advantage on the board and, before the man can incorporate it, says: "Looks like it's yours."

And then the two of them leave.

Just after noon, when Ray has gone across the street for lunch and Mickey has wandered off until evening, a young man looks in the door. A massive black tiara of hair encircles his head; his matching light green shirt and bell-bottom trousers advertise his wealth. Butler flashes his most hospitable smile and rises from his chair.

"How much for a quick one?" the young man asks from the door.

"For all that, two-fifty, maybe three dollars," Butler says.

The young man snorts and throws back his arms in playful amazement. "Just for a *trim?* You wouldn't wanna mess up my vibrations, would you?"

Butler loosens the smile and lowers his voice. "No," he says. "Better go somewhere else. I got me some heavy hands."

The young man laughs. "A heavy hand make a rusty register in your business, don't it?" And backs out the door before the barber can form an answer.

At the end of the day some regulars do come in; but they are losing more hairs than Butler clips. Still, they lower their heads, more from respect than necessity, and allow him limited operations around the edges. These balding faithfuls—John Gilmore or Dick Kendricks or Willie Russell—the backbone of his Sunday congregation, fold their hands beneath the white sheet-square and abide, in their turn, his wandering frustrations. "These whites have bullshitted our young men," he says. "Now, me, I'm as proud as the next man. But our boys didn't stop gettin' haircuts until these white boys started that mess. That's a fact. Wasn't no more than a couple years ago, they'd be lined up against that wall on a Saturday night, laughin' at the white boys. But soon as they see these white kids runnin' round wild, all at once they hair ain't long enough no more."

John Gilmore keeps his head lowered, his lips tight, his eyes watching his hands work beneath the sheet.

Ray, sitting in his own chair, looks up from the paper he has been reading and says: "Hey, I see where they arrested a big shot for tax evasion. First of the year they bound to hamstring *one* for example." But no one picks it up. Ray rattles and folds the paper, and eases back into his reading.

Once, there had been violent betting and spit-infested verbal battles and crowded-round checker games and hot clothes and numbers passing through; once, Butler would hum radio spirituals as he went about his work, or else trade righteous homilies with Ray, busy in the other chair. The men who remember those days—Gilmore, Kendricks, and the others—would like to have them back; but there is an unspoken fear of being too possessive about the past, and a determination not to allow the present to slip out of focus. They recognize another world outside the shop door, and find it much easier to pay up and walk away when Butler is done with his work.

"If it wasn't for you belonging to his church," John Gilmore tells his wife after each visit, "I wouldn't go in there."

"Now don't you be no trouble to him," Marie Gilmore reminds her husband. "He ain't got much longer to go."

On Sundays Butler now converts his sermons. The themes still resemble something familiar to his congregation, but lately the images have been doing different work. The relative few who still come into the church to hear it are growing bored. Some have already visited Reverend Tarwell and his more magical thumpings over on 138th. They like what they hear. There is talk that Tarwell plans to have himself crucified next month at Easter Sunrise Service and preach the entire sermon from the cross. Such resurrected remnants of the South appeal to them; the oldest have ever been homesick. Besides, Butler seems to have an obsession with a single theme: "I was walkin' down here this mornin', brothers and sisters," he begins, his rising voice mellowing into a comfortable chant, "thinkin' about the rift there is these days between father and son; thinkin' about the breach there is between son and son and daughter and daughter. I'm thinkin' this mornin' about old bloody Cain and his guiltless brother; about old man Abraham castin' his son out into the wilderness; about that old rascal Saul, lettin' his *wine* turn him against young David. I see little Joseph tossed in the dark pit, strip naked of his garment by his brothers. And hungry Esau, just a-droolin' at the mouth, sellin' his birthright for a mess of *pottage*. There's old slick Jacob now, a-crawlin' in to blind Isaac's bedside underneath the *fleece* of a wild and woolly animal; and Esau standin' outside the door, just a-weepin' away. Next to him is old rebellious Absalom, up in an *oak* tree, swingin' by his hair with Joab ridin' *down* on him. Just look at that boy cuss. I want to cut him down, Church, but I ain't got the strength. My arm is raised up to him, but my *razor's* kind of rusty. So can I git an *amen* over here . . . ?"

Some of the people on his left say a weak "a-men."

"Can I hear an *a-men* over there . . . ?"

Some few on the right say "a-men."

"My razor growin' *sharper* by the second . . ."

"You better lay off that stuff," Ella, his wife, tells him at Sunday dinner. "The church done got tired of that one record you keep playin'." They have not been invited out for Sunday dinner in over five months.

"They ain't got no cause to complain," Butler tells her.

"I give them a good service. Besides, most of them don't even listen to nothin' but the names."

"Just the same you better lay off it for a while. It ain't their fault you goin' out of business."

Butler looks over at her. She is chewing with a deliberation calculated to enrage him into an argument. "Whose fault you reckon it is?" he demands.

She continues chewing, looking wise.

Butler looks at his own food. "All right," he says. "It's *my* fault."

"It ain't that you *have* to do Afros. Ray could do that and you could do your old customers. There ain't nothin' wrong with dividin' up the work thataway."

"Ray ain't go'n do fancy cuts in *my* place. First thing you know, these young fellows come hangin' round there and drive the old customers away."

She chews for a while, sips her coffee, and watches him. She takes her time in swallowing, smacks her lips, and then says: "Then you won't have a place for much longer."

He scrapes at his own plate, trying to avoid her eyes.

"And the way *you* goin'," she adds, "you won't be preachin' much longer either."

This thought he takes to bed with him, while she lingers in the kitchen and sips, with irritating emphasis, another cup of coffee.

On another slow Monday morning, Ray, shaping his own mustache at the mirror, says: "You know, Reverend, I been thinking. Maybe we ought to go into processes. Nobody can say *now* that's imitating the white man. And there's guys on the block still wearing them."

Butler turns from the window, his face twitching.

Images of winos and hustlers flash through his mind. "That's what you been thinkin', huh?" he says to Ray.

"Yeah, Reverend," Ray says, laughing to himself in the mirror. "Since the white folks always imitating us, maybe we could even process some of them."

"I don't process," Butler answers.

"It's work," Ray says, dropping the laugh and looking serious.

"It's devil's work," Butler says.

"Right now, I'd say we ain't got much of a choice."

Butler stands behind him. They exchange looks in the mirror. Ray works the scissors in his right hand, shaking off the hairs. Then he begins to clip his mustache again, drawing in his chin. Butler watches. After a while he says: "Ray, I know you think I'm a fool. I can't help that. But when you get to be my age, change is just hard. You can shape a boy's life by what you do to his hair," he says, looking over at Mickey tossing coins against the wall. "Now everybody can't do that, but I'm proud to say I done it more than once in my lifetime. And I want to do it some more. But scrapin' a few loose hairs off every Tom, Dick, and Harry that come in here, just to get the money, why, anybody can do that. You understand what I'm sayin'?"

Ray lowers the scissors but does not answer.

"You, Mickey? You understand?"

Mickey thinks it over, tossing another coin to the wall. After a while he says, "Naw, suh," and nods his head.

Butler walks back to the window. "That's what I figured," he finally says, looking out.

A little after one o'clock John Gilmore comes in for a quick shave during his lunch hour. Lying almost horizontal in the chair, his rust brown lips and eyelids showing through the lather, he makes careful conversation while Butler exercises the repressed magic in his hands. "Times being what they is in religion and all," he says, "I been wonderin' what you been plannin' to do."

"About what?" Butler says, not pausing in his work.

"Well," Gilmore begins, "Marie say Second Calvary ain't drawin' no stronger membership. In fact, a lot of folks thinkin' about plain quittin'.."

"That's their business." he answers, holding back Gilmore's ear. "They git what they pay for."

Gilmore waits until his ear is allowed to fall back into place. Then he says: "I hear Reverend Tarwell thinkin' 'bout *you* for assistant pastor of his place. Times bein' good for the colored like they is, he thinkin' 'bout goin' into politics in a few years. When he step down, there sure go'n be a crowd over at his place for somebody."

Butler paused to wipe the razor. "Ain't most of his people from South Carolina?" he asks.

"Some."

"Well, most of mine from Alabama. There's two different styles."

Gilmore licks some lather off his lips with a delicate flicker of his tongue. He moistens both lips in the process. "That don't make a difference no more," he says. "People thinkin' 'bout *unity* these days. All of us in the same boat no matter where we from."

"Guess so," Butler says lightly. But after cleaning his razor again he says: "Where you from?"

"Alabama."

"Then why you worryin' about Tarwell's church? Why don't he bring his people over to *mine*?"

Gilmore tightens his lips.

"He's the one plannin' to leave the community, not me."

"I'll tell him that," Gilmore says, closing his eyes tight and easing into a resolved silence.

Late on Thursday afternoon, Ray, his eyes averted, says he has to go. "It was a good shop, Reverend," he says, "but I got me a family to support."

"Where you goin' to?" Butler asks.

"This new parlor over on 145th."

"It's all set up, huh?"

Rays says, "Yeah."

"Well," Butler says, forcing a smile, "maybe my luck will change some now with you gone."

Ray looks sad. His fat jaws break out in sweat. He wipes it away, turning up the edge of his mustache. Lately he has taken to wearing his hair long about his ears: a steady warning, but of unsuspected proportions. "It ain't nothing to do with *luck*, Reverend," he sighs. "God*damn!* Everybody done switched over but *us*. Even the *barber schools* don't teach them old down-home cuts no more. You just *plain stubborn!*" Now he pauses, checking a great part of what has been building up in him. "Look, you want to get in on the money? It's easy as pie. There ain't no work involve in it. All you have to do is trim. *Trim!*" He sighs, smoothing down his ruffled mustache while stroking his face again. "You getting to be an old man, Reverend. You should be looking ahead. That's what I'm doing. That's *all* I'm doing."

"I'll take over your regulars."

"What regulars?" Rays says. "There ain't no regulars to divide. I cut your hair, you cut mine. Sometime Willie Russell or Jack Gilmore come in here out of guilt and let you burn their ears. What's gonna happen when they get tired? Who you go'n cut then, your*self?*"

"You can take your stuff with you," Butler tells him, oblivious of Ray's exasperation. "But mind you don't take the goodwill over there to 145th."

Ray, locking his mouth against more hot words, sprawls into his own chair, penitent and brooding. Mickey, smoking a cigarette and listening in the john, blows a stream of smoke into the air and thinks his own thoughts.

"Now old Isaac," he tells his people on another Sunday morning, "he's a-layin' down to die. He done followed out God's directions and now ain't worried about but one thing: makin' his dyin' bed comfortable. He done married to Rebekah, accordin' to his *father's* will; he done planted, in his old age, the *seed* of a great nation in her womb. But now he's tired, Church, his eyesight is a-failin' and he's hungry for *red meat.* He's just about ready to lay his blessin' on anybody, just as long as he can get a taste of venison steak. But God—Glory, Glory—is a-workin' against him, as he always works against the *unwise. He* can't run the risk of that blessin' fallin' on Esau, who is all covered with hair. So he has to make Rebekah his instrument, one more time, to see that his work gits done. I want you to picture old Isaac now, just layin' in his darkness, pantin' for meat. And Jacob, God's beloved, sneakin' in to blind Isaac's bedside, a goatskin on his head, a service tray in his hand. But look here, Church: yonder, over there, runnin' up from the woods with his hair holdin' him down, here come old Esau just a-hustlin' home. It's gonna be a close one, Church; both these boys is *movin' fast.* Now who go'n put money down on Esau?

I say who go'n *bet* on Jacob? Both these boys is hustlin' on in. Who go'n lay somethin' on Esau this mornin' now . . .?"

No one responds.

"Well, then, who go'n *bet* on Jacob . . .?"

Most of them are confused. But some of the oldest, and most faithful, lay uninspired "a-mens" on Jacob.

"The race is gettin' closer by the minute . . ."

Marie Gilmore, dressed in her best white usher's uniform, gets up and leaves the room.

There is John Butler, the barber, on another Monday morning; again loitering by the window, again considering the rhythm of the street. He has not housed a complete checker game for almost a month.

"How do you do one of these Afros?" he asks Mickey, turning from the window.

"Nothin' to it, Rev," says Mickey, a careful boy who bears the jokings of his buddies concerning his own close-cut hair in order to keep some steady work. "Nothin' to it," he repeats, anticipation in his wise eyes. "You just let it grow, put some stuff on it, and keep it even all the time."

"What kind of stuff? Sound like a process to me."

"Naw, Rev," Mickey says.

"What is this *stuff?*"

"It's just to keep dandruff out."

"You think I could do one?"

"Hell, Rev, *any*body can do it."

Butler thinks a bit. "Mickey, what does it do for these kids?"

Mickey looks up at him, his face suggesting the fire of

deeply held knowledge. "What *don't* it do for you?" is his answer.

Butler considers this.

Just before closing time that same day John Gilmore comes in. He does not need a shave or even a trim. Nor does he offer much conversation. Butler waits. Finally Gilmore musters sufficient courage.

"Marie says she ain't comin' back to Second Calvary no more."

"Gone over to Tarwell, I bet."

Gilmore nods. His large hands dangle between his legs as he sits on the green metal chair across from Butler.

"She was a fine usher," Butler says. "Now Tarwell done beat me out of somethin' fine."

"You beat your*self*," Gilmore says. "She didn't no more want to go over there than I want to stop comin' in here."

Butler looks at him. Gilmore looks down at his hands.

"So that's how it is?"

Gilmore nods again.

"And you call yourself a *Alabama* boy."

"That's been over a long time ago. Things change."

"I suppose you fixin' to grow yourself an Afro too, with that bald spot on your head."

Gilmore grows irritated. He gets up and moves toward the door. "I ain't fixin' to do *nothin'*," he says. "But if I was you I'd be fixin' to close up shop for a while so's I could reread my Bible for a spell."

"I know the Good Book," Butler says. "Thank you kindly."

Gilmore turns at the door, his long right hand holding it open. "Or maybe give up the Good Book and go back down home where you can cut the kind of hair you want."

"Maybe *all* of us ought to go back," Butler calls after him. But John Gilmore has already closed the door.

Through the ebb of the afternoon Butler slumps in his chair, taking inventory of his situation. He is not a poor man: the title to the shop is clear; the upper floor of his duplex is rented out to a schoolteacher; and there is, besides, a little money in the bank. But there is Mickey to consider if Butler were to close up shop; the boy's salary comes to three-fifty a week. He would not like to see Mickey leave, too. He would not like to see Mickey over on 145th, picking up ideas that have always been alien to his shop. He thinks some more about Mickey. Then he thinks about the South. Closing time comes, and goes. Mickey, passing down the street, sees him there and comes in. Butler sends him for coffee and then leans back again and closes his eyes. He thinks about going home, but again he thinks about the South. His feet braced against the footrest, the chair swinging around on its own, he recalls the red dirt roads of Alabama.

"Gimme a 'fro."

Having lost all sense of direction, he has to raise himself before the sound can be connected.

"Gimme a 'fro, please?"

A boy is standing next to his chair. He is Tommy Gilmore, youngest son of his former customer. Butler once baptized him during the heat of a summer revival. Tommy's hair is gray black and tightly curled, his mouth is open, his dungarees faded and torn at the knee; a dollar bill is held up to Butler in the edge of his fist.

"What you want?"

"A haircut."

"It's after closing time," Butler tells him. Then he sees the dollar. "And anyway, it's gonna cost you one-fifty. You got that much?"

The boy hands up the dollar.

"That ain't enough," Butler says, handing it back. "What else you got in your pocket? How much Marie give you?"

"Ain't got no more," the boy mumbles.

Greed lifts its thumb, but charity quickly waves it away. "You sure that's all you got?"

"Yes, sir."

Butler moves over to the hot-water heater and takes the board from behind it. He lays it across the armrests of his chair, takes a fresh cloth from the drawer and gives it a decisive snap. "Sit down, mister," he tells the boy. "I'm gonna give you the nicest schoolboy you ever seen."

Tommy does not move. His fist tightens around the dollar. Part of it disappears into the vise. His eyes narrow cynically. "A schoolboy ain't no 'fro," he states.

"Git up on the board, son."

"You go'n *gimme* one?"

"I'm a barber, ain't I?"

The boy mounts.

Butler secures him, and then ties the cloth.

Mickey comes in with the coffee, surveys the room, and then sets the steaming cup on the counter below the mirror.

Butler fastens the safety pin in the knot behind the boy's neck. "Now look here, Mickey, and you'll learn something," he says, as Mickey stands back to inspect the boy in the chair.

Mickey's eyes flicker over the scene, the curiosity in him slowly changing to doubt. "How you go'n do it, Rev?

You ain't got no *comb*, you ain't got no *stuff*, and it ain't even *long* enough yet."

The boy begins to wiggle in the chair. The board shifts under him. "It is *too* long enough," he says.

"Naw, it ain't," says Mickey, malice in his eyes, his eyes on the younger boy's face, his head solemnly swaggering. "You got to go four, five months before you get enough. And you ain't got but one or two yet."

"Shut your trap, Mickey," Butler orders. He straightens the board with one hand and places the other on the struggling boy's shoulder. "I'm goin' to work on it now," he says, pressing down.

"But it ain't go'n do no *good!*"

"Shut up or go on home!" Butler says.

Mickey struts over to his own green chair at the end of the row, his face beaming the detachment of a protected bettor on a fixed poker game. He sits, watching with great intensity. The boy sees him and begins to squirm again.

"Quiet down, now," the barber says, this time pressing down on the boy's head. "I know what I'm doin'."

The boy obeys, whimpering some. Butler begins to use his shears. The hair is hard and thick, tightly curled and matted; but, deep inside it, near the scalp, he sees red dust rising. He is furious in his work, a starved man; turning and clipping and holding and brushing and shaping and holding and looking and seeing, beyond it all, the red dust rising. In ten minutes it is done. He stands back for a final look, then opens the pin, undoes the knot. Again he shapes the white sheet-square; again he brushes. The boy steps down, still whimpering softly. The board goes back behind the hot-water tank. And Butler lifts him up to the long mirror. The last whiffs of steam curl out from the cooling coffee. Mickey tightens his mouth and reaches into his pocket for a coin to toss against the wall. The boy looks into the mirror.

There is the barber, under the single bulb that sends light out through the windows of his shop. Gesturing, mouthing, making swift movements with his hands in the face of the shouting John Gilmore, who stands between him and the window. The boy is clinging to the man, crying softly. There is Mickey, still in his green chair against the wall, his own eyes, his open mind deciding.

"If you didn't call yourself a minister of God, I'd *kick your ass!*" the tightfisted John Gilmore is saying. His bottom lip is pushed far out from his face.

"Didn't you ever have a schoolboy when you was his age? Just answer me that."

"I went to a different school. But my son ain't no *plantation* Negro."

"He didn't have nothin' but a dollar anyhow."

"Then you should of sent him somewhere else!"

Tommy's mouth is open. He is crying without sound.

"*Look* at him! You can't *tell* me he don't look better now."

"We go'n close you down, old man. You hear what I'm sayin'? We go'n close this joint down and your church, *too!*"

"You go'n close us *all* down."

"We go'n run all you Toms from the community..."

Mickey slides his hands into his pockets, rattling the coins.

On still another Sunday morning he stands, tired now, old, facing the last few strays of a scattered flock. It is almost Easter. Word is going around that Tarwell has already nailed the cross together in the basement of his church. Some say they have seen it. Others, some of those who are sitting here, are still reserving judgment. Marie Gilmore is back; but she has not come for the sermon. She sits at the back of the room in a purple dress, her eyes cast down. Butler, looking fierce and defensive, stares at the six or so faces peering up at him. Some look sheepish, some impatient; some look numb as always, waiting to be moved. He stands before them, his two hands gripping the edges of the pulpit. They wait. Several plump ladies fan themselves, waiting. One, Betty Jessup, sitting on the front pew, leans forward and whispers: "You fixin' to preach, or what?"

He does not answer.

Now the people begin to murmur among themselves: "What's wrong with him?" "When's he gonna start?"

"We are a stiff-necked people," he begins, his voice unusually steady, the music gone. "Our heads turn thisaway and thataway, but only in one direction at a time." He pauses. "We'll be judged for it."

"Who go'n judge us?" Marie Gilmore suddenly fires from the back of the room. They all turn, their mouths hanging loose. Marie Gilmore rises. "Who's to say what's to be judged and what ain't?" she says through trembling lips. "Who's left to say for certain he knows the rules or can show us where they written down?" she says.

The people are amazed. Several of them wave their hands and nod their heads to quiet her. Marie Gilmore does not notice. Her eyes are fixed on Butler.

He stands behind the pulpit and does not say anything.

At Sunday dinner Ella says: "Well, what you go'n do now?"

"Send that truant officer after Mickey," Butler says quietly.

"What else?"

He shifts his eyes about the room, looking for something.

Ella sighs and strikes her chest. "Lord, why I had to marry a man with a *hard head?*"

Butler looks her in the face. "Because you couldn't do no better," he tells her.

Problems of Art

I

SEATED rigidly on the red, plastic-covered sofa, waiting for Mrs. Farragot to return from her errand, Corliss Milford decided he did not feel comfortable inside the woman's apartment. Why this was he could not tell. The living room itself, as far as he could see around, reflected the imprint of a mind as meticulous as his own. Every item seemed in place; every detail meshed into an overriding suggestion of order. This neatness did no damage to the image of Mrs. Farragot he had assembled, even before visiting her at home. Her first name was Mary, and she was thin and severe of manner. He recalled that her walnut-brown face betrayed few wrinkles; her dark eyes were quick and direct without being forceful; her thin lips, during conversation, moved with precision and resolve. Even her blue summer dress, with pearl-white buttons up its front, advertised efficiency of character. The bare facts of her personal life, too, argued neatness and restraint; he had them down on paper, and the paper rested on his knee. Milford jiggled his knee; the paper shifted, but did not fall. That, too, he thought. It was part of why he felt uneasy. For a few seconds, he entertained the notion that this living room was no more than a sound stage on a movie lot. Somehow, it seemed too calculated.

Milford's suspicion of an undisclosed reality was heightened by the figure in the painting on the wall across the room. It was the portrait of a sad-eyed Jesus. Immaculate in white and blue robes, the figure held a pink hand just above the red, valentine-shaped heart painted at the center of its chest. Bright drops of red blood dripped from the valentine. Such pictures as this Milford had seen before in dime stores. Though it had a certain poignancy, he thought, it was . . . cheap. It conveyed the poverty of the artist's imagination and tended to undermine the sophistication of those who purchased such dimensionless renditions. Did not the Latin poor build great cathedrals? Even country Baptists wheeled their preachers about in Cadillacs. Why then, Milford asked himself, would a poor black woman compound an already bleak existence by worshiping before a dime-store rendition of a mystery? He recalled having heard someplace something about the function of such images, but could not recall exactly what he had heard.

The plastic crinkled as he shifted on the sofa to review Mrs. Farragot's papers. She had been born in Virginia, but had lived for many years in Los Angeles. She was a widow, but received no compensation from her husband's Social Security. She had been arrested for driving under the influence of alcohol, although she insisted that she was a teetotaler. About the only consistent factual evidence about her that Milford knew was her insistence, over a period of two weeks, that no one but a white lawyer could represent her at the license revocation hearing.

For her firm stand on this she was now notorious in all the cubbyhole offices of Project Gratis. Milford looked again at the portrait. Perhaps that explains it, he thought. Then he thought, perhaps it does not.

He leaned back on the sofa, impatient now for Mrs. Farragot to return. According to his watch it was 11:45 A.M. The hearing was scheduled for 1:30 P.M. The day was already humid and muggy, and would probably grow tense as events developed in the afternoon. But Milford was used to it. For want of a better rationalization, he liked to call such occasions "invigorating." Now he sighed and glanced again about the room, wondering just who would return with her to act as witness and corroborator. But his mind was trained to focus on those areas where random facts formed a confluence of palatable reality, and he was restless for easy details. His eyes swept over the brown coffee table; above the red, plastic-covered armchair across the room; past the tall glass china closet, packed with jade green and brandy red and sunset orange cut glass ashtrays and knickknacks, whose scalelike patterns sparkled in the late morning sunlight, streaming lazily through the open window on bright particles of dust; beyond the china closet to the yellowish white door leading into the quiet, smell-less kitchen from which sounded the hum of a refrigerator; past the doorframe, quickly, and the sofa's edge, to where a group of pictures in cheap aluminum frames stood grouped on a brown plywood coffee table. These he examined more closely.

The largest one was of Mrs. Mary Farragot. It was a close-up of her face as it must have looked years ago. There were fewer wrinkles and no strains of gray in her ebony-black hair. She was smiling contentedly. This, Milford thought, was not the face of an alcoholic. It reflected strength and motherly concern. Next to this picture was a small color print of two white children. Both were smiling. One, a blond boy seated in a blue high chair, grinned with his spoon raised above a yellow dish of cereal, as if about to strike. A little girl, with dark brown hair, posed extravagantly beside the chair, her skinny right arm raised in anticipation of the falling spoon. The picture was inscribed: "To Aunt Mary, Love, Tracy and Ken." Corliss Milford did not pause to examine their faces. Instead, his eyes were drawn to the third picture. This was a faded black-and-white enlargement of a very weak print. Behind the glass stood a robust black man in army uniform, saluting majestically. His grin was mischievous and arrogant; his nostrils flared. The thumb of his raised hand stood out prominently from his temple; a few inches above the hand, the edge of an army private's cap hung casually over his forehead, like an enlarged widow's peak.

This is a good picture, Milford decided. He picked it up and examined its details more closely. The man stood in what was obviously an exaggeration of attention. He saw that the man's left brogan was hooked nonchalantly around his right ankle. In the background a flagpole raised up some six or eight feet above the man's head. The flag was snapping briskly in what may have been the morning breeze, although the faded condition of the print obscured the true direction of the sun. Milford counted the number of stars in the flag. Then he peered deeper into the background, beyond the pole, and saw what may have been palm trees, and beyond these, mountains. His eyes moved from the mountains back to the flagpole and down the pole past the saluting soldier, to the bottom of the picture, where the grass was smooth as a billiard table. His eyes fastened on a detail he had missed before:

a bugle stood upright on its mouth just at the soldier's feet; in fact, the man's left brogan was pointing slyly at the bugle. This was why the man was grinning. Near the bugle, at an angle, someone, probably the soldier, had written: "To Mary Dear, Lots of Love, 'Sweet Willie'." There was a flowing line just below this inscription, as if the signer had taken sudden inspiration.

Corliss Milford shifted his eyes to the papers on the sofa beside him. Mrs. Farragot had reported that she was a widow. He had written that down. But now he recalled she had actually said "grass widow," which meant that Sweet Willie was still around. It also accounted for why she was not drawing Social Security. Perhaps, he thought, it also justified her frustration if, indeed, she had been drunk when arrested. There was no doubt that it accounted completely for the bitterness that had compelled her to request specifically the services of a white lawyer. From his picture, Milford concluded, Willie Farragot seemed to reek of irresponsibility. Perhaps all the men Mrs. Farragot knew were like him. This would account for the difficulty she seemed to be having in getting a witness to corroborate her story that she had not been drunk when arrested.

Now he shifted his eyes to the print on the wall, but this time with more understanding. He had reentered the living room on another level, and now he could sympathize. Still, he did not like the painting. A disturbing absence of nuance undermined the face: the small brown eyes were dimensionless, as if even they did not believe the message they had been calculated to convey. The pigeon nose had no special prominence, no irregularity suggestive of regality; even the lips, wafer-thin and pink, suggested only a glisten of determination. In the entire face, from forehead to chin, there was not the slightest hint of tragedy or transcendence. To appreciate it, Milford concluded, required of one an act of faith. The robes, though enamel white and royal blue, drooped without majesty from shoulders that were round and ordinary. And the larger-than-life valentine heart seemed to have been merely positioned at the center of the figure's chest. The entire image suffered badly from a lack of calculation. It did not draw one into it. Its total effect did no more than suggest that the image, at the complete mercy of a commercial artist, had resigned itself to being painted. The face reflected a nonchalant resignation to this fate. If the mouth was a little sad, it was not from the weight of this world's sins, but rather from an inability to comprehend the nature of sin itself.

Milford was beginning to draw contrasts between the figure and the picture of Sweet Willie, when Mrs. Mary Farragot opened the door and stepped quickly into the room. A heavy-set brown-skinned man followed behind her. "May Francis Cripps wouldn't come," she announced in a quiet, matter-of-fact voice, "but Clarence was there, too. He seen it all. Clarence Winfield, this here's Mr. Milford from that free law office round there."

Milford stepped to the center of the room and extended his hand.

"How do?" the man named Winfield boomed. He grasped Milford's hand and squeezed it firmly. "Everything Miss Mary told you, she told you the truth. I was there and I seen it all. Them cops had no call to arrest her. She warn't drunk, and I know damn well she warn't going nowheres in that car." While saying this Winfield ran the thumb of his left hand around the inside of his belt, tucking his shirt more neatly into his trousers. "Like

I say," he continued, dropping Milford's hand, "I was there and I seen the whole thing."

Milford stepped back and considered the man. He wore a light brown seersucker suit and a red shirt. A red silk handkerchief flowered from the pocket of his jacket. A red silk tie dangled in his left hand. He had obviously just finished shaving, because the pungent scent of a cheap cologne wafted from his body each time he moved. There was something familiar about the cologne, Milford thought; he imagined he had smelled it before, but could not remember when or where. He turned and sat on the plastic-covered sofa, crossing his legs. "I'm from Project Gratis," Milford announced. "Did Mrs. Farragot tell you about my interest in her case?"

Clarence Winfield nodded. "When Miss Mary told me what happen, I put on my business clothes and rush right on over here. I told her—" and here he threw a comforting glance at Mrs. Farragot, who stood several feet behind him—"I told her, I say, 'Miss Mary, you don't have to beg May Francis and Big Boy and them to testify for you.' Anyway, that nigger Big Boy couldn't hit a crooked lick with a straight stick."

"Speak good English now, Clarence, for the Lord's sakes," Mrs. Farragot called. "We got to go downtown. And there's one thing I learnt about white people: if they don't understand what you saying, they just ain't gonna hear it." She looked conspiratorially at Milford.

The lawyer did not say anything.

Clarence Winfield glanced again at Mrs. Farragot. "I knows good English," he said. "Don't you forget, I worked round white folks, too. They hears what they wants to hear." Then he looked at Milford and said, "No offense intended."

The lawyer studied the two of them. Over Winfield's broad shoulder he saw Mrs. Farragot leaning against the wall, directly under the painting. Both hands placed firmly on her hips, she stood surveying the two men, with something close to despair playing over her face. Milford noticed her high brown cheeks twitch slightly. Her lips were drawn and thin. She seemed about to say something to Winfield, but no words came from her mouth. The big, middle-aged black man remained standing in the middle of the room, as if waiting for something to happen. The longer Milford studied him, the more he became convinced that it was not the smell of the cologne but something else, possibly something about his carriage, that made him seem so familiar. The man seemed eager to be in motion. He seemed self-conscious and awkward standing at attention. Milford took up the papers from the sofa. He flipped a page to the statement of facts he had typed before leaving the office. "Now Mr. Winfield," he said, "please tell me what you saw the night of August seventh of this year."

Clarence Winfield cleared his throat several times, then glanced once more at Mrs. Farragot. "That there's a night I remember well," he began slowly. "It was hot as a sonofabitch. I was setting on my porch with May Francis Cripps and Buster Williams. It warn't no more than eight-thirty, 'cause the sun had just gone down, and the sky up the street was settlin' in from pink to purple to black. I remembers it well. We had us some beer and was shootin' the shit, and the only sound was the crickets scrapin' and a few kids up the block raisin' hell, when all at once there come this loud honkin'. I look 'cross the street and seen Miss Mary here come runnin' out her door and down the stairs. I knowed it was her 'cause she left

the door open, and the light from in here come out
through the screen and spotlight her porch like a stage.
Yeah, come to think of it, just like a stage. See, there was
this car light behind hers that was park so close the headlights was burning right into Miss Mary's tail end, and
right up close behind *him* was another car. Well, the guy
was trap and couldn't get out. I don't know who was in
that car, but that guy kept honkin' his horn, 'cause he
couldn't move without scratchin' against Miss Mary's car.
I never found out who that guy was, but man, he played
'Dixie' on that horn. See, he couldn't back-back either,
'cause that car behind had him squeezed in like a Maine
sardine. That's the way it is round here in summertime.
There's so many big cars park end to end, it look like
some big-time *Eye*-talian gangsters was having a convention. For folks poor as these round here, I don't know
where in the *hell* all these here cars come from. Me, I
drive . . ."

"You see what I mean, Clarence?" Mrs. Farragot interrupted. She walked toward Winfield, her hands still on
her hips. "The man didn't ask about no *gangsters!* All he
want is the *facts!*" Then she threw up her hands, cast a
look of exasperation at Milford, and dropped into the
plastic-covered armchair beneath the painting.

"It's all right," Milford told the two of them. He set
down his notes and watched Mrs. Farragot. She was
sprawled in the armchair; her arms were folded, her legs
were crossed, and there was great impatience in her face.
Milford attempted to communicate to her, with a slight
movement of his pencil, that he had no objection to the
mode of Winfield's presentation.

For his own part, Clarence Winfield grinned bashfully.
Then he said, " 'Scuse me, Miss Mary; you right." Then

he swallowed again and proceeded, this time pausing tentatively before each sentence. "Well, me and May Francis and Buster listen to all this racket, and we seen Miss Mary here, plain as day, open up her car and start it up and cut on the headlights. Now *her* car was lighting up the taillights of the car in front of her, and it reflect back on her behind the wheel. I seen that. And I heard this guy steady honking on his horn. Well, just about then, who should drive up the street in his new Buick but Big Boy Ralston. He lives up the block there, 'bout five houses down from me. Big Boy a security guard down to the bank, and I guess he just naturally take his work serious. I mean, he bring it home when he come. Anyway, he drives up just about even with this guy that's honking, and he stops and calls out, 'Who that making all that motherfuckin' racket?' Well, this makes the other guy mad, and then he *really* tore into that horn. By this time the street is all lit up like a department store. All three of 'em got they headlights and brake lights on, so the street's all white and yellow and red, and Big Boy car is fire engine red, and the sky is black and purple now, with just a little bit of pink way over west, yonder where the sun done gone down. But this guy is still playing 'Chopsticks' on that horn. Big Boy holler, 'If you don't quit that racket, I'ma put my foot up your ass as far as your nose!' Well, that there just shell old Buster's peanuts. He scream out, 'Stomp on his ass, Big Boy!' Big Boy lean out the window and look over at us setting on the porch. He holler, 'That go for you, too, Buster. I'm tired of this shit every night. Ain't y'all got nothing else to do but set out on them motherfuckin' steps sellin' wolftickets?' But this fella is honkin' hard and strong now, and he don't pay Big Boy no mind. So Big Boy scream, 'You blowin' your own fu-

neral music, *chump!*' And he throwed open the door to
his Buick. But right about then I seen Miss Mary here
pull out of her spot and go *faward* 'bout three feet. I seen
that, 'cause my eyes got pull in that direction when her
brake lights went off and the red in the back of her car
went all yellow and white. Well, Big Boy leaves his motor runnin' and he jumps out of his car and slam the door.
Old Buster, settin' by me on the porch, he laugh and say
to me and May Francis, 'Now watch old Big Boy *bo*gart
this motherfucker. I ain't seed a Friday go by yet, he
don't floor somebody.' Buster was tellin' the truth. When
Big Boy round his car, his shoulders was hunched like he
was fixin' to clean him some house. The light was shinin'
on his brown uniform and that red Buick, and I tell you
the truth, you couldn't hardly tell the steel in that Buick
from the steel in him."

Here Winfield paused to sigh. "Sonofa*bitch!*" he said,
to no one in particular, "that there was a *night!* We just
set and watch and drunk our beer. People run out they
houses. Some throw up they windows. These bad kids
round here commence to sic Big Boy on. Well, this fella
warn't no dummy. He must of seen he didn't have a
Chinaman's chance 'gainst Big Boy. He cut his wheels
sharp and shoot out of that space like a shot. Fact is, he
just miss swattin' Big Boy as he wheel round that Buick.
Well, Big Boy rush back round his front end to get in his
car and go after the guy. But just then, who should I see
but Miss Mary here come back-backin' up real slow-like
into her old parkin' space. Well, just then *four* things happen, all at the same time. Them wild kids yell; Miss
Mary's brake lights come on fast and red; there was a real
loud *scrruunch!;* and Big Boy scream, 'Mother-*fuck!*' See,

Miss Mary here done back-back right into the side of his red Buick."

Milford sat transfixed. He leaned forward on the sofa, oblivious to anything but the big man in the brown seersucker suit standing quietly in the center of the room. He did not notice Mrs. Mary Farragot, seated in the armchair beneath the picture of Jesus, draw her crossed arms tighter about her breasts.

"*Now,*" Clarence Winfield continued, wetting his lips slowly, "now we come to the part *you* interested in. See, when Big Boy mad, he don't have no respect for *nobody!* He run over to Miss Mary's car, pull open the door, and commence to give her hell. Buster Williams spit on the sidewalk and said to us, 'Oh shit! Now they go'n be some *real* trouble. The one thing *nobody* can do is mess with Big Boy Buick. Me, I seen the time he near killt a guy for puttin' a dent in his *bumper,* so you know they's hell to pay now with the side all smash in. Somebody better run and call up the *po-*lice!' He nudge May Francis and she take and run up to her place to call up the law. And just in time, too. I heard Big Boy tell Miss Mary here, 'Woman, what the fuck you mean back-backin' into my car that way? If you was a man I'd kick your ass to kingdom come!' Lawd, he cuss this poor woman here somethin' awful . . ."

"Please, Clarence," Mrs. Farragot called from behind him. "Just get the thing told." She looked at Milford while saying this. "This man ain't got all day."

Milford said nothing. Nor did he allow his eyes to respond to Mrs. Farragot's searching expression. Instead, he kept his face turned toward the big man standing before him and touched his pencil to the paper on his lap.

Clarence Winfield smiled, as if the gesture had reas-

sured him. "Okay," he said, to no one in particular. "Me
and Buster run on over before Big Boy could swing on
Miss Mary here. Like I say, Big Boy don't much care
who he swing on when he gets mad. Poor Miss Mary here
just standin' there in her *pee*-jays, cryin' and carryin' on,
she so excited, and there was dogs barkin', and them wild
kids was runnin' round, whoopin' and hollerin' in the
floodlights of them two cars, and by this time the sky was
all black and purple with no pink. I tell you, man, it was
a sight. Buster, he run down the corner for more beer,
and Miss Bessie Mayfair, up the block, lean out her window and scream, '*Fish sandwiches! Hot fresh fish sandwiches*, just out the *pan!* Don't *rush*, they's *plenty. Fifty
cents!*' Miss Bessie don't miss a chance to make a dollar.
Anyway, 'long about then a squad car come screamin' up
with red and white lights flashin', and it screech to a stop
right 'longside Big Boy's red Buick, and this white cop
lean out the window and holler, 'Stand back! Don't nobody touch the body. The law is here to take *charge!*' Big
Boy push me away from him and look at that cop. He
stare him dead in the face and say, 'Drop dead yourself,
creampuff!' Hot damn! That's what I heard him say. That
street was all lit up like a department store, with red and
white lights flashin' on all them people in blue and brown
and pink clothes. Lawd, it was a sight! But even in all
them lights I saw this white cop turn red in the face; his
own strobe lights made his face look like it was bleedin'. I
seen that. I seen the driver get out of the car. It was a
colored fellow, and he walk like he was ready to do somebody in. He walk up real close to Big Boy and look him
dead in the eye. He say, real cool-like, 'What it is, feller?'
And Big Boy say, 'Plenty! This here woman done *ruin* my
Buick Electra with *push*-button drive and *black leather*

bucket seats! There ain't a worser thing that could of happen to me.' So the colored cop begin to question Miss Mary. She was so mad and angry and cryin' so much I guess he thought she was drunk, 'cause he ask her to walk the line. He just walk over to the sidewalk and point the toe of his shoe to a crack. Well, Miss Mary here look at him and say, 'No. No, *sah*. N-O. *Naw!*' That's what I recollect she said. Then I heard him tell her the law was writ so that if she refuse she was bound to lose her license. Well, by this time there was so much commotion goin' on till I suspect Miss Mary here was too embarrassed to even *think* about walkin' no line. Folks was laughin', drinkin' beer, grabbin' for fish sandwiches and raisin' so much hell, till I reckon a private person like Miss Mary here would rather lose her license than walk the line in her *pee*-jays. So she refuse. Well, them two cops put her in the car and taken her off to jail. Like I said, I seen it all, and I done told you the truth of all I seen. And I'm ready anytime to go down and tell the same thing to the judge."

Milford completed his notes. He had scribbled sporadically during the recitation. Now he looked up at Clarence Winfield, who shifted impatiently as though confirming his eagerness to be on his way downtown. Then he looked at Mrs. Mary Farragot, still seated in the armchair behind Winfield, her arms locked tightly across her breasts. "His story corroborates yours in all essential details," Milford called to her.

"Of course it do," Mrs. Farragot answered. "That ain't the problem." She shrugged, "The problem is how in the *hell* can I tell a white judge something like all that Clarence just said without being thrown out of court?" She paused and sighed, raising her head so that her hair almost touched the edge of the picture frame. "What I wanted me in the first place," Mrs. Farragot added slowly, "was a white boy that could make some *logic* out of all that."

Now both she and Winfield looked imploringly at Corliss Milford.

II

At 1:45 P.M. the three of them sat waiting outside the hearing room of the Department of Motor Vehicles. During the drive downtown, Milford had attempted to think through the dimensions of the situation; now he decided that Mrs. Farragot had been right all along. Since this was not a jury case, there was no way a judge would allow Clarence Winfield to tell his version of the story. As Mrs. Farragot had anticipated, any defense she offered would have to be confined to the facts. Milford cast a sideways glance at the woman seated on the bench beside him, with new appreciation of her relative sophistication. In the car she had disclosed that she did domestic work for a suburban stockbroker; from listening in on conversations between the broker and his wife, she would have discerned how a bureaucracy, and the people who made it function, must of necessity be restricted to the facts. And as colorful as were the circumstances of her case, there was not the slightest possibility that any responsible lawyer could include them in her defense.

A pity, too, Milford thought, turning his gaze to Clarence Winfield. Despite the imprecision of his language, the man possessed a certain rough style. He watched Winfield pacing the waxed tile floor of the corridor. The black man had put on his tie now, but because of the excessive heat, allowed it to hang loosely about his red collar. At one point, with Milford looking on, Winfield lifted his right foot and polished the pointed toe of his shoe against the cloth of his left trouser leg. When he saw Milford watching, Winfield grinned. A pity, the lawyer concluded. Now he would have to restrict the man's statement to yes or no answers to specific questions. He motioned for Winfield to come over to the bench. "Now listen," Milford said, "when you talk to the hearing officer restrict your statement to the *last* part of your story, the part about her *not* being drunk when she was arrested. You understand?"

Clarence Winfield nodded slyly.

"And don't volunteer anything, please. I'll ask all the questions."

Winfield nodded again.

"Do like he tell you now, Clarence, hear?" Mrs. Farragot said, leaning sideways on the bench. "Don't mess up things for me in front of that man in there." Then she said to Milford, "Clarence one of them from down-home. He tend to talk around a point."

"Ah hell!" Winfield said, and was about to say more when the door to the hearing room opened and a voice called, "Mary Farragot?"

It was a woman's voice.

The lawyer stood. "I'm representing Mrs. Farragot," he said. "I'm with Brown and Barlow's Project Gratis."

"Well, we're ready," the woman called, and she stepped out into the corridor. She was short and plump, but not unattractive in a dark green pantsuit. Her silver blond hair was cut short. Dark eyelashes, painted, Milford suspected, accentuated her pink face. "I'm Hearing Officer Harriet Wilson," she announced.

As she stood holding open the door, Milford noticed Mrs. Farragot staring intently at Hearing Officer Harriet Wilson. The expression on her face was one he had not seen before. Suddenly he remembered the photograph of Mrs. Farragot on her plywood coffee table, and the expression seemed more familiar. He touched her shoulder and whispered, "Let's go on in." They filed into the hearing room, Mrs. Farragot leading and Clarence Winfield bringing up the rear. Over his shoulder, Milford saw the hearing officer sniffing the air as she shut the door. The room was humid. Over on the windowsill a single electric fan rotated wearily, blowing more humid air into the small place. They seated themselves in metal chairs around a dark brown hardwood table. Only Hearing Officer Harriet Wilson remained standing.

"Now," Hearing Officer Wilson said, "we're ready to begin." She smiled around the table pleasantly, her eyes coming to rest on the red silk handkerchief flowering out of Clarence Winfield's coat pocket. It seemed to fascinate her. "Now," she said again, moving her eyes slowly away from the handkerchief, "I'll get the complaining officer and we'll begin." She moved toward a glass door at the back of the room.

"Lawyer Milford," Mrs. Farragot whispered, as the glass door opened and shut. She tugged his coat. "Lawyer Milford, I thought it was men that handled these hearings."

Milford shrugged. "Times change," he answered.

Mrs. Farragot considered this. She glanced at the glass door, then at Winfield seated on her right. "Tell you what, Lawyer Milford," she said suddenly. "Actually,

Clarence don't do too bad when he talk. Maybe you ought to let him tell his story after all."

"I thought we had already agreed on procedure," the lawyer muttered. He found himself irritated by the mysterious look that had again appeared in Mrs. Farragot's eyes. She looked vaguely amused. "We can't change now," he told her.

"Miss Mary," Winfield volunteered, "I can't tell it exactly like I did before."

"Clarence, that don't matter, long as you hit on the facts. Ain't that right?" she asked Milford.

He had no choice but to nod agreement.

"Good," Mrs. Farragot said. She straightened in her chair and brushed her hand lightly across her sweating forehead.

It seemed to Milford she was smiling openly now.

Hearing Officer Harriet Wilson reentered the room. Behind her, carrying a bulky tape recorder, stepped the arresting officer. He was a tall, olive-brown-skinned man who moved intently in a light gray summer suit. Cool dignity flashed in his dark brown eyes; his broad nose twitched, seeming to sniff the air. He placed the recorder on the table near Hearing Officer Wilson's chair, then seated himself at the head of the table. He crossed his legs casually. Then he gazed at the three seated on his right and said, "Officer Otis S. Smothers."

"How do?" Winfield called across the table.

Milford nodded curtly.

Mrs. Farragot said nothing. Her eyes were fixed on the tape recorder.

Hearing Officer Harriet Wilson noticed her staring and said, "This is not a jury matter, dear. At this hearing all we do is tape all relevant testimony and forward it on to the central officer at the state capital. The boys up there make the final decision."

Milford felt a knee press against his under the table. "I should of knowed," Mrs. Farragot whispered beside him. "Won't be long they gonna give you a lie detector and railroad you that way."

Milford shushed her into silence.

From the head of the table Officer Smothers seemed to be studying them, quiet amusement playing at the corners of his plump lips.

Officer Wilson placed a finger on the record button and looked around the table. Milford felt Mrs. Farragot tense beside him. A desperate warmth seemed to exude from her body. Officer Wilson smiled cheerily at Clarence Winfield, but sobered considerably as her eyes came to rest on Officer Smothers. She pressed the record button. After reciting the date and case record into the microphone, she swore in the parties. Then she motioned for Officer Smothers to make his statement.

It seemed to Milford that Smothers, while taking his oath, had raised his right hand a bit higher than had Mrs. Farragot and Winfield. Now he told his version of the story, presenting a minor masterpiece of exactness and economy. His vocabulary was precise, his delivery flawless. When he reached the part of his testimony concerning the sobriety test, he pulled a sheet of paper from his coat pocket and recited, ". . . Suspect was informed of her legal obligation to submit to the test. Suspect's reply was—" and he touched a lean brown finger to the page "—'I ain't go'n do *nothin'!*'" These words, delivered in comic imitation of a whine, stung Milford's ears. Even Mrs. Farragot, he noticed, winced at the sound. And Clarence Winfield, slouching in his chair, looked sheepish and threatened. To Milford the action seemed especially cruel when Smothers looked over at Hearing Officer Wilson and said in crisp, perfect English, "That's all I have to say," as though he intended to end the recital of facts without any account of his own response to Mrs. Farragot's refusal. Milford watched Smothers as he leaned back in his chair, looking just a bit self-righteous.

"If you have no questions," Hearing Officer Harriet Wilson said to Milford. Her finger was already on the off button of the recorder.

"You *did* offer her a test, then?" Milford asked, stalling for time to reconsider his position.

"Of course," Smothers replied, his fingers meshed, his hands resting professionally on his knee.

"And you had already concluded there was probable cause to believe she was drunk?"

"Certainly."

"How?"

"Her breath, her heavy breathing, and her slurred speech."

"Could you have mistaken a Southern accent for slurred speech?"

"No, I couldn't have," Smothers answered nonchalantly. "I'm from the South myself."

Across the table, Hearing Officer Harriet Wilson smiled to herself. Her finger tapped the metal casing just above the off button on the recorder.

"Let me say something here," Clarence Winfield interrupted. "I was there. I seen the whole thing. It warn't like that at all."

Hearing Officer Wilson looked at Winfield out of the

corner of her eye. "Do you want this witness to testify now?" she asked Milford.

But before the lawyer could answer, he felt the pressure of Mrs. Farragot's hand on his shoulder. Looking up, he saw her standing over him. "No'm, thank you," he heard her say in a voice very much unlike her own. She was facing Hearing Officer Wilson, but looking directly at the recorder. Her face was expressionless. Only her voice betrayed emotion. "I'm innocent," Mrs. Farragot began. "But who go'n believe me, who go'n take my word against the word of that officer? Both of us black, but he ain't bothering hisself with that, and I ain't concerning myself with it, either. But I do say I'm innocent of the charges he done level against me. The night this thing happen I was inside my house in my pajamas, minding my own business. I wasn't even *fixing* to drive no car . . ."

She told her side of the story.

While she talked, in a slow, precise tone, Milford watched the two officers. It was obvious that Hearing Officer Harriet Wilson was deeply moved; she kept her eyes lowered to the machine. But Officer Smothers seemed impervious to the woman's pleadings. His meshed fingers remained propped on his knee; his eyes wandered coolly about the room. At one point he lifted his left hand to rub the side of his nose.

When Mrs. Farragot had finished speaking, she eased down into her chair. No on spoke for almost a minute; the only sounds in the room were the soft buzz of the recorder and the hum of the window fan. Then Clarence Winfield cleared his throat noisily. Officer Harriet Wilson jumped.

"Tell me something, Officer Smothers," Milford said, "If you did offer a test, which one was it?"

"I asked her to walk the line, as both of us have already testified," Smothers answered.

"That was the only test you offered?"

"That's right," Smothers said in a tired voice.

"But doesn't the statute provide that a suspect has the right to choose one of *three* tests: *either* the breathalyzer, the blood or the urine? As I read the statute, there's nothing about walking the line."

"I suppose that's right," Officer Smothers said.

"Are you authorized to choose, arbitrarily, a test of your own devising?"

"My choice was *not* arbitrary!" Smothers protested. "The policy is to use that one on the scene. Usually, the others are given down at the station."

Now Milford relaxed. He smiled teasingly at the olive-skinned oficer. "*Was* this lady offered one of the other tests down at the station before being booked?"

"I don't really know," the officer answered. "I didn't stay around after filing the report."

Milford turned to Mrs. Farragot, new confidence cooling his words. "*Were* you offered any other tests?"

"No, suh," she said quietly, her voice almost breaking. "They didn't offer me nothing in front of my house and they didn't offer me nothing down to the jail. They just taken me in a cell in my pajamas."

"We've had enough," Hearing Officer Harriet Wilson said. Her pink face seemed both sad and amused. She pressed the off button. "You'll hear from the board within thirty days," she called across the table to Mrs. Farragot. "In the meantime, you can retain your license."

They all stood abruptly. Milford smiled openly at Officer Smothers, noting with considerable pleasure the man's hostile glare. Milford offered his hand. They barely touched palms. Then the lawyer took Mrs. Farragot's arm and steered her toward the door. Clarence Winfield came behind, tearing off his tie. Just before Winfield closed the door, Hearing Officer Harriet Wilson's voice came floating after them on the moist heat of the room: "Otis, tell the boys that in the future . . ."

Milford and Clarence Winfield waited by the bench while Mrs. Farragot rushed down the corridor toward the ladies' room. Winfield walked around, adjusting his trousers. Milford felt pleased with himself. He had taken command of a chaotic situation and forced it to a logical outcome. He had imposed order. Absently, he followed Clarence Winfield over to the water fountain and waited while Winfield refreshed himself. "This meant a lot to her," Milford observed.

Winfield kept a stiff thumb on the metal button. The cold water splashed his brown cheek, as he turned his face upward and nodded agreement. "Yeah," he said. "Many's the time I told Miss Mary about that drinkin'."

In his imagination Milford had long conceded the possibility of a beer. But what was that on a hot night? He now said this to Winfield, as he bent to drink.

Clarence Winfield chuckled. "Man, Miss Mary don't drink no *beer!*" He leaned close to Milford's ear. "She don't drink nothin' but Maker's Mark." He laughed again. "I thought you *knowed* that."

Turning his head, Milford saw Mrs. Farragot coming up the hall. Her blue dress swished gaily. It seemed to him that she was strutting. He observed for certain that she was smiling broadly, not unlike the picture of her next to Sweet Willie on the coffee table in her home.

Clarence Winfield nudged him, causing the cold water to splash into his eyes. "Don't you pay it no mind," Winfield was saying. "Between you and me, why, we ought to be able to straighten her out."

The Story of a Scar

S INCE Dr. Wayland was late and there were no recent newsmagazines in the waiting room, I turned to the other patient and said: "As a concerned person, and as your brother, I ask you, without meaning to offend, how did you get that scar on the side of your face?"

The woman seemed insulted. Her brown eyes, which before had been wandering vacuously about the room, narrowed suddenly and sparked humbling reprimands at me. She took a draw on her cigarette, puckered her lips, and blew a healthy stream of smoke toward my face. It was a mean action, deliberately irreverent and cold. The long curving scar on the left side of her face darkened. "I ask *you*," she said, "as a nosy person with no connections in your family, how come your nose is all bandaged up?"

It was a fair question, considering the possible returns on its answer. Dr. Wayland would remove the bandages as soon as he came in. I would not be asked again. A man lacking permanence must advertise. "An accident of passion," I told her. "I smashed it against the headboard of my bed while engaged in the act of love."

Here she laughed, but not without intimating, through heavy, broken chuckles, some respect for my candor and the delicate cause of my affliction. This I could tell from the way the hardness mellowed in her voice. Her appetites were whetted. She looked me up and down, almost approvingly, and laughed some more. This was a robust woman, with firm round legs and considerable chest. I am small. She laughed her appreciation. Finally, she lifted a brown palm to her face, wiping away tears. "You *cain't* be no married man," she observed. "A wife ain't worth *that* much."

I nodded.

"I knowed it," she said. "The best mens don't git married. They do they fishin' in goldfish bowls."

"I am no adulterer," I cautioned her. "I find companionship wherever I can."

She quieted me by throwing out her arm in a suggestion of offended modesty. She scraped the cigarette on the white tile beneath her foot. "You don't have to tell me a thing," she said. "I know mens goin' and comin'. There ain't a-one of you I'd trust to take my grandmama to Sunday school." Here she paused, seemingly lost in some morbid reflection, her eyes wandering across the room to Dr. Wayland's frosted glass door. The solemnity of the waiting room reclaimed us. We inhaled the antiseptic fumes that wafted from the inner office. We breathed deeply together, watching the door, waiting. "Not a-one," my companion said softly, her dark eyes wet.

The scar still fascinated me. It was a wicked black mark that ran from her brow down over her left eyelid, skirting her nose but curving over and through both lips before ending almost exactly in the center of her chin. The scar was thick and black and crisscrossed with a network of old stitch patterns, as if some meticulous madman had first attempted to carve a perfect half-circle in her flesh, and then decided to embellish his handiwork. It was so grotesque a mark that one had the feeling it was the art of no human hand and could be peeled off like so much soiled putty. But this was a surgeon's office and the scar was real. It was as real as the honey-blond wig she wore, as real as her purple pantsuit. I studied her approvingly. Such women have a natural leaning toward the abstract expression of themselves. Their styles have private meaning, advertise secret distillations of their souls. Their figures, and their disfigurations, make meaningful statements. Subjectively, this woman was the true sister of the man who knows how to look while driving a purple Cadillac. Such craftsmen must be approached with subtlety if they are to be deciphered. "I've never seen a scar quite like that one," I began, glancing at my watch. Any minute Dr. Wayland would arrive and take off my bandages, removing me permanently from access to her sympathies. "Do you mind talking about what happened?"

"I *knowed* you'd git back around to that," she answered, her brown eyes cruel and level with mine. "Black guys like you with them funny eyeglasses are a real trip. You got to know everything. You sit in corners and watch people." She brushed her face, then wiped her palm on the leg of her pantsuit. "I read you the minute you walk in here."

"As your brother..." I began.

"How can you be my brother when your mama's a man?" she said.

We both laughed.

"I was pretty once," she began, sniffing heavily. "When I was sixteen my mama's preacher was set to leave his wife and his pulpit and run off with me to *Dee*troit City. Even with this scar and all the weight I done put on, you can still see what I had." She paused. *"Cain't* you?" she asked significantly.

I nodded quickly, looking into her big body for the miniature of what she was.

From this gesture she took assurance. "I was twenty when it happen," she went on. "I had me a good job in the post office, down to the Tenth Street branch. I was a sharp dresser, too, and I had me my choice of mens: big ones, puny ones, old mens, married mens, even D. B. Ferris, my shift supervisor, was after me on the sly—don't let these white mens fool you. He offered to take me off the primaries and turn me on to a desk job in hand-stampin' or damaged mail. But I had my pride. I told him I rather work the facin' table, *every shift,* than put myself in his debt. I shook my finger in his face and said, 'You ain't foolin' me, with your *sly self!* I know where the *wild goose went;* and if you don't start havin' some *respect* for black women, he go'n come *back!*' So then he turn red in the face and put me on the facin' table. Every shift. What could I do? You ain't got no rights in the post office, no matter what lies the government tries to tell you. But I was makin' good money, dressin' bad, and I didn't want to start no trouble for myself. Besides, in them days there was a bunch of good people workin' my shift: Leroy Boggs, Red Bone, 'Big Boy' Tyson, Freddy May . . ."

"What about that scar?" I interrupted her tiresome ramblings. "Which one of them cut you?"

Her face flashed a wall of brown fire. "This here's *my* story!" she muttered, eyeing me up and down with suspi-

cion. "You dudes cain't stand to hear the whole of anything. You want everything broke down in little pieces."
And she waved a knowing brown finger. "That's how
come you got your nose all busted up. There's some
things you have to take your time about."

Again I glanced at my watch, but was careful to nod
silent agreement with her wisdom. "It was my boyfriend
that caused it," she continued in a slower, more cautious
tone. "And the more I look at you the more I can see you
just like him. He had that same way of sittin' with his legs
crossed, squeezin' his sex juices up to his brains. His
name was Billy Crawford, and he worked the parcel-post
window down to the Tenth Street branch. He was nine
years older than me and was goin' to school nights on the
GI Bill. I was twenty when I met him durin' lunch break
down in the swing room. He was sittin' at a table against
the wall, by hisself, eatin' a cheese sandwich with his nose
in a goddamn book. I didn't know any better then. I sat
down by him. He looked up at me and say, 'Water seeks
its own level, and people do, too. You are not one of the
riffraff or else you would of sit with them good-timers and
bullshitters 'cross the room. Welcome to my table.' By riffraff he meant all them other dudes and girls from the back
room, who believed in havin' a little fun playin' cards and
such durin' lunch hour. I thought what he said was kind
of funny, and so I laughed. But I should of knowed better. He give me a cheese sandwich and started right off
preachin' at me about the lowlife in the back room. Billy
couldn't stand none of 'em. He hated the way they
dressed, the way they talked, and the way they carried on
durin' work hours. He said if all them tried to be like him
and advanced themselfs, the Negro wouldn't have no

problems. He'd point out Eugene Wells or Red Bone or
Crazy Sammy Michaels and tell me, 'People like them
think they can homestead in the post office. They think
these primaries will need human hands for another twenty
years. But you just watch the Jews and Puerto Ricans
that pass through here. *They* know what's goin' on. I bet
you don't see none of them settin' up their beds under
these tables. They tryin' to improve themselfs and get out
of here, just like me.' Then he smile and held out his
hand. 'And since I see you're a smart girl that keeps a
cold eye and some distance on these bums, welcome to
the club. My name's Billy Crawford.'

"To tell you the truth, I liked him. He was different
from all the jive-talkers and finger-poppers I knew. I liked
him because he wasn't ashamed to wear a white shirt and
a black tie. I liked the way he always knew just what he
was gonna do next. I liked him because none of the other
dudes could stand him, and he didn't seem to care. On
our first date he took me out to a place where the white
waiters didn't git mad when they saw us comin'. That's
the kind of style he had. He knew how to order wine with
funny names, the kind you don't never see on billboards.
He held open doors for me, told me not to order rice
with gravy over it or soda water with my meal. I didn't
mind him helpin' me. He was a funny dude in a lot of
ways: his left leg was shot up in the war and he limped
sometimes, but it looked like he was struttin'. He would
stare down anybody that watched him walkin'. He told
me he had cut his wife loose after he got out of the army,
and he told me about some of the games she had run on
him. Billy didn't trust women. He said they all was after a
workin' man's money, but he said that I was different. He
said he could tell I was a God-fearin' woman and my

mama had raised me right, and he was gonna improve my
mind. In those days I didn't have no objections. Billy was
fond of sayin', 'You met me at the right time in your life.'

"But Red Bone, my co-worker, saw what was goin'
down and began to take a strong interest in the affair.
Red was the kind of strong-minded sister that mens just
like to give in to. She was one of them big yellow gals,
with red hair and a loud rap that could put a man in his
place by just soundin' on him. She like to wade through
the mail room, elbowin' dudes aside and sayin', 'You
don't wanna mess with *me*, fool! I'll *destroy* you! Anyway, you ain't nothin' but a dirty thought I had when I
was three years old!' But if she liked you she could be
warm and soft, like a mama. 'Listen,' she kept tellin' me,
'that Billy Crawford is a potential punk. The more I
watch him, the less man I see. Every time we downstairs
havin' fun I catch his eyeballs rollin' over us from behind
them goddamn books! There ain't a rhythm in his body,
and the only muscles he exercises is his eyes.'

"That kind of talk hurt me some, especially comin' from
her. But I know it's the way of some women to bad-
mouth a man they want for themselfs. And what woman
don't want a steady man and a good provider?—which is
what Billy was. Usually, when they start downgradin' a
steady man, you can be sure they up to somethin' else
besides lookin' out after you. So I told her, 'Billy don't
have no bad habits.' I told her, 'He's a hard worker, he
don't drink, smoke, nor run around, and he's gonna git a
college degree.' But that didn't impress Red. I was never
able to figure it out, but she had something in for Billy.
Maybe it was his attitude; maybe it was the little ways he
let everybody know that he was just passin' through;
maybe it was because Red had broke every man she ever

had and had never seen a man with no handholes on him. Because that Billy Crawford was a strong man. He worked the day shift, and could of been a supervisor in three or four years if he wanted to crawl a little and grease a few palms; but he did his work, quiet-like, pulled what overtime he could, and went to class three nights a week. On his day off he'd study and maybe take me out for a drink after I got off. Once or twice a week he might let me stay over at his place, but most of the time he'd take me home to my Aunt Alvene's, where I was roomin' in those days, before twelve o'clock.

"To tell the truth, I didn't really miss the partyin' and the dancin' and the good-timin' until Red and some of the others started avoidin' me. Down in the swing room durin' lunch hour, for example, they wouldn't wave for me to come over and join a card game. Or when Leroy Boggs went around to the folks on the floor of the mail room, collectin' money for a party, he wouldn't even ask me to put a few dollars in the pot. He'd just smile at me in a cold way and say to somebody loud enough for me to hear, 'No, sir; ain't no way you can git quality folk to come out to a Saturday night fish fry.'

"Red squared with me when I asked her what was goin' down. She told me, 'People sayin' you been wearin' a high hat since you started goin' with the professor. The talk is you been throwin' around big words and developin' a strut just like his. Now I don't believe these reports, being your friend and sister, but I do think you oughta watch your step. I remember what my grandmama used to tell me: "It don't make no difference how well you fox-trot if everybody else is dancin' the two-step." Besides, that Billy Crawford is a potential punk, and you

gonna be one lonely girl when somebody finally turns him
out. Use your mind, girl, and stop bein' silly. Everybody
is watchin' you!'

"I didn't say nothin', but what Red said started me to
thinkin' harder than I had ever thought before. Billy had
been droppin' strong hints that we might git married after
he got his degree, in two or three years. He was plannin'
on being a high school teacher. But outside of being married to a teacher, what was I go'n git out of it? Even if we
did git married, I was likely to be stuck right there in the
post office with no friends. And if he didn't marry me, or
if he was a punk like Red believed, then I was a real
dummy for givin' up my good times and my best days for
a dude that wasn't go'n do nothin' for me. I didn't make
up my mind right then, but I begin to watch Billy Crawford with a different kind of eye. I'd just turn around at
certain times and catch him in his routines: readin',
workin', eatin', runnin' his mouth about the same things
all the time. Pretty soon I didn't have to watch him to
know what he was doin'. He was more regular than Monday mornings. That's when a woman begins to tip. It ain't
never a decision, but somethin' in you starts to lean over
and practice what you gonna say whenever another man
bumps into you at the right time. Some women, especially
married ones, like to tell lies to their new boyfriends; if
the husband is a hard worker and a good provider, they'll
tell the boyfriend that he's mean to them and ain't no
good when it comes to sex; and if he's good with sex,
they'll say he's a cold dude that's not concerned with the
problems of the world like she is, or that they got married
too young. Me, I believe in tellin' the truth: that Billy
Crawford was too good for most of the women in this

world, me included. He deserved better, so I started lookin' round for somebody on my own level.

"About this time a sweet-talkin' young dude was transferred to our branch from the 39th Street substation. The grapevine said it was because he was makin' woman trouble over there and caused too many fights. I could see why. He dressed like he was settin' fashions every day; wore special-made bell-bottoms with so much flare they looked like they was starched. He wore two diamond rings on the little finger of his left hand that flashed while he was throwin' mail, and a gold tooth that sparkled all the time. His name was Teddy Johnson, but they called him 'Eldorado' because that was the kind of hog he drove. He was involved in numbers and other hustles and used the post office job for a front. He was a strong talker, a easy walker, that dude was a *woman* stalker! I have to give him credit. He was the last *true* son of the Great McDaddy—"

"Sister," I said quickly, overwhelmed suddenly by the burden of insight. "I *know* the man of whom you speak. There is no time for this gutter-patter and indirection. Please, for my sake and for your own, avoid stuffing the shoes of the small with mythic homilies. This man was a bum, a hustler and a small-time punk. He broke up your romance with Billy, then he lived off you, cheated on you, and cut you when you confronted him." So pathetic and gross seemed her elevation of the fellow that I abandoned all sense of caution. "Is your mind so *dead*," I continued, "did his switchblade slice so *deep*, do you have so little *respect* for yourself, or at least for the idea of *proportion* in this sad world, that you'd sit here and *praise* this brute!?"

She lit a second cigarette. Then, dropping the match to the floor, she seemed to shudder, to struggle in contention with herself. I sat straight on the blue plastic couch, waiting. Across the room the frosted glass door creaked, as if about to open; but when I looked, I saw no telling shadow behind it. My companion crossed her legs and held back her head, blowing two thoughtful streams of smoke from her broad nose. I watched her nervously, recognizing the evidence of past destructiveness, yet fearing the imminent occurrence of more. But it was not her temper or the potential strength of her fleshy arms that I feared. Finally she sighed, her face relaxed, and she wet her lips with the tip of her tongue. "You know everything," she said in a soft tone, much unlike her own. "A black mama birthed you, let you suck her titty, cleaned your dirty drawers, and you still look at us through paper and movie plots." She paused, then continued in an even softer and more controlled voice. "Would you believe me if I said that Teddy Johnson loved me, that this scar is to him what a weddin' ring is to another man? Would you believe that he was a better man than Billy?"

I shook my head in firm disbelief.

She seemed to smile to herself, although the scar, when she grimaced, made the expression more like a painful frown. "Then would you believe that I was the cause of Billy Crawford goin' crazy and not gettin' his college degree?"

I nodded affirmation.

"Why?" she asked.

"Because," I answered, "from all I know already, that would seem to be the most likely consequence. I would expect the man to have been destroyed by the pressures placed on him. And, although you are my sister and a

woman who has already suffered greatly, I must condemn
you and your roughneck friends for this destruction of a
man's ambitions."

Her hardened eyes measured my face. She breathed
heavily, seeming to grow larger and rounder on the red
chair. "My brother," she began in an icy tone, "is as far
from what you are as I am from being patient." Now her
voice became deep and full, as if aided suddenly by some
intricately controlled wellspring of pain. Something aristocratic and old and frighteningly wise seemed to have
awakened in her face. "Now this is the way it happened,"
she fired at me, her eyes wide and rolling. "I want you to
write it on whatever part of your brain that ain't already
covered with page print. I want you to *remember* it every
time you stare at a scarred-up sister on the street, and
choke on it before you can work up spit to condemn her.
I was *faithful* to that Billy Crawford. As faithful as a
woman could be to a man that don't ever let up or lean
back and stop worryin' about where he's gonna be ten
years from last week. Life is to be *lived*, not traded on
like *dollars!* . . . All that time I was goin' with him, my
feets itched to dance, my ears hollered to hear somethin'
besides that whine in his voice, my body wanted to press
up against somethin' besides that facin' table. I was young
and pretty; and what woman don't want to enjoy what she
got while she got it? Look around sometime: there ain't
no mens, young nor old, chasin' *no older womens*, no
matter how pretty they *used to be!* But Billy Crawford
couldn't see nothin' besides them *goddamn books* in front
of his face. And what the Jews and Puerto Ricans was
doin'. Whatever else Teddy Johnson was, he was a dude
that knowed how to live. He wasn't out to *destroy* life,
you can believe *that!* Sure I listened to his rap. Sure I give

him the come-on. With Billy workin' right up front and watchin' everything, Teddy was the only dude on the floor that would talk to me. Teddy would say, 'A girl that's got what you got needs a man that have what I have.' And that ain't all he said, either!

"Red Bone tried to push me closer to him, but I am not a sneaky person and didn't pay her no mind. She'd say, 'Girl, I think you and Eldorado ought to git it on. There ain't a better lookin' dude workin' in the post office. Besides, you ain't goin' *nowheres* with that professor Billy Crawford. And if *you* scared to tell him to lean up off you, I'll do it *myself*, bein' as I am your sister and the one with your interest in mind.' But I said to her, 'Don't do me no favors. No matter what you think of Billy, I am no sneaky woman. I'll handle my own affairs.' Red just grin and look me straight in the eye and grin some more. I already told you she was the kind of strong-minded sister that could look right down into you. Nobody but a woman would understand what she was lookin' at.

"Now Billy wasn't no dummy durin' all this time. Though he worked the parcel-post window up front, from time to time durin' the day he'd walk back in the mail room and check out what was goin' down. Or else he'd sit back and listen to the gossip durin' lunch hour, down in the swing room. He must of seen Teddy Johnson hangin' round me, and I know he seen Teddy give me the glad-eye a few times. Billy didn't say nothin' for a long time, but one day he pointed to Teddy and told me, 'See that fellow over there? He's a bloodletter. There's some people with a talent for stoppin' bleedin' by just being around, and there's others that start it the same way. When you see that greasy smile of his you can bet it's soon gonna be a bad day for somebody, if they ain't careful. That kind of fellow's been walkin' free for too long.' He looked at me with that tight mouth and them cold brown eyes of his. He said, 'You know what I mean?' I said I didn't. He said, 'I hope you don't ever have to find out.'

"It was D. B. Ferris, my shift supervisor, that set up things. He's the same dude I told you about, the one that was gonna give me the happy hand. We never saw much of him in the mail room, although he was kinda friendly with Red Bone. D. B. Ferris was always up on the ramps behind one of the wall slits, checkin' out everything that went down on the floor and tryin' to catch somebody snitchin' a letter. There ain't no tellin' how much he knew about private things goin' on. About this time he up and transferred three or four of us, the ones with no seniority, to the night shift. There was me, Red, and Leroy Boggs. When Billy found out he tried to talk D. B. Ferris into keepin' me on the same shift as his, but Ferris come to me and I told him I didn't mind. And I didn't. I told him I was tired of bein' watched by him and everybody else. D. B. Ferris looked up toward the front where Billy was workin' and smiled that old smile of his. Later, when Billy asked me what I said, I told him there wasn't no use tryin' to fight the government. 'That's true,' he told me— and I thought I saw some meanness in his eyes—'but there are some other things you can fight,' he said. At that time my head was kinda light, and I didn't catch what he meant.

"About my second day on the night shift, Teddy Johnson began workin' overtime. He didn't need the money and didn't like to work nohow, but some nights around ten or eleven, when we clocked out for lunch and sat around in the swing room, in would strut Teddy. Billy would be in school or at home. Usually, I'd be sittin' with

Red and she'd tell me things while Teddy was walkin' over. 'Girl, it *must* be love to make a dude like Eldorado work overtime. *He* needs to work like *I* need to be a Catholic.' Then Teddy would sit down and she'd commence to play over us like her life depended on gittin' us together. She'd say, 'Let's go over to my place this mornin' when we clock out. I got some bacon and eggs and a bottle of Scotch.' Teddy would laugh and look in my eyes and say, 'Red, we don't wanna cause no trouble for this here fine young thing, who I hear is engaged to a college man.' Then I'd laugh with them and look at Teddy and wouldn't say nothin' much to nobody.

"Word must of gotten back to Billy soon after that. He didn't say nothin' at first, but I could see a change in his attitude. All this time I was tryin' to git up the guts to tell Billy I was thinkin' about breaking off, but I just couldn't. It wasn't that I thought he needed me; I just knew he was the kind of dude that doesn't let a girl decide when somethin' is over. Bein' as much like Billy as you are, you must understand what I'm tryin' to say. On one of my nights off, when we went out to a movie, he asked, 'What time did you get in this mornin'?' I said, 'Five-thirty, same as always.' But I was lyin'. Red and me had stopped for breakfast on the way home. Billy said, 'I called you at six-thirty this morning, and your Aunt Alvene said you was still out.' I told him, 'She must of been too sleepy to look in my room.' He didn't say more on the subject, but later that evenin', after the movie, he said, 'I was in the war for two years. It made me a disciplined man, and I hope I don't ever have to lose my temper.' I didn't say nothin', but the cold way he said it was like a window shade flappin' up from in front of his true nature, and I was scared.

"It was three years ago this September twenty-second that the thing happened. It was five-thirty in the mornin'. We had clocked out at four-forty-five, but Red had brought a bottle of Scotch to work, and we was down in the swing room drinkin' a little with our coffee, just to relax. I'll tell you the truth: Teddy Johnson was there, too. He had come down just to give us a ride home. I'll never forget that day as long as I live. Teddy was dressed in a pink silk shirt with black ruffles on the sleeves, the kind that was so popular a few years ago. He was wearin' shiny black bell-bottoms that hugged his little hips like a second coat of skin, and looked like pure silk when he walked. He sat across from me, flashin' those diamond rings every time he poured more Scotch in our cups. Red was sittin' back with a smile on her face, watchin' us like a cat that had just ate.

"I was sittin' with my back to the door and didn't know anything, until I saw something change in Red's face. I still see it in my sleep at night. Her face seemed to light up and git scared and happy at the same time. She was lookin' behind me, over my shoulder, with all the smartness in the world burnin' in her eyes. I turned around. Billy Crawford was standin' right behind me with his hands close to his sides. He wore a white shirt and a thin black tie, and his mouth was tight like a little slit. He said, 'It's time for you to go home,' with that voice of his that was too cold to be called just mean. I sat there lookin' up at him. Red's voice was even colder. She said to me, 'You gonna let him order you around like that?' I didn't say nothin'. Red said to Teddy, 'Ain't *you* got something to say about this?' Teddy stood up slow and swelled out his chest. He said, 'Yeah. I got somethin' to say,' looking hard at Billy. But Billy just kept lookin'

down at me. 'Let's go,' he said. 'What you got to say?'
Red Bone said to Teddy. Teddy said to me, 'Why don't
you tell the dude, baby?' But I didn't say nothin'. Billy
shifted his eyes to Teddy and said, 'I got nothing against
you. You ain't real, so you don't matter. You been strutting the streets too long, but that ain't my business. So
keep out of this.' Then he looked down at me again.
'Let's go,' he said. I looked up at the way his lips curled
and wanted to cry and hit him at the same time. I felt like
a trigger bein' pulled. Then I heard Red sayin', 'Why
don't you go back to bed with them *goddamn books,
punk!* And leave decent folks *alone!*' For the first time
Billy glanced over at her. His mouth twitched. But then
he looked at me again. 'This here's the *last time* I'm
asking,' he said. That's when I exploded and started to
jump up. 'I ain't goin' *nowhere!*' I screamed. The last
plain thing I remember was tryin' to git to his face, but it
seemed to turn all bright and silvery and hot, and then I
couldn't see nothin' no more.

"They told me later that he sliced me so fast there
wasn't time for nobody to act. By the time Teddy jumped
across the table I was down, and Billy had stabbed me
again in the side. Then him and Teddy tussled over the
knife, while me and Red screamed and screamed. Then
Teddy went down holdin' his belly, and Billy was comin'
after me again, when some of the dudes from the freight
dock ran in and grabbed him. They say it took three of
them to drag him off me, and all the time they was pullin'
him away he kept slashin' out at me with that knife. It
seemed like all the walls was screamin' and I was floatin'
in water, and I thought I was dead and in hell, because I
felt hot and prickly all over, and I could hear some

woman's voice that might of been mine screamin' over and over, 'You devil! . . . You *devil!*' "

She lit a third cigarette. She blew a relieving cloud of smoke downward. The thin white haze billowed about her purple legs, dissipated, and vanished. A terrifying fog of silence and sickness crept into the small room, and there was no longer the smell of medicine. I dared not steal a glance at my watch, although by this time Dr. Wayland was agonizingly late. I had heard it all, and now I waited. Finally her eyes fixed on the frosted glass door. She wet her lips again and, in a much slower and pained voice, said, "This here's the third doctor I been to see. The first one stitched me up like a turkey and left this scar. The second one refused to touch me." She paused and wet her lips again. "This man fixed your nose for you," she said softly. "Do you think he could do somethin' about this scar?"

I searched the end table next to my couch for a newsmagazine, carefully avoiding her face. "Dr. Wayland is a skilled man," I told her. "Whenever he's not late. I think he may be able to do something for you."

She sighed heavily and seemed to tremble. "I don't expect no miracle or nothin'," she said. "If he could just fix the part around my eye I wouldn't expect nothin' else. People say the rest don't look too bad."

I clutched a random magazine and did not answer. Nor did I look at her. The flesh around my nose began to itch, and I looked toward the inner office door with the most extreme irritation building in me. At that moment it seemed a shadow began to form behind the frosted glass, signaling perhaps the approach of someone. I resolved to put aside all notions of civility and go into the office before her, as was my right. The shadow behind the door darkened, but vanished just as suddenly. And then I remembered the most important question, without which the entire exchange would have been wasted. I turned to the woman, now drawn together in the red plastic chair, as if struggling to sleep in a cold bed. "Sister," I said, careful to maintain a casual air. "Sister . . . what is your name?"

I Am an American

IT was not the kind of service one would expect, considering the quality of the hotel. At eight o'clock both Eunice and I were awakened by a heavy pounding on the door of our room that sounded once, loud and authoritatively, then decreased into what seemed a series of pulsing echoes. I staggered across the dirty rug, feeling loose grit underfoot, and opened the door. Halfway down the hall a rotund little man, seeming no more than a blur of blue suit and red tie, was pounding steadily on another door and shouting, "American girlies, wake up! Breakfast!"

"Telephone?" I called to him.

"Breakfast!" he shouted cheerily, turning his face only slightly in my direction. I could not see the details of his face, although it seemed to me his nose was large and red, and his hair was close-cropped and iron gray. For some reason, perhaps because of the way his suit was cut, I nursed the intuition that he was a Bulgarian; although there are many other eastern Europeans who wear the same loose style of suit. Just then the door before him opened. "Breakfast, American girlies!" he called into the room. From where I stood in my own doorway, stalled by sleepiness as much as by lingering curiosity, I glimpsed a mass of disarranged blond hair leaning out the door toward the man. "We'll be right down," a tired voice said. But the man was already moving down the hall toward the next door.

"Who was it?" Eunice asked from the bed.

"Time for breakfast," I said, and slammed the door. I had been expecting something more than a call for breakfast. We had come over from Paris to London in hopes of making a connection. All during the hot train ride the previous afternoon, from Gare du Nord to Calais, from Dover to Paddington Station, we had built up in our imaginations X, our only local connection, into a personage of major importance and influence in matters of London tourism. But so far he had not called.

While Eunice unpacked fresh clothes, I sat on the bed smoking a cigarette and assessed our situation. We could wander about the city on our own, call X again, or wait politely for him to call on us. But the thought of waiting in the room through the morning was distasteful. Looking around, I saw again what I had been too reluctant to perceive when we checked in the evening before. The room was drab. Its high ceiling, watermarked and cracked in places, seemed a mocking reminder of the elegance that might have once characterized the entire building. The rug was dusty and footworn from tramping tourists and the sheer weight of time. The thin mattress, during the night, had pressed into my back the history of many bodies it had borne. This was not Dick Whittington's magic London.

"Hurry up!" Eunice ordered. "They stop serving breakfast at nine o'clock." She opened the door, pulling her robe close about her neck. "I'll use that john down the hall, and then you get out until after I wash up in the face bowl." As she went out, I glanced over at the yellowing face bowl. The sight of it provided another reason for giving up the room. After digging out my toothbrush from my suitcase, I stood over the bowl brushing my teeth and trying to remember just why we had come to London.

One reason might have been our having grown tired of being mere tourists. In the Louvre two mornings before, among a crowd of American tourists standing transfixed before the Old Masters of Renaissance painting, I had suddenly found myself pointing a finger and exclaiming to Eunice, "Hey, didn't they name a cheese after that guy?"

"Leroy, they did no such a-thing!" Eunice had hissed.

The other tourists had laughed nervously.

Eunice had pulled me out of the Louvre, though not by the ear.

That same morning I had decided to wire one of a list of London people suggested to us by friends back home in Atlanta. Their advice had been the usual in such matters: "Be sure to look up X. We're good friends. He showed us a good time when we were in London, and we showed him a good time when he came to Atlanta. Be sure to tell him all the news about us." My wire to X had been humble: "We are Leroy and Eunice Foster from Atlanta, friends of Y and Z. Will be in London on weekend. Would like to see you." X's reply, which arrived the next morning, was efficient: "Call at home on arrival. X." And so we had raced from Paris to London. Upon arrival, as I instructed, I called up X.

"Y and Z who?" he asked, after I introduced myself.

I gave their full names. "They send warm regards from Atlanta," I added smoothly.

"Yes," X said. "They're fine people. I always regretted I never got to know them well."

"They're fine people," I said.

"Yes," X allowed. "I've got a bit of a flu right now, you know."

So we were in London. We located a room a few blocks from the train station and were content to let be. The room was in a neat, white Georgian house that, at some point during that time when American tourists first began arriving en masse, had been converted into a hotel. Such places abound in London; many of them are quite pleasant. But the interior of this one was bleak, as was the room we secured on the fourth floor. To compound our displeasure, the landlady had insisted that we declare exactly how long we planned to stay, and then pay for that period in advance. This was one of those periodic lapses of faith in the American dollar. American tourists suffered with it. But watchful landlords from Lyons to Wales refused to show the slightest mercy. "These are class rooms, love," the landlady had declared, inspecting our faces over the tops of her glasses. She was a plump woman who fidgeted impatiently inside a loose gray smock. "There's lots of people callin' for rooms," she reminded us. "All the time," she added.

We had been in no position to haggle. Having entered London on the eve of a bank holiday weekend, we had no choice but to cash more traveler's checks and pay rent through the following Monday morning. Only then did the landlady issue us a single set of keys: one for the street door, which was always locked, and one for our room. To further frustrate us, I found that the lobby pay telephone did not work. This required me to walk back to the station to ring up X and supply him with our address. He did not seem enthusiastic about getting it, but said he might call on us the next day, if his flu showed signs of abating. Discovering, finally, that the toilet on our floor barely flushed, and that the bathtub was unhealthily dirty, we went to bed with curses rumbling in us and the dust of the road still clinging to our skins.

Considering the many little frustrations that marred our arrival in London, we were very pleased to have been awakened for breakfast by the house porter. After Eunice returned to the room, I went out into the hall and waited in line for my turn in the john. I was not even perturbed that the two Orientals, occupying the room next to ours, took long chances at the toilet. While one occupied the stall, the other stood outside the door as if on guard. Standing behind him, I noted that he was tall and slim and conservatively dressed in a white shirt and black trousers. He seemed aloof, even reserved, though not inscrutable. This I could tell from the way his brows lifted and his ears perked, like mine, each time his companion made a vain attempt to flush the slowly gurgling toilet. Indeed, the two of us outside the door tried with the companion: we strained to apply our own pressures to the loose handle, to join in his anticipation of a solid and satisfying flush. But, unlike me, the Oriental did not shift from foot to foot each time his companion's failure was announced by strained gurgles and hisses from behind the closed door. Standing straight as a Samurai, he seemed more intent on studying my movements, without seeming to, than on commandeering the john. I wanted to communicate with him, but did not want to presume that he spoke English. To further compound the problem, I could

not tell if he was Japanese or Chinese. In Paris I had seen
Chinese tourists, but they had been uniformed in the
colors of Chairman Mao. This fellow wore western
clothes. The problem became academic, however, when I
recalled that the only Oriental phrases I knew were
derived from a few sessions in a class in Mandarin I had
once attended. I could never hope to master the very in-
tricate and delicate degrees of inflection required, but I
had managed to bring away from the class a few phrases
lodged in memory, one of which was a greeting and the
other introducing me as an American.

"Ni hau ma?" I inquired with a broad smile.

At first the Oriental stared at me in silence. Then he
pointed a finger at his chest. "I next," he said. Then he
pointed a finger at my chest. "You next."

He was right. I shifted from one foot to the other until
finally there came the welcome sound of his companion's
mastery of English hydraulics. As the companion stepped
out of the stall and my acquaintance went in, I wanted to
caution him that he need not be as concerned with a matter as ephemeral as decorum. But the desire died aborn-
ing. I did not have the language, and could only continue
to shift from foot to foot. And sadly, very shortly afterward, while the second Oriental waited by the stairs, there
came the same dry, strained sound of the very same difficulty. The situation was hopeless.. I brushed past the companion and raced down the stairs to the third floor. But
that stall too was in use. The one on the second floor offered even less hope: an elderly couple and a young man
stood shifting in front of it.

On the ground floor, off the lobby, I ran into the same
little man, still seeming to me like nothing if not a Bulgarian, still knocking on doors and shouting, "Americans!

Americans! Get up for breakfast!" When he saw me he turned, again ever so slightly, and said, "That way," pointing toward the door to the street. "Hurry! Hurry! Only served from eight to nine." I nodded my thanks and, seeing no stall on that floor, raced back up the stairs. Just below the third floor the two Orientals passed me on their way down. "Ni hau ma?" I called to them. They stopped and looked at each other, then at me. The taller man spoke in a high, hurried tone to the other. Then his companion nodded enthusiastically and said, "Oh!" He looked at me, pointed a finger up the stairs and said, "Open now."

He was right.

Going down for breakfast, finally, Eunice and I passed the little blue-suited man in the lobby. He seemed about to go out the door, but as we approached he stepped aside and held the portal open for us. "Breakfast that way," he said, smiling. "In the basement." We thanked him and walked out the door, along a few feet of pavement, and down into the basement of the adjoining house. The little room was dank and smelled of rancid bacon. About a score of people, mostly Americans, were seated at the cloth-covered tables. We could tell they were Americans by the way they avoided eye contact. One girl was speaking halting French with a West Texas accent to two male companions who only listened. Over against the wall a middle-aged couple was poring over a *Herald-Tribune* stretched out beside their plates of bacon and eggs. "You just wait till we get back," the man was saying in a loud voice. "I'll *get* the sonofbitches for doin' this to me!" His wife kept looking up from her reading and saying, "Now Bob . . . now Bob . . ." Eunice and I went to a table at the far side of the room. At the table next to

ours a rather attractive girl was eating rapidly and saying
to the young man with her, "Cadiz was an utter bore.
Madrid was an utter bore. . . . There's too many kids in
Copenhagen. . . . Italian men are the *nastiest* men on
earth! . . ."

"Aw, shut up and eat," her friend said.

Across the room, seemingly at a distance, the two Orientals ate their meal in silence, looking only at each other.

The landlady's assistant brought our plates out from
the kitchen. She was pale and dumpy, with dull auburn
hair done up in a ragged bun. She seemed immune to all
of us in the room. She slid two plates onto our table,
plunked down a dish of jam, and sashayed back into the
kitchen.

"You know," Eunice said, inspecting the food, "it's
kind of funny."

"What?" I asked.

"That a place as sloppy as this can afford to have
somebody wake you up for breakfast. This kind of place,
the more people miss breakfast, the more food they save."

"You know," I said, after reflecting a moment, "it *is*
kind of funny that that little Bulgarian was heading *out*
the door when we came down, but stepped back *inside*
the second we went out."

Eunice laid down her fork. "It's more than funny," she
said. "It's pure-dee suspicious."

"It's more than suspicious," I added. "It could be
downright slick."

Both of us looked round the room. Everyone was
eating.

"I been telling you, Leroy," Eunice said. "It's good
sense to riff in a place where you don't know the score."

She fished the keys from her purse. "Which one of us go'n go up?"

But I had already eased out of my seat and was on my way. In a few seconds I had unlocked the front door and stepped quickly into the hall. Although I ran up the three flights of stairs on tiptoe, the aged boards betrayed my presence. And just as I reached the fourth floor landing, I saw the little blue-suited man backing quickly out the door of the room next to ours. I paused. He turned and smiled at me, shutting the door and giving a theatrical turn to the doorknob. Then he walked calmly over to the linen closet, opened it, and peered inside. At first he frowned in exasperation, then he patted a stack of folded sheets and smiled reassuringly at me. Turning, he waltzed slowly to the stairs and went down. By this time I had opened my own door. Nothing in the room seemed to have been disturbed. I checked our suitcases. Eunice's camera was still there, as were the gifts she had purchased in Paris. But my suspicions were not eased. After locking the door, I rushed down to the breakfast room and directly to the table where the two Orientals were eating their meals. "Ni hau mau?" I said hurriedly. Again they stared at each other, then at me. "Not open?" the one who had the better command of English, the shorter of the two, said to me. He was dressed like his companion, except that his short-sleeved shirt was light green. And he carried a row of pens on a plastic clip in the breast pocket of his shirt.

"I think you had better check your room," I said as slowly as my excitement would allow. "I-think-you-had-better-check-your-room," I repeated even more slowly. "I-just-saw-a-man-com-ing-out-of-it."

He screwed up his face. "English is not good to us," he said. "Please to speak more slow."

I pointed to my keys and then raised a finger in the direction of the other building. "I-think-your-room-may-have-been-*robbed!*" I said.

"*Rob?*" he said.

"I saw a man come out of there."

"Rob," he repeated slowly to his companion.

To avoid seeming to caricature a fine and extremely proud people, I will not attempt to relate the development of their conversation after that point. They consulted extensively across the table in their own language. From their gestures and eye movements I could tell that the discussion included references to me, Eunice, the landlady, the quality of the meal, and the lazy toilet way up on the fourth floor. Then one word of their own language, sounding like "New Sunday," seemed to come suddenly into focus. It bounded back and forth between them across the table. The word excited them, made them anxious, perhaps even angry. The spokesman repeated "New Sunday" to me with sufficient force to make me know that my suspicion had been absorbed, and then run through their own language until it settled around a corresponding thought. "New Sunday—*robbed*," I said in answer, nodding my head.

Both of them leaped up from the table and rushed toward the door. Most people in the room turned to look after them. Only after the two had vanished did the tourists turn their eyes on me. I slipped back to where Eunice waited at our table. By this time my eggs had hardened into a thin layer of yellow mush encrusted in bacon fat. I sipped the cup of cold tea and waited.

"Leroy, maybe it was a false alarm," Eunice said.

"Those Chinese don't think so," I told her.

Eunice frowned. "Those aren't Chinese."

"Well, they ain't Koreans," I observed.

"They're Japanese," Eunice said. "How could you be so dumb?"

"How can *you* be so sure?"

"All you have to do is *look* at them," Eunice told me. "Japanese are like upper-class people down home. They don't look around much because they *know* who *they* are in relation to everybody else."

"Bullshit," I said. "They're Chinese. Whoever saw Japanese without cameras?"

"Leroy, you're a black bigot," Eunice told me. "And a *dumb* one at that," she added.

"But not in *public!*" I whispered through my teeth. Over at the next table the young man was watching us intently. But soon he turned back to his companion and her complaints—this time against Etruscan art.

We waited.

In a few minutes the two Orientals came rushing back into the room. The taller one pointed at me and spoke hurriedly to his companion. Then the two of them came over to our table. "Please to say Japanese students are . . . rob in hotel."

"New Sundayed?" I asked.

The young man nodded.

I said I was sorry to hear it.

"You see doorrobber?" He breathed excitedly.

I admitted that both of us had seen the man, although I was careful not to say that to me he seemed to be a Bulgarian.

The taller student spoke to his companion.

"He complains for police," the spokesman translated.

I agreed that should be done. Leaving Eunice at the table gloating pridefully over the sharpness of her insight, I led the two students back into the kitchen. The landlady was scraping bacon fat off the top of her black range. She glanced up at the three of us over her glasses and said, "What you want, love?"

The man in the green shirt, the shorter of the two, attempted to explain; but he seemed unable to muster sufficient English, or sufficient interest on the landlady's part, to make her appreciate how seriously he viewed the situation. While he was speaking, the service lady came in from the breakfast room with a stack of plates. She squeezed past the three of us, further upsetting the student in his recital. "Pity what these blokes does to the language," she muttered.

At this point I interrupted the student with a bow intended to be polite. I explained to the landlady the ploy used in the robbery and a description of the man whom I suspected of the deed. But I did not volunteer my suspicion that he looked to me to be a Bulgarian.

"What was took off you?" the landlady asked the two, and I thought I detected suspicion in her voice. They did not understand, so I translated as best I could, using sign language and the smallest part of pig Latin. Between the three of us it was finally determined that the thief had taken two Eurail passes, two Japanese passports, and about one hundred dollars in traveler's checks drawn on the bank of Tokyo.

"Shssss!" whispered the landlady. "Don't talk so *loud*, love! You want the other guests to hear?" Then she turned to the service lady, who leaned against a cupboard with her thick arms folded, and said, "Think they'd know enough to lock up their valuables." Then she faced the three of us again and said. "We can't be *responsible* for all that, duckies. There's signs on a'l the doors tellin' you to keep valuables under padlock. Regulations, you know."

Even without understanding fully what had been said, both students seemed to sense they could make more progress into the theft on their own. "Go search doorrobber," the short man said.

The electricity of their excitement sparked into me. As they left the basement I stepped quickly behind them, recalling all the scenes dealing with personal honor I had viewed in Japanese movies. I had the feeling of being part of a posse. As one of the students was unlocking the door, his companion suddenly gave out a shrill cry and jumped several feet in the air. He kept repeating, *"Aa! Aa! Aa!"* and pointed down the street with a quick movement of his arm. I looked immediately where he pointed, but did not see the man whom I suspected of being the thief. But the other student looked in the same direction, and what he saw made him shout back to his comrade. Looking again, I saw the cause of their excitement: a rather chubby Oriental man was walking up the street toward us. The two students rushed toward the man. After greeting him, and after a few gestures, the three of them, shouting something that sounded like "Waa Waa! Waa!" swept past me and into the building. The spokesman paused beside me long enough to say, "Please to watch door."

Waiting excitedly on the bottom step, I imagined them searching the building from attic to basement, peering into keyholes, dark stairwells, the johns on each floor, trying doors, linen closets, open windows. I pictured the little Bulgarian cornered in the hall, trying to understand what they could possibly mean when they said in cultured

Japanese, "You have dishonored the hospitality of this house. You will please commit hara-kiri." And the little fellow, sneak thief that he was, would echo the counter-code; *"Why? I want to live!"* I expected to see at any moment the little blue-suited fellow come pumping out the door, his red tie trailing in the wind he made, with the three Japanese in hot pursuit. When Eunice came up from the basement, I urged her to take a long walk around the block. I advised that I anticipated horrors from which her modesty should be protected. But Eunice refused to budge from where she stood on the sidewalk.

"Leroy, you're overreacting," she said.

Eunice was right as usual.

Instead of three Samurai bearing the head of the thief, only the two Japanese students and their newfound tourist ally emerged from the building. They sighed and looked up and down the street, perhaps looking for additional Samurai, perhaps looking for bobbies. I sighed, and looked with them. But there was nothing else on the street we could add to our resources. The three conversed among themselves in Japanese, and then the stranger turned to me. "This Japanese salaryman from Osaka," the English-speaking student announced.

"Ni hau ma?" I said, offering my hand as the man bowed smartly.

"You are African?" the man asked, smiling pleasantly as we shook. "Nigerian, yes?"

"Woo sh Meei-gworen," I said.

He looked perplexed. "I do not know this tribe," he confessed finally. "But now I must go. They should get the officials to help them," he told me. He turned and made a short statement to the students in Japanese. Then he shook my hand again, bowed smartly to the students, and went on his way up the block.

"What was that foolishness you were talking?" Eunice asked.

The English-speaking student strolled closer to me. He looked deep into my face and said, "All *open* upstair."

"You ought to be horsewhipped for carryin' on such foolishness at a serious time like this," Eunice said.

Of course Eunice was right.

For the second time we crowded into the kitchen to register our complaint with the landlady. "Pipe *down*, love!" she muttered. "We don't want the others to hear, now do we?"

"Why not?" I asked.

She stood with her back against the black gas range. "What can *I* do?"

"Call up the bobbies."

She mumbled some more to herself, gave us a cold stare, then fished around in the pocket of her gray smock and produced a shilling and a few pence for the telephone. As we passed again through the breakfast room, the other tourists stared at us as though we were entertainers employed by the landlady to make the breakfast hour less monotonous. I wondered how many of them had been robbed while they sat leisurely over their bacon and eggs. And I wondered whether the little Bulgarian had anticipated they would have this blind spot.

I glanced at the table Eunice and I had occupied. It had been cleared and another couple, who looked German, now occupied it. They ate in silence and looked only at each other. But at the next table the little brunette was still preaching over cold tea to her companion: "Spain was *so* depressing. The French ignore you in August. Zurich looks like a big computer. Greek men . . ."

We were inside the lobby before I remembered the telephone did not work.

After getting directions from a passerby and advising Eunice to wait outside, lest the Bulgarian should be lurking in our room, the two Japanese and I walked toward a bobby station, said to be about a mile from the hotel. During the walk they managed to communicate to me their names and the outline of their dilemma. The spokesman's name was Toyohiko Kageyama. His tall companion, who apparently knew little English, was Yoshitsune Hashima. I told them to call me Lee. Toyohiko explained that without the traveler's checks, passports and rail passes they could not get to Amsterdam, where their flight back to Japan would depart in a few days. And with the bank holiday in effect, they would not be able to obtain more traveler's checks until Monday, when the banks reopened. Unfortunately, Monday was also the day their flight was to leave Amsterdam.

They talked between themselves in Japanese, working through the problem. They decided that with help from the Japanese embassy they might be able to obtain money for a flight to Amsterdam. But there was still the matter of the missing passports. I did not learn this by listening to their conversation, but through the pains taken by Toyohiko Kageyama to explain the problem to me in English. So far as I could tell, neither of them made any unkind remarks about the thief. Instead, they seemed to have accepted the loss and were working toward solution of the problem it caused. As we talked, Yoshitsune Hashima looked at the two of us, nodding occasional, though hesitant, agreement with whatever Kageyama said to me. But neither one of them smiled.

When we arrived at the bobby station, a bleak little building containing almost no activity, I excused myself and sat in the waiting room while the two Japanese stood at the reception desk and reported the robbery to the desk officer. He was a pale, elderly man with a gray-speckled pencil-line mustache. He listened carefully, occasionally drumming his pen on a report form, while suggesting words to Toyohiko Kageyama. The student had difficulty making the bobby recognize the name of the hotel and the street on which it was located, as well as the items that had been stolen. After many trials and errors by the bobby, Kageyama came over to me. "Please tell," he said.

I went to the desk and reported to the bobby as much as I knew about the robbery. I gave him a description of the man whom I suspected of being the thief, but I did not volunteer my suspicion that to me he seemed to be a Bulgarian. The bobby wrote it all down on a report form, then questioned us again for corroboration. Afterward, he wrote something of his own at the bottom of the form, perhaps a private comment, perhaps his own name. Then the students and I sat in the waiting room, while a pair of bobbies was summoned to accompany us back to the hotel. These were somewhat younger men, although one of them sported the same kind of thin mustache as the bobby at the desk. The other was plump, with tufts of bright red hair showing beneath his tall hat. He had a cold manner that became evident when he motioned us out of the building and into the back seat of their patrol car. The gesture was one of professional annoyance.

During the drive back to the hotel, the students and I

were silent, but the two bobbies in the front seat discussed a recent rally of homosexuals in Trafalgar Square.

"What a hellish sight that one was," the redhead observed.

"No doubt," the other said. "No doubt."

"At least five hundred of them parading round like the Queens of Elfin."

"No doubt," said the other. "Any trouble?"

The redhead laughed. "No," he said grimly.

The two Japanese students sat next to each other, their eyes looking past the bobbies and through the windshield of the car. Only I concentrated on the conversation. And after a while, I found myself wondering about how I had come to be driving through the streets of London in the back seat of a bobby car listening to commentary on a rally of homosexuals, when my major purpose in coming over from Paris had been to contact X, that elusive knower of London nightlife, and give him the warm regards of Y and Z, friends of his who lived in Atlanta.

The two bobbies searched the hotel from top to bottom, but they did not find the man. No one else had reported anything missing. The landlady flitted around with a great show of sympathy, explaining to the bobbies that this sort of thing had not happened in her place since the boom in American tourists back in '65. Both bobbies were cool and efficient, asking questions in a manner that suggested their suspicion of everyone and of no one in particular. But the redhead, it seemed to me, was more than probing in his questions concerning the part Eunice and I had played in the drama. He said finally, "There's little else we can do now except get a notice out. You'll have to go over to the station for the Paddington district and make a report there. This isn't our district, you know; so they'll need a bit of a report over there."

"People should be careful of these things," the landlady said, wiping her hands on her apron.

"It's ten-thirty," Eunice said. "We want to go sightseeing."

The redhead smiled cryptically. "He'll have to go along to make a proper description," he advised Eunice. "It would be quite helpful to these two chaps here."

"I'm sick and tired of all the running around," Eunice said.

The bobby smiled.

The two Orientals stood watching all of us.

The drive to the other district station was short. The bobbies did not talk more about the rally of homosexuals. They let us out in front of the station and wished us luck. I wished them a happy bank holiday. Inside the station the routine was the same as before: while the students explained their predicament as best they could, I stayed in the waiting room until I was needed. Waiting, I amused myself by studying the wanted posters on the bulletin board hanging between the windows. Walking close to the board for a closer inspection, I saw that four of the seven wanted men were black. Moreover, one of them, a hardcase named Wimberly Lane, priced at fifty pounds and wanted for extortion, looked somewhat familiar. I studied his face. Lane had high cheekbones, prominent eyes, and a dissolute look about him. I looked closer and saw that he resembled, especially in profile, my cousin Freddy Tifton back home in Atlanta. But Lane was a desperado, probably hiding out in the London underworld, and my cousin was a world away in Atlanta, probably at that moment eating fried chicken on Hunter Street.

"Please tell about . . . doorrobber," someone said. Toyohiko Kageyama was standing behind me.

I turned and followed him back to the desk. This bobby's pale blue eyes flickered over my face. He and another man, a clerk who had obviously been helping him piece together the story told by the students, glanced quickly at each other and then back at me. "You saw the alleged robber?" the bobby asked.

"I did."

"Can you describe him?"

I gave what I thought was an accurate description. But this time I was sure not to venture my suspicion that he seemed to me to be a Bulgarian. The bobby wrote with his left hand. He wrote beautiful script with his pen turned inward toward his wrist. I watched his hands.

The two students stood behind me, one on each side.

"Just what is your relation to the complainants?" the bobby asked.

"I am an American," I said. "My room is next to theirs."

The bobby stopped writing and frowned. "You are the only person who actually *saw* this man, you know?" His eyes narrowed.

"What about it?" I said.

"A friend indeed, what?" the clerk said. He looked at the bobby and winked.

The two students stood behind me, conversing between themselves.

"Now let's go through this *once* more," the bobby said.

Suddenly Yoshitsune Hashima stepped from behind me and up to the desk. "Lee . . . good . . . de*tail*," he said, pointing firmly at me. "Japanese students . . . take *Lee* detail . . . doorrobber."

The bobby stopped smiling and began writing again. He wrote a beautiful script.

Yoshitsune Hashima did not speak again.

The bobby advised them to go quickly to the Japanese embassy.

I wanted to go quickly and see the rest of London.

We saw the two students again in the late afternoon at Madame Tussaud's. Eunice and I had wandered down into one of the lower chambers with exhibits commemorating the French Revolution. When I saw them I was standing beside a rusty guillotine that had been used to behead Marie Antoinette. The Japanese were standing together, peering into a lighted showcase containing wax replicas of famous murderers who had once plagued London. I motioned to Eunice, then walked over and touched Kageyama on the shoulder. He started, as if intruded upon too much by the mood of the place. But when they saw who we were, both of them smiled nervously and bowed. Toyohiko Kageyama reported that the Japanese embassy had secured temporary passports for them, had ordered the checks cancelled, and had lent them enough money for living expenses and a flight to Amsterdam. Now that business had been taken care of, they were seeing the sights of London. Both of them thanked us for our help. Kageyama in English and Hashima in Japanese. Both of them bowed politely. Then Yoshitsune Hashima pulled a notebook from the pocket of his trousers, leafed through it to a certain page, and read in a slow voice, "Please-to-give-Japanese-students-name-and-house-number."

I wrote them for him.

Yoshitsune Hashima accepted back the notebook, leafed through several more pages, and read in an uncertain voice: "I thank you kindness at New Sunday to help Japanese students. . . . I hope Lee visit Nihon one day. . . . Please visit home of Yoshitsune Hashima in suburb of Tokyo."

Then he handed me a packet of Japanese stamps.

The two of them bowed again.

"You see?" Eunice said, as we walked away. "The Japanese ain't nothing but part-time Southerners."

I had to concede that once again Eunice was right.

But it was too dark inside the wax museum. The colored lights shining on the exhibits did not improve the mood of the place. "Let's get out," I said to Eunice.

Toward dusk we stood in a crowd of tourists on a green outside the Tower of London. We had spent about ten minutes inside the tower. Before us on the green was an old man, encased in a white sack crisscrossed with chains and padlocks. He wriggled and moaned inside the sack while the crowd laughed. Standing beside him was a muscular, bald-headed man who beat himself on the naked chest with a sledge-hammer. In certain respects this man resembled the thief, but he not at all resembled a Bulgarian. From time to time this strong man marched with a tin cup around the inside of the circle, holding it out to onlookers. He collected pence and shillings from some of those standing closest to the recreation. He said things like, "Me old daddy left near a thousand pound when he died; but I ain't yet found out where he left it." When the crowd laughed, he laughed with them. But he cursed those who put slugs and very small change in his cup. He seemed to be a foreigner, but he spoke with the accents of the British lower class. "A man 'as got to live!" he shouted at us while rattling the cup. "The old man there can't get out the sack till you pay up."

"Leroy," Eunice said beside me. "I don't think X will ever call. Now that we've seen London, let's please go home."

As usual, Eunice was right.

Widows and Orphans

Turning his back to the noisy crowd in the banquet room, Louis Clayton gripped the back of his chair, laughed to himself, and thought, "Someone is getting the Academy Award." He glanced down at Mrs. Richards and decided it was not her. She seemed outdated. Her expression, as she looked up at him from the table, reminded Louis of a café scene from a movie made back in the 1940s. The title of the movie was in her smile. Whether Bette Davis or Barbara Stanwyck played the heroine in the scene, Louis could not remember. But unlike the heroine, Mrs. Richards was old. Instead of a smartly tailored gown, she wore a blue satin dress with a white orchid pinned to its bosom. When he bent over to kiss her cheek, the orchid pressed its fragile petals against his face. Louis felt the slippery coolness of the flower, but there was no smell. Mrs. Richards laughed delightedly, her tired brown eyes glowing, and kissed him on the mouth. "You looked *so* good when you had that beard," she told him. "I can't see why you went and cut it off." Louis stood holding her hand. While his eyes lingered on her face, he tried to recall the outcome of this lovers' rendezvous. He could not be sure. But in her face he saw that familiar mixture of pain and intrigue with which older women suggest to young men the wickedness of their own youth. Mrs. Richards slapped his face.

Louis sat down at the table in the chair beside hers. The scene he was recalling had gone completely out of his mind.

"Wouldn't he look better with a beard?" Mrs. Richards asked the other people at the table.

The two women interrupted their eating of green garden salads long enough to nod agreement. Mrs. Richards introduced Mrs. Loretta Burton, an elderly, plump woman with a slight mustache. She wore a pink dress with a white orchid. She nodded graciously at Louis. Seated next to Mrs. Burton, facing the head table and the platform, sat a young, heavily made-up but quite beautiful coffee-brown girl. This was Mrs. Burton's daughter, Fredricka. She smiled briefly at Louis. Her heavy eyelids fluttered once as she took his measurements. Louis averted his eyes.

Mrs. Richards, watching him, said to the others, "He's one of them shy ones." Then she laughed mischievously. Mrs. Burton grinned. Fredricka was staring intently at the head table where the guest of honor sat.

Louis ate his salad and watched the people at other tables. Many were young men, some bearded, some clean shaven, with dates or their wives. There were also older men with their wives. But, unlike the young men, they seemed less intense in conversation, less focused on the spirit of the occasion. Their wives too seemed distracted. But the younger women seemed perfectly at home. All the men were watching them and they seemed to know it. This was a testimonial banquet for the Progressive Association of Greater Watts, and as far as Louis knew he was the only outsider in attendance. He also seemed to be the only man without a woman, and the thought of this made him lonely; almost lonely enough to turn his head and look with Fredricka toward the platform and the head table, where Clair was sitting. But he ate his salad and refused to turn in that direction.

"I never dreamt you would be here," Mrs. Richards said to him. She laid a warm palm on the back of his left hand and pressed it hard against the table. She leaned her face close to his ear and sighed. "You know, you and Clair looked so good together," she whispered. "I just don't know why things didn't work out better. And you looked so *fine* with that beard." She appraised him with eyes moist and warm, yet cool and knowing in their deepest recesses of brown.

Louis rested his fork in the salad. He felt she wanted him to say something. He remembered this scene, too, from an old movie, but could not remember the lines. He decided to not say anything.

"You done put on a little weight, too," Mrs. Richards said.

"A little," he answered.

"A little, *hell!*" Mrs. Richards chuckled. She waved her finger. "I'll bet some woman is fattenin' you up for the fry."

He remembered the married woman with whom he was having an affair. He would have to call her later. Her husband was a very agreeable man. He would be able to talk for as long as he wanted. He would be able to say everything he felt. He lived in a very sophisticated world. Thinking about this, he jumped suddenly.

Mrs. Richards was pinching his chin. "You bad boy," she said, and grinned wickedly. "Don't you know you broke my baby's heart?"

"These mixed marriages don't always work out," Louis told her. But in his private thoughts he was thinking very hard about movies.

Mrs. Richards laughed. "You bad boy," she said.

They were in the penthouse of a skyscraper. The entire room was enclosed by glass. Through these almost invisible walls Louis could see thousands of tiny yellow, red, and white lights, sparkling like exotic lightning bugs on the glass and cement sides of surrounding skyscrapers in the cool Los Angeles night. There was a sense of wealth outside the glass walls. Inside the room a similar richness was reflected in the white-on-white suits, tailored black dinner jackets, handmade ties colored like rainbows, jeweled tie clasps, exotic scents and manners of the people at the tables surrounding his. In his memory was a sense of having seen it all before in other scenes. His imagination became engaged, and while the Chicano waiters placed the main course on the tables, he inspected closely the faces of the other guests.

To his left, several tables away, sat a thin man, whose tight-pressed mouth and steady-eyed expression of understated strength reminded Louis of Gregory Peck. Across the room, at a table near the glass wall, he watched a plump little brown woman, whose bulging eyes and nervously waving cigarette, while she talked, recalled to his mind the abysmally lonely intensity of Bette Davis. Seated with her, but looking elsewhere, Louis thought he saw a man whose face expressed the corruption-comfortable

look and the energetic meanness of Edward G. Robinson.
Louis closed his eyes and laughed to himself. When
he opened his eyes again he glimpsed, at the very next
table, a familiar intense gaze that emanated raw, animal power. He saw Marlon Brando's full cheeks, set
mouth, and unabashed eyes. He was convinced it
was Brando as he looked in his prime. But just then the
man laughed, and he heard the irrepressible rhythms
of the barbershop. Then Louis remembered that this
was only a banquet honoring the achievements of the
Progressive Association of Greater Watts. Everyone in
the room had accepted, and defined himself in terms
of, the caste definition. They all were black, except for
the guest speaker and his wife seated at the head
table.

He was turning toward the head table to get his bearings
when he sensed Fredricka watching him. When he looked
at her she was laughing.

The Chicano waiters hauled away the dinner plates and
then brought out trays loaded with desserts. Blue, pink and
white crème-de-menthe ices in tall, frosted glasses, yellow
cake, and pots of coffee were placed on the tables. The
Chicanos were sullen but efficient. They circled the tables
in their red coats. Voices rose into higher-pitched conversation as the eating eased. Mrs. Richards wiped her
mouth and cheeks with a pink handkerchief. Mrs. Burton
smiled around the table and sipped her coffee. She laid a
gentle hand on Fredricka's shoulder. The girl looked
straight at the head table. "You be sure to see that
movie," Mrs. Burton was saying. "Ricky does a dynamite
job." Mrs. Richards was nodding agreement. The girl
shrugged off her mother's hand and said, her eyes still on
the platform, "Please, Mother. I told you it's Fredricka!"

Both Mrs. Burton and Mrs. Richards grinned sheepishly. Louis did not know what they were talking about.

"We're ready to begin," Clair's voice called from the head table.

He did not turn to look with the others.

"May I have your attention, please," Clair's voice called again. There was a rapping of glasses, a clearing of throats, all from the same direction. The noise in the room did not abate. "We're ready to begin, ladies and gentlemen!" Clair's voice said again. And then it broke its authority and lapsed into a giggle. "Oh, wow!" Louis heard her say, and she followed this with more good-humored, but exquisitely controlled, bursts of exasperated laughter. Her voice was lovely, but he still refused to turn his head and look toward her.

Mrs. Richards's brown eyes glowed with the most intense pride. "That there's my heart," she whispered, nudging him with her shoulder. "Don't Clair look *fine?* Oh, don't my baby look *fine,* though?"

He turned his head and Clair looked beautiful. Her smooth brown face had rounded some, but it still projected, when she smiled, an aura of careless energy, promising the most subtle excitement to anyone on whom she looked. The second this energy made contact with his eyes he knew he loved her. Clair's dress was of burnished red. Around her neck, hugging snugly against her full breasts, a string of pearls, matching her teeth in whiteness, glistened in the glare of the overhead lights. Her dark, sparkling eyes settled on her mother's face, then on his, and seemed to say an intimate "Hello." This was a call to an energy in him, and when he felt it rising to respond he became frightened, then excited, then frightened again. He turned his face away from the head table.

"Ain't she something, now?" Mrs. Richards was saying to Mrs. Burton and Fredricka. "That there's my heart up there."

"That dress is not the best she could do," Fredricka said.

Clair rapped firmly on a water glass. Then she struck a pose with the spoon upraised. Someone near the back of the room snapped a picture. Clair giggled. Many of the people in the room laughed. "All right, ladies and gentlemen," she said in a crisp, more formal tone of voice. "I am ready to introduce our speaker, Mr. Maltz."

The room hushed.

Clair's introduction of the speaker was rousing. Louis had learned from Mrs. Richards that Clair now had a reputation as a very shrewd businesswoman. In a few years she might run for political office. Louis was proud of her command of rhetoric. As she spoke, everyone sat transfixed, Fredricka Burton fluttered her eyelids thoughtfully. Occasionally, Mrs. Richards dabbed quickly at her eyes with the pink handkerchief. Louis tried to remember the rhythm of her in bed. Clair was saying: ". . . defeats as opportunities, adversary relationships as covert friendships, the drive to combat, in light of a corresponding drive to conserve all that is best and good about the processes through which we strive toward excellence. This was, and still is, his message to us. This, then, should be our greatest goal; to aspire toward excellence in such a way that, despite our various . . ."

Louis retained the rhythm of a good many women, but he could not remember Clair in this way. He tried very hard while watching her, but nothing resembling passion recalled itself to his conscious mind. He recalled only an image of her full-breasted shadow, floating on the wall of his dark bedroom. The tone of the shadow grew sharp and then hazy, as the orange glow of her cigarette brightened and dimmed between her lips. This image, and a single sentence, "What do you want from me?", closed out all he could remember of her passion.

He found himself looking at Fredricka. Her mouth had the same set as Clair's had. She was smoking a cigarette with the same deliberate, almost mechanical efficiency. She was just as lovely. He could not see her body below her breasts. Behind him Clair was saying: ". . . not by luck or accident, but by perseverance toward a goal outlined in sweat and sheer vision, years and years before the ultimate arrival. This is the true path of excellence. And only the dedicated make it to the . . ."

"Don't she talk good, though?" Mrs. Richards was leaning close to his ear. "I wish to God things had of work out better between you and my Clair. She got her faults, but my baby is a good, hardworking girl." She glanced toward the head table, breathed heavily, and then sighed. "She's lonely. I don't like to see her like that."

"Isn't she close to somebody now?" Louis whispered.

Mrs. Richards laughed quietly. "My Clair ain't never been close to anybody in her life."

Louis thought about this and knew that it was true. There had been a toughness in her, seemingly so assured of itself that it tested relentlessly the toughness of others. This was an aspect of her beauty. Instead of crying when angry, he remembered, Clair would back off and nod aggressively, like a pretty little bulldog, too cute to charge. He had loved that about her. He had developed the practice of patting her on the head when angry. His strategy had been to soften her with absolute support, to break through her emotional armor by showing he could match her, strength for strength. He had been convinced that someone, long before, had hurt her deeply in that place where she had felt most vulnerable. She had simply closed herself off. His desire had been to have her, after a final proof of his restrained devotion, walk into his arms and declare with a certainty formed by fully evolved trust, "I love you." This had not happened. And after reflecting more he had determined that it was because he was from the South and she was at least two generations removed from the place. He concluded that he was trying to make her seem more like his own mother than like herself. He backed off some and changed tactics. This did not help. She seemed completely self-sustained. Now, watching her perform before the audience, a certain scene came back into his mind. On her birthday, five years before, he had given her a ring suggesting the movement of his thoughts toward engagement. She had accepted the ring with an exclamation of complete happiness, her hand pressed excitedly to her mouth. This gesture made his heart swell. He held her books while she slipped the ring onto her finger. He kissed her, and in his excitement dropped the books. Bending to retrieve them, his eyes lighted on a green and pink card that had fallen from the pages of a literature text. While she stood above him smiling, he read the inscription in her large handwriting: *"Happy Birthday, My Dearest, Darling, Me!"* This had happened back in Chicago, when he was still a very young man just four years out of the South. He had been at that time convinced that there were certain mysteries in the world. He had been fascinated by what he read. She was from California, and he sensed in the writing that quality of ego said to be produced by the broadness of the sky in the West. He fell deeper in love with her, in love with the mystery of California.

The speaker was taking his place at the lectern. He was thanking Clair for the introduction. Everyone applauded. The speaker kissed Clair on the cheek. Everyone applauded. Clair tossed her head and smiled broadly and beautifully. She said something to the speaker in a voice too low for the mircophone to share. Louis thought she said, "Oh, wow!"

"Viola, you ought to be proud," Mrs. Burton was saying to Mrs. Richards. "Your Clair is settin' the example for my Ricky."

"It's *Fredricka*, Mother!" the pretty girl said. "You do that just to embarrass me." She pouted prettily, but kept her eyes on the speaker at the head table.

Both mothers laughed. Mrs. Burton winked at Louis. "They can say what they want about Watts," she said. "But if Clair and my Ricky come out of Watts, we got to be doing *something* right."

"I live out in *Hollywood*," Fredricka said. She said this with a defensive tone in her voice.

"Hollywood, Watts, Baldwin Hills," Mrs. Burton said, "it's all the same. Look like everywhere you go, the young people ain't happy with nothin'. That's why I'm so happy to hear Clair talkin' so strong about positive things."

Fredricka lit a cigarette. "Those pearls don't go with that dress," she said. "They should have been dark blue."

At the head table, the speaker, Lester Maltz, was talking about the necessity of having ideals.

Fredricka seemed bored. Louis could sense her eyes moving over his face. She was very pretty. Everything about her seemed calculated and neat. When she exhaled she blew the smoke from her nose toward the ceiling. He figured he had ten years on her. He was content to wait, listening to the speaker, until she said: "Where you from?"

"Chicago," he answered in a whisper.

She smiled. "And before that?"

"North Carolina," he answered.

"I thought so," Fredricka said.

"Why?" he asked.

"You dress funny."

"I thought so," he said. He paused a while and then asked, "What's the name of that movie you're in?"

She leaned across the table, her breasts moving loosely beneath the thin, green dress. *"The Syncopated Buck,"* she answered. "But it won't be out till next year."

"I'll see it," he told her.

She smiled, her large eyes flirting with a controlled intensity familiar to him. "You married?"

"No," he answered.

"It's just as well," she said. "Marriage is a bore."

The vacant look in her eyes reminded him of a Swedish actress he had seen in a recent movie about the domestic difficulties of the European elite. He thought, "If I keep talking to her, anything is possible after this show. She is just as lost as I am. I have only to remember my lines." But while thinking this he was looking around at Mrs. Richards and Mrs. Burton. Their eyes were fastened on the speaker at the head table. He listened to the words, and felt ashamed. He thought, "I'm lost. I am trying to remember the responses to lines this child has already memorized."

At the head table, the speaker was saying: ". . . one pays for what one gets. Nothing—love, recognition,

money, power, even a soul at peace with itself—comes
without its price. There is, therefore, no such animal as
the successful man. There is only a mass of people looking, sometimes in ignorant envy, at the *evidence* of prices
paid that will forever remain secret. *Everyone* pays. But
no one is telling the cost, because sometimes the terms
can be too frightening for others to contemplate . . ."

"Do Lord!" Mrs. Richards was saying beside him.

Clair sat at the head table with her eyes fixed on the
speaker. His name was Lester Maltz and everyone present
seemed to respect him. Maltz was a thin, elderly man, obviously successful in his profession if not wealthy. He had
that peaceful, not quite hungry look that Louis had come
to associate with people who had their appetites under
firm control. He spoke with a gentleness and rapport with
his audience, as if he understood completely their frame
of mind. They were marginal winners in a game they did
not really understand, and he seemed patient and content-
ed, like a good teacher, with helping them to understand
the rules. He was obviously a professional. The audience
looked at him with admiration. For Louis, he resembled
Cesar Romero in his prime. Thinking this, he felt guilty.
He thought, "If *he* is Cesar Romero, who am *I?*"

He had been born in North Carolina and now he lived
in Chicago. Louis was certain of at least this much. He
had been born in one kind of world and now lived in another, but in this new world all the old world rules had
been changed. His name was Louis Clayton and he was
from Baxter, North Carolina. His father's name was also
Louis Clayton but he had stayed, and died, in Baxter,
North Carolina. The father had been a textile worker.
The son was a college teacher. The father had been
barely literate. The son wrote bawdy poems, in the Eliza-

bethan style, to the broad and truant wife of a departmen-
tal colleague. For the past six months, reciting snatches of
his verse to her in bed, he had, inside his secret self, considered this a kind of triumph. It was an affirmation of
something, but of what, before now, he had not asked
himself. But now, listening to the speaker, half his mind
began to put the question. There was no response from
the other half. That part of his mind was occupied with
the speaker, and with Clair, up on the platform.

But he remembered part of the pathway to Chicago.
He remembered being drawn out of North Carolina and
pulled eastward and westward by forces still unclear to
him. From a distance, via television, he had seen that old
world disintegrate, and understood emotionally there was
little left to which he could return. From New York he
had looked around and seen a much larger world, one
clouded in mystery. He had moved toward it. He went
from New York to Boston, from Boston to Chicago—at
each stop resting, learning, growing always into something
more than he had been. It had seemed to him an easy
process, much like shedding old skins. He took care to
say his prayers at night so the process would not end. He
was twenty-five, and not at all embarrassed to pray on his
knees. He was all-confident, restless, overflowing with
courage. His mind was vibrant and alive. After taking his
degree, he got a job teaching at a small college. But he remained restless and curious about the rest of the world.
The year Clair Richards walked into his classroom, he
had looked at her, seen a mystery in her, and determined
to trace it all the way to California.

Louis had adored Clair's mystery. In a wintry Chicago
she wore red knee-high boots, daring in their thinness
against the snow-crusted ground. When it snowed heavily,

she dressed like a spring garden. He liked to watch her from the window, struggling, red-booted and blue-coated, through the stinging wind, a red-green shawl around her face, her eyes peeping through tiny slits. When she entered class and stamped the snow from her boots and body, she was always laughing. He remembered a movie, in Technicolor, in which it had snowed at Christmas in Los Angeles. In the whiteness of her teeth and the greenness of her shawl, while she stood in the doorway laughing, he could see that scene. In spring she wore white. She was very beautiful, and giddy-gay in a sense different from any girl he had ever known, in the South or elsewhere. When she came to his office she was always in a rush; she seemed always breathless, bursting with an energy not so much restless as carefree. He was intrigued by this. The ideas expressed in her papers were badly organized, suggesting a curious, untamed intellect bedazzled by affection for too many minds, or perhaps one unwilling to settle permanently on any single idea. Her mind seemed like a butterfly in a summer garden. He took great care while printing notes in the margins of her themes, comments suggesting his own sense of humor, a hint of his own sense of freedom calculated to correspond to her own. Whenever they discussed these notes, in his office, she leaned her smooth brown face close to his, and he smelled, in her perfume, the mystery that was California.

Lester Maltz was saying: "... values to hold onto. The choices are many. We all strive toward the good things of life, but unfortunately only a few achieve these goals. But this is no cause for despair. I say to you that out of twenty junkies on the corner of 243rd and Cypress, there is likely to be one with a little backbone, and a little imagination. If he can free himself, that is the man for the

other junkies to watch. What he chooses to reify—what
he selects to value—remains implanted in the imaginations of the others. They will not forget him, no matter
how forcefully they dismiss what he does. But achieving
this image is a matter of discipline, and also a matter of
love. We . . ."

"Amen!" Mrs. Richards said. She was crying.

Mrs. Burton was also moved by the speech. Louis saw
her reach over quickly and pluck a stray thread from
Fredricka's dress. Fredricka fluttered her eyelids rapidly,
acknowledging the touch, but did not avert her eyes from
the head table. She was watching Clair. Louis looked
around. The younger men gazed at the speaker with rapt
attention. The women looked sober. But the older men,
Louis saw, fidgeted uncomfortably, like little boys in
church accused of mischief. Plump, round-faced, stylishly
dressed, they seemed to him now sullen, now bored, then
restless. The man who looked like Marlon Brando sat
with his eyes closed. The one resembling Gregory Peck
was chewing on a cigar. Louis glanced suddenly at Fredricka and saw her following the movement of his eyes
with a playful, pouting smile. He felt apprehended, as if
he had been caught looking under her dress. He leaned
toward her and said, "What is the name your mother said
you're using in that movie?"

"Iola Fedd," Fredricka answered. Then she laughed
quietly. "What is the name you're using in yours?"

It was a harmless flirtation, but he saw the irony. Louis
laughed. "I forget," he told her. "I was in it a long time
ago."

Fredricka continued laughing. "Was it a hit?"

He turned his head and looked at Clair. She was very,

very beautiful sitting at the head table. Without turning back to face Fredricka, he whispered, "No."

His first trip to Los Angeles, five years before, had been at Clair's invitation to meet her mother. On several occasions the invitation had been withdrawn. She was wearing his ring. He felt he had the right to press her. But when prodded she grew sullen and depressed. Just before she left Chicago to return home for the summer, he had insisted on a firm date. Clair laughed and said, "Oh, wow!" At O'Hare, when he again insisted, her eyes had narrowed; a metallic toughness had crept into the tone of her voice. She lost much of her animation; her movements had become heavy, slow, like those of a man. When he kissed her goodbye, she had said, "I know you don't think I love you, but I do. Maybe I'm just too complex for you to understand."

A few weeks later she had called long-distance and invited him out in early August.

From the plane, the first view of the city was magnificent. Looking down he saw millions of green, blue, white, yellow, and red lights coalescing into lines, squares, triangles, and stars in the rust-brown light of dusk. A blue and brown sky hung neatly over the city like a warm blanket. There was a feeling of space one had to take inside oneself. Louis had felt completed. At the gate, when he kissed Clair again, he felt the mystery calling him on. It seemed to be saying, *"Here. Here."* It was a quiet sound speaking secretly inside him. In the airport coffee shop they sat quietly and looked each other over. They had been apart almost two months and something in Clair had changed. She wore green pants with pink sequins, a red halter and much makeup. She said little outside of small talk. Her eyes narrowed several times while they talked. Her mouth was firm and set, almost mannish in its determination. "I want you to meet some friends later," she told him. "But first, why don't you change your pants?"

He said that all his pants had narrow legs and cuffs.

She drove him around the city in her convertible. They parked in Hollywood and strolled several blocks down Sunset Boulevard. At Grauman's they paused while she pointed out the names and handprints and footprints frozen in the dirty cement. She stared long at the concrete, as if searching for something she could not find. Louis waited, watching addicts, pimps, whores, and outlandish homosexuals strolling with the tourists along the boulevard. Then Clair drove him up into Baldwin Hills, then down into the humid flatlands of Watts. There was a Santa Ana condition that night, and people lounged on the street corners or around checkerboards in vacant, garbage-strewn lots. They looked surly, and without hope. He told Clair that Watts reminded him of a Southern town dressed up in cement and neon and streetlights. Instead of red-necks on the inside keeping watch, the residents had television and police helicopters to remind them of who maintained the status quo. Clair nodded. "I would have rioted, too," he told her. Clair pointed out the many kinds of cars. They drove to her home on the outskirts of Watts. When Louis met her mother, Mrs. Viola Richards, the woman looked at him. embraced him, and then slapped him hard on the left cheek.

Louis heard Lester Maltz saying, ". . . honor . . ."

Mrs. Richards's eyes glistened. She was smiling radiantly.

But she had slapped him. He raised his hand to his

cheek and remembered. He had felt ashamed. But also he had felt confused, because then she had laughed and treated him royally. She had poured all her skills into preparing the dinner. And afterward, while Clair changed in her bedroom for the party with her friends, Mrs. Richards had chased him out of the kitchen while she washed dishes. She hummed hymns familiar to him. He listened to them while he waited in the living room for Clair. The living room contained familiar items: a vase of plastic flowers, a yellowed cretonne lambrequin hanging from the mantel, on one wall a blue, framed placard with the Golden Rule spelled out in silver glitter. Above the sofa hung a cheap painting of Martin Luther King. On the top of the television were two pictures, placed side by side on a pink crocheted doily. One was of a thin-faced, brown-skinned man, more Indian than African in his features. It was a very old and discolored print. The man was smiling grimly. This was Clair's father, Dominion Richards, a product of Virginia, Detroit, and Los Angeles. Clair had told him he had died when she was just a baby. The other picture was of a very attractive white woman. Her blond hair was set in the curly style of the 1940s. She did not smile. Her narrow eyes glared from beneath heavily painted brows; her thin lips, shining with rouge, were pressed into a determined set. She looked arrogant. He read the inscription at the bottom of the photograph: "To Viola, from Charlotta Curry." She looked somewhat familiar.

"That there's a woman I worked for a long time ago." Mrs. Richards had come quietly into the room and was standing behind him. She reached past him and took the picture from atop the television and looked longingly at it. She sighed. "She was a good child," Mrs. Richards said, "but she had hard luck. She would of been great if the Lord had been with her, but I guess it just wasn't her time." She looked up from the picture, her eyes warm and knowing. "You know, movies is a hard business."

Then Louis saw that the woman was made up to resemble Barbara Stanwyck.

"Mama, where did you put my red pants?" Clair called from the bedroom. "Mama, where are those red pants with the *ruffles?*"

Mrs. Richards quickly wiped her hands on her apron. "Look in that closet," she called.

"*What* closet?" Clair yelled. "Mama, I've *told* you about handling my things. Now I want you to *find those pants!*"

Mrs. Richards looked sheepishly at Louis and sighed. "She treat me wrong," she whispered. "But that's my heart. That's all I got in the world. What else can I do but *love her?*"

Suddenly she took his hand, squeezed it, and pulled him after her toward Clair's room.

The place was congested. Trunks, suitcases, hat and shoe boxes, discarded clothes, and books were strewn on the bed, the chairs, the dressers, and the floor. The larger dresser, with pictures and postcards stuck into its mirror, was covered with bottles of perfume, lotion, tubes of eye shadow, lipstick, hose. Before a walk-in closet occupying one side of the room stood Clair, her fox terrier Marty yapping at her feet, with her hands pressed determinedly against her hips. Inside the closet Louis saw hundreds of dresses arranged by color, style, length, fabric. Wire hangers strained under the load of pants. On the floor of the closet, and hanging from racks against its walls, were dozens, perhaps hundreds, of shoes of different styles. "*I want those pants!"* Clair was saying. "I *told* you when I *left* not to *touch* my things!" The dog, Marty, barked fiercely along with Clair's voice.

Mrs. Richards stood behind her daughter before the closet. She seemed flustered and embarrassed, almost like a child caught in error. She said to Louis, "See, she don't treat me right. No, she don't treat her mama right. I have work my fingers to the bone, and she *still* don't treat me right." She looked from Clair to Louis, then from Louis to Clair. Her eyes seemed to be imploring one of them. Louis could not be sure. Mrs. Richards moaned, "But what can you do when it's the only baby you got?"

Louis felt called upon to act. The look in the mother's face seemed to be begging him. He stepped past Clair, grabbed a dress from its hanger, and threw it at her. "Wear this!" he shouted. "There's so many lights in this city, a mismatched one won't dull the glow of things. Wear this and be for one night *less* than a star!"

Marty, the little brown fox terrier, snarled at him and dug its claws into the carpet. Then it jumped at him and barked. Clair turned quickly from Louis. She bent and swept the dog into her arms. And while it barked and snapped at him, she pressed it to her breast, her face, her neck, allowing its tiny nails to scratch her in its struggle to break free and avenge its mistress. Red welts appeared on her arms, her cheeks; loose threads appeared on her halter. Clair hugged the dog closer. Then she turned her head and looked up at Louis, her face enraged and stubbornly set, like a pretty little bulldog.

"That's all I have in the world," Mrs. Richards was sobbing. "I have work my fingers to the bone. She *don't* treat me right. She *don't treat me right.* But it's my *heart!"*

Mrs. Richards rushed toward Louis and slapped him hard on the face.

At the party much later, among Clair's friends, a young man high on marijuana came up to Louis and said, "I see by the marks on your lady, my man, that you have plans to settle in. I think you was a little rough, but I also think you doin' the right thing. They're barracudas, my man, *barracudas!* I don't know how in the *fuck* it happen, but that's the way things is."

This young man, with a full belly protruding from inside his white suit, explained, with considerable embarrassment, that in reality he was a refugee from a little country town in Florida. Since other people were crowded around, he spoke softly while disclosing this. Still later in the night, when he passed Louis again, he winked, paused with a drink in his hand, and sang in a low voice: "If I live, see next fall, I ain't go'n pick no cotton at *all!*" He laughed then, rolling his eyes toward the crowd, and continued in a slower voice, his left foot beating out the rhythm: "If I live, don't get kill, *I'm* goin' back . . . I'm goin' . . . I'm goin' *back* . . ."

Louis watched Clair on the other side of the room. She was surrounded by people and smiling radiantly. *"Jacksonville!"* Louis heard himself saying to the chubby young man.

The young man laughed. He jabbed a knowing finger at Louis, as if the two of them shared a great, comic secret. Both of them then laughed hysterically.

Lester Maltz was presenting Clair with the award for civic achievement. The audience applauded loudly when he finished reading the citation. Beside him, Louis heard Mrs. Richards weeping. Mrs. Burton was patting her hand. Fredricka's eyelids fluttered, like a camera lens being shifted into closer focus. She seemed to Louis positively jealous. "My baby was always a hard worker," Mrs. Richards was saying. She turned to Louis. "Don't you think my baby's smart?"

"She's smart," he whispered back.

Clair was also very beautiful. Standing at the lectern, she smiled around the room with a quality of control in her radiance that made his heart jump with desire. He began planning what he would say to her later, after they had sent her mother home. "Ladies and gentlemen," Clair said. "Colleagues, platform guests, and members of the Progressive Association of Greater Watts." She looked from table to table while saying this, moving her eyes in a natural, intimate sweep that seemed to promise something special to each person in the audience. She clutched the silver plaque against her breasts. "The road to achievement is always rough and strewn with the mis- . . ."

She spoke very beautifully. She seemed confident, shining, alive. But although Louis tried very hard, he could not recall the rhythm of her in bed. Watching her, he resolved to try harder.

". . . This is only just," Clair was saying, "because self-interest, finally, is at the heart of every individual effort. So I am very proud to accept this award as a tribute from my friends and colleagues in the Progressive Association of Greater Watts. But having achieved, one must not forget from whence one came, or the influences that have shaped one's ambitions." Clair paused a beat and looked down toward the table where Louis sat. She smiled magnificently. "Mom?" she said.

Mrs. Richards stood, dabbing at her eyes with the pink handkerchief.

"For those of you who don't know her, this is my mom. More than anyone else, she is responsible for my success." Again Clair paused a beat. Then she smiled and said, "Oh, wow! That's my *mom!*"

Everyone applauded enthusiastically. Even the Chicano waiters, leaning with their trays against the glass walls, seemed touched. Lester Maltz seemed deeply moved. He bowed his head chivalrously toward the elderly woman. Mrs. Richards bravely faced the audience and blushed through her tears. The man who looked like Marlon Brando, seated at the next table, whistled loudly and shouted, "Speech! *Speech!*" This shout was taken up by many others in the room. Several Chicano waiters pounded tamely against their trays. Mrs. Richards trembled, breathed deeply, and closed her eyes. "I just wants to say," she began in a tearful tone of voice, "that that there's my heart up there. I have slaved many's the day to put her through school and give her all the things I never could have, bein' a widow-woman and all. And I have work all my life for white people that have been more than nice to me. Why, I remember when my Clair was a teeny, fatherless baby, a woman told me she was just too *pretty* to not be great. And that has been my solace and my inspiration. So I want all of y'all to remember, it don't make no nevermind *where* you come from, just so you get somewheres. Jesus Christ was born in a manger, and thanks to my prayers to Him all these years, tonight I'm the happiest mother in the world. Thank you. Thank you all."

People were extraordinarily moved. There was complete silence for a full minute after Mrs. Richards sat down. Then there were many rounds of applause.

During all this Louis kept his eyes on Clair. Framed by

the platform, smiling beautifully while she drank in the
applause, she looked the way she should have looked all
her life. She looked like the woman in the picture who
resembled Barbara Stanwyck. Louis smiled to himself. He
watched Clair. But in his imagination he created the face
behind the picture as a farmer's daughter from Iowa, Ne-
braska, perhaps Missouri; a young girl with imagination
and a harsh-sounding German name. Twenty-five or
thirty years ago, perhaps, she might have been seized by a
fantasy of a more glamorous life. She had escaped the
prairies, racing to Los Angeles to claim her possibilities.
Perhaps she glowed for an instant in this light-infected
city, established a starlet's cottage somewhere in the hills,
hired a black maid who listened intently to the fantasies
she spun while waiting for her break. And then, just as
suddenly, she had become one of the countless losers, dis-
placed by the actress who brought most force to the pre-
vailing image. Of her career, the only parts surviving on
film were probably the tough-talking barmaid, the ambitious flapper, the young girl with grit on the wagon train,
the gangster's moll, the competitive businesswoman in a
brutal world rigged in favor of men.

Clair saw him watching her and winked at him. She
was beautiful.

Louis waved.

"Also in the audience tonight," Clair said, "is another
person of great importance to my career. Ladies and
gentlemen, my former teacher, Mr. Louis Clayton, from
the great city of Chicago. He just happened to be in LA
tonight attending the MLA convention and was delighted
that he could join us." Clair was pointing toward him, in-
dicating he should stand. "My former teacher," she told

the crowd, her voice rising. "How about a warm LA round of applause for *Mr.* Louis *Clayton?* Lou?"

Louis stood.

People applauded politely.

A Loaf of Bread

IT was one of those obscene situations, pedestrian to most people, but invested with meaning for a few poor folk whose lives are usually spent outside the imaginations of their fellow citizens. A grocer named Harold Green was caught red-handed selling to one group of people the very same goods he sold at lower prices at similar outlets in better neighborhoods. He had been doing this for many years, and at first he could not understand the outrage heaped upon him. He acted only from habit, he insisted, and had nothing personal against the people whom he served. They were his neighbors. Many of them he had carried on the cuff during hard times. Yet, through some mysterious access to a television station, the poor folk were now empowered to make grand denunciations of the grocer. Green's children now saw their father's business being picketed on the Monday evening news.

No one could question the fact that the grocer had been overcharging the people. On the news even the reporter grimaced distastefully while reading the statistics.

His expression said, "It is my job to report the news, but sometimes even I must disassociate myself from it to protect my honor." This, at least, was the impression the grocer's children seemed to bring away from the television. Their father's name had not been mentioned, but there was a close-up of his store with angry black people, and a few outraged whites, marching in groups of three in front of it. There was also a close-up of his name. After seeing this, they were in no mood to watch cartoons. At the dinner table, disturbed by his children's silence, Harold Green felt compelled to say, "I am not a dishonest man." Then he felt ashamed. The children, a boy and his older sister, immediately left the table, leaving Green alone with his wife. "Ruth, I am not dishonest," he repeated to her.

Ruth Green did not say anything. She knew, and her husband did not, that the outraged people had also picketed the school attended by their children. They had threatened to return each day until Green lowered his prices. When they called her at home to report this, she had promised she would talk with him. Since she could not tell him this, she waited for an opening. She looked at her husband across the table.

"I did not make the world," Green began, recognizing at once the seriousness in her stare. "My father came to this country with nothing but his shirt. He was exploited for as long as he couldn't help himself. He did not protest or picket. He put himself in a position to play by the rules he had learned." He waited for his wife to answer, and when she did not, he tried again. "I did not make this world," he repeated. "I only make my way in it. Such people as these, they do not know enough to not be exploited. If not me, there would be a Greek, a Chinaman, maybe an Arab or a smart one of their own kind. Believe me, I deal with them. There is something in their style that lacks the patience to run a concern such as mine. If I closed down, take my word on it, someone else would do what has to be done."

But Ruth Green was not thinking of his leaving. Her mind was on other matters. Her children had cried when they came home early from school. She had no special feeling for the people who picketed, but she did not like to see her children cry. She had kissed them generously, then sworn them to silence. "One day this week," she told her husband, "you will give free, for eight hours, anything your customers come in to buy. There will be no publicity, except what they spread by word of mouth. No matter what they say to you, no matter what they take, you will remain silent." She stared deeply into him for what she knew was there. "If you refuse, you have seen the last of your children and myself."

Her husband grunted. Then he leaned toward her. "I will not knuckle under," he said. "I will *not* give!"

"We shall see," his wife told him.

The black pickets, for the most part, had at first been frightened by the audacity of their undertaking. They were peasants whose minds had long before become resigned to their fate as victims. None of them, before now, had thought to challenge this. But now, when they watched themselves on television, they hardly recognized the faces they saw beneath the hoisted banners and placards. Instead of reflecting the meekness they all felt, the faces looked angry. The close-ups looked especially intimidating. Several of the first pickets, maids who worked in the suburbs, reported that their employers, seeing the activity on the afternoon news, had begun treating them with new respect. One woman, midway through the weather report, called around the neighborhood to disclose that her employer had that very day given her a new china plate for her meals. The paper plates, on which all previous meals had been served, had been thrown into the wastebasket. One recipient of this call, a middle-aged woman known for her bashfulness and humility, rejoined that her husband, a sheet-metal worker, had only a few hours before been called "Mister" by his supervisor, a white man with a passionate hatred of color. She added the tale of a neighbor down the street, a widow-woman named Murphy, who had at first been reluctant to join the picket; this woman now was insisting it should be made a daily event. Such talk as this circulated among the people who had been instrumental in raising the issue. As news of their victory leaked into the ears of others who had not participated, they received all through the night calls from strangers requesting verification, offering advice, and vowing support. Such strangers listened, and then volunteered stories about indignities inflicted on them by city officials, policemen, other grocers. In this way, over a period of hours, the community became even more incensed and restless than it had been at the time of the initial picket.

Soon, the man who had set events in motion found himself a hero. His name was Nelson Reed, and all his adult life he had been employed as an assembly-line worker. He was a steady husband, the father of three children, and a deacon in the Baptist church. All his life he had trusted in God and gotten along. But now something in him capitulated to the reality that came suddenly into focus. "I was wrong," he told people who called him. "The onliest thing that matters in this world is *money*.

And when was the last time you seen a picture of Jesus
on a dollar bill?" This line, which he repeated over and
over, caused a few callers to laugh nervously, but not
without some affirmation that this was indeed the way
things were. Many said they had known it all along. Others argued that although it was certainly true, it was one
thing to live without money and quite another to live
without faith. But still most callers laughed and said,
"You right. You *know* I know you right. Ain't it the
truth, though?" Only a few people, among them Nelson
Reed's wife, said nothing and looked very sad.

Why they looked sad, however, they would not communicate. And anyone observing their troubled faces
would have to trust his own intuition. It is known that
Reed's wife, Betty, measured all events against the
fullness of her own experience. She was skeptical of everything. Brought to the church after a number of years
of living openly with a jazz musician, she had embraced
religion when she married Nelson Reed. But though she
no longer believed completely in the world, she nonetheless had not fully embraced God. There was something in
the nature of Christ's swift rise that had always bothered
her, and something in the blood and vengeance of the Old
Testament that was mellowing and refreshing. But she
had never communicated these thoughts to anyone, especially her husband. Instead, she smiled vacantly while
others professed leaps of faith, remained silent when
friends spoke fiercely of their convictions. The presence of
this vacuum in her contributed to her personal mystery;
people said she was beautiful, although she was not out-
wardly so. Perhaps it was because she wished to protect
this inner beauty that she did not smile now, and looked
extremely sad, listening to her husband on the telephone.

Nelson Reed had no reason to be sad. He seemed to
grow more energized and talkative as the days passed. He
was invited by an alderman, on the Tuesday after the initial picket, to tell his story on a local television talk show.
He sweated heavily under the hot white lights and attempted to be philosophical. "I notice," the host said to
him, "that you are not angry at this exploitative treatment. What, Mr. Reed, is the source of your calm?" The
assembly-line worker looked unabashedly into the camera
and said, "I have always believed in *Justice* with a capital
J. I was raised up from a baby believin' that God ain't
gonna let nobody go *too* far. See, in *my* mind God is in
charge of *all* the capital letters in the alphabet of this
world. It say in the Scripture He is Alpha and Omega, the
first and the last. He is just about the *onliest* capitalizer
they is." Both Reed and the alderman laughed. "Now,
when *men* start to capitalize, they gets *greedy*. They put a
little *j* in *joy* and a littler one in *justice*. They raise up a
big *G* in *Greed* and a big *E* in *Evil*. Well, soon as they
commence to put a little *g* in *god*, you can expect some
kind of reaction. The Savior will just raise up the *H* in
Hell and go on from there. And that's just what I'm doin',
giving these sharpies *HELL* with a big *H*." The talk show
host laughed along with Nelson Reed and the alderman.
After the taping they drank coffee in the back room of
the studio and talked about the sad shape of the world.

Three days before he was to comply with his wife's request, Green, the grocer, saw this talk show on television
while at home. The words of Nelson Reed sent a chill
through him. Though Reed had attempted to be philosophical, Green did not perceive the statement in this light.
Instead, he saw a vindictive-looking black man seated be-

tween an ambitious alderman and a smug talk-show host. He saw them chatting comfortably about the nature of evil. The cameraman had shot mostly close-ups, and Green could see the set in Nelson Reed's jaw. The color of Reed's face was maddening. When his children came into the den, the grocer was in a sweat. Before he could think, he had shouted at them and struck the button turning off the set. The two children rushed from the room screaming. Ruth Green ran in from the kitchen. She knew why he was upset because she had received a call about the show; but she said nothing and pretended ignorance. Her children's school had been picketed that day, as it had the day before. But both children were still forbidden to speak of this to their father.

"Where do they get so much power?" Green said to his wife. "Two days ago, nobody would have cared. Now, everywhere, even in my home, I am condemned as a rascal. And what do I own? An airline? A multinational? Half of South America? *No!* I own three stores, one of which happens to be in a certain neighborhood inhabited by people who cost me money to run it." He sighed and sat upright on the sofa, his chubby legs spread wide. "A cab driver has a meter that clicks as he goes along. I pay extra for insurance, iron bars, pilfering by customers and employees. Nothing clicks. But when I add a little overhead to my prices, suddenly everything clicks. But for someone else. When was there last such a world?" He pressed the palms of both hands to his temples, suggesting a bombardment of brain-stinging sounds.

This gesture evoked no response from Ruth Green. She remained standing by the door, looking steadily at him. She said, "To protect yourself, I would not stock any more fresh cuts of meat in the store until after the give-

away on Saturday. Also, I would not tell it to the employees until after the first customer of the day has begun to
check out. But I would urge you to hire several security
guards to close the door promptly at seven-thirty, as is
usual." She wanted to say much more than this, but did
not. Instead she watched him. He was looking at the
blank gray television screen, his palms still pressed against
his ears. "In case you need to hear again," she continued
in a weighty tone of voice, "I said two days ago, and I say
again now, that if you fail to do this you will not see your
children again for many years."

He twisted his head and looked up at her. "What is the
color of these people?" he asked.

"Black," his wife said.

"And what is the name of my children?"

"Green."

The grocer smiled. "There is your answer," he told his
wife. "Green is the only color I am interested in."

His wife did not smile. "Insufficient," she said.

"The world is mad!" he moaned. "But it is a point of
sanity with me to not bend. I will not bend." He crossed
his legs and pressed one hand firmly atop his knee. *"I will
not bend,"* he said.

"We will see," his wife said.

Nelson Reed, after the television interview, became the
acknowledged leader of the disgruntled neighbors. At first
a number of them met in the kitchen at his house; then,
as space was lacking for curious newcomers, a mass meeting was held on Thursday in an abandoned theater. His
wife and three children sat in the front row. Behind them
sat the widow Murphy, Lloyd Dukes, Tyrone Brown, Les
Jones—those who had joined him on the first picket line.

Behind these sat people who bought occasionally at the store, people who lived on the fringes of the neighborhood, people from other neighborhoods come to investigate the problem, and the merely curious. The middle rows were occupied by a few people from the suburbs, those who had seen the talk show and whose outrage at the grocer proved much more powerful than their fear of black people. In the rear of the theater crowded aging, old-style leftists, somber students, cynical young black men with angry grudges to explain with inarticulate gestures. Leaning against the walls, huddled near the doors at the rear, tape-recorder-bearing social scientists looked as detached and serene as bookies at the track. Here and there, in this diverse crowd, a politician stationed himself, pumping hands vigorously and pressing his palms gently against the shoulders of elderly people. Other visitors passed out leaflets, buttons, glossy color prints of men who promoted causes, the familiar and obscure. There was a hubbub of voices, a blend of the strident and the playful, the outraged and the reverent, lending an undercurrent of ominous energy to the assembly.

Nelson Reed spoke from a platform on the stage, standing before a yellowed, shredded screen that had once reflected the images of matinee idols. "I don't mind sayin' that I have always been a sucker," he told the crowd. "All my life I have been a sucker for the words of Jesus. Being a natural-born fool, I just ain't never had the *sense* to learn no better. Even right today, while the whole world is sayin' wrong is right and up is down, I'm so dumb I'm *still* steady believin' what is wrote in the Good Book . . ."

From the audience, especially the front rows, came a chorus singing, "Preach!"

"I have no doubt," he continued in a low baritone, "that it's true what is writ in the Good Book: 'The last shall be first and the first shall be last.' I don't know about y'all, but I have *always* been the last. I never wanted to be the first, but sometimes it look like the world get so bad that them that's holdin' onto the tree of life is the onliest ones left when God commence to blowin' dead leafs off the branches."

"Now you preaching," someone called.

In the rear of the theater a white student shouted an awkward "Amen."

Nelson Reed began walking across the stage to occupy the major part of his nervous energy. But to those in the audience, who now hung on his every word, it looked as though he strutted. "All my life," he said, "I have claimed to be a man without earnin' the right to call myself that. You know, the *average* man ain't really a man. The average man is a *boot-licker*. In fact, the *average* man would *run away* if he found hisself standing alone facin' down a adversary. I have done that *too many a time* in my life! But *not no more.* Better to be *once* was than *never* was a man. I will tell you tonight, there is somethin' *wrong* in being average. *I intend to stand up!* Now, if your average man that ain't really a man stand up, two things gonna happen: *One,* he g'on bust through all the weights that been place on his head, and, *two,* he g'on feel a lot of pain. But that same hurt is what make things fall in place. That, and gettin' your hands on one of these slick four-flushers tight enough so's you can squeeze him and say, *'No more!'* You do that, you g'on hurt some, but *you won't be average no more . . .*"

"No *more!*" a few people in the front rows repeated.

"I say *no more!*" Nelson Reed shouted.

"*No more! No more! No more!*" The chant rustled through the crowd like the rhythm of an autumn wind against a shedding tree.

Then people laughed and chattered in celebration.

As for the grocer, from the evening of the television interview he had begun to make plans. Unknown to his wife, he cloistered himself several times with his brother-in-law, an insurance salesman, and plotted a course. He had no intention of tossing steaks to the crowd. "And why should I, Tommy?" he asked his wife's brother, a lean, bald-headed man named Thomas. "I don't cheat anyone. I have never cheated anyone. The businesses I run are always on the up-and-up. So why should I pay?"

"Quite so," the brother-in-law said, chewing an unlit cigarillo. "The world has gone crazy. Next they will say that people in my business are responsible for prolonging life. I have found that people who refuse to believe in death refuse also to believe in the harshness of life. I sell well by saying that death is a long happiness. I show people the realities of life and compare this to a funeral with dignity, *and* the promise of a bundle for every loved one salted away. When they look around hard at life, they usually buy."

"So?" asked Green. Thomas was a college graduate with a penchant for philosophy.

"So," Thomas answered. "You must fight to show these people the reality of both your situation and theirs. How would it be if you visited one of their meetings and chalked out, on a blackboard, the dollars and cents of **your** operation? Explain your overhead, your security fees, all the additional expenses. If you treat them with respect, they might understand."

Green frowned. "That I would never do," he said. "It would be admission of a certain guilt."

The brother-in-law smiled, but only with one corner of his mouth. "Then you have something to feel guilty about?" he asked.

The grocer frowned at him. *"Nothing!"* he said with great emphasis.

"So?" Thomas said.

This first meeting between the grocer and his brother-in-law took place on Thursday, in a crowded barroom.

At the second meeting, in a luncheonette, it was agreed that the grocer should speak privately with the leader of the group, Nelson Reed. The meeting at which this was agreed took place on Friday afternoon. After accepting this advice from Thomas, the grocer resigned himself to explain to Reed, in as finite detail as possible, the economic structure of his operation. He vowed to suppress no information. He would explain everything: inventories, markups, sale items, inflation, balance sheets, specialty items, overhead, and that mysterious item called profit. This last item, promising to be the most difficult to explain, Green and his brother-in-law debated over for several hours. They agreed first of all that a man should not work for free, then they agreed that it was unethical to ruthlessly exploit. From these parameters, they staked out an area between fifteen and forty percent, and agreed that someplace between these two borders lay an amount of return that could be called fair. This was easy, but then Thomas introduced the factor of circumstance. He questioned whether the fact that one serviced a risky area justified the earning of profits, closer to the forty-percent edge of the scale. Green was unsure. Thomas smiled. "Here is a case that will point out an analogy," he said, licking a cigarillo. "I read in the papers that a family wants to sell an electric stove. I call the home and the man says fifty dollars. I ask to come out and inspect the merchandise. When I arrive I see they are poor, have already bought a new stove that is connected, and are selling the old one for fifty dollars because they want it out of the place. The electric stove is in good condition, worth much more than fifty. But because I see what I see I offer forty-five."

Green, for some reason, wrote down this figure on the back of the sales slip for the coffee they were drinking.

The brother-in-law smiled. He chewed his cigarillo. "The man agrees to take forty-five dollars, saying he has had no other calls. I look at the stove again and see a spot of rust. I say I will give him forty dollars. He agrees to this, on condition that I myself haul it away. I say I will haul it away if he comes down to thirty. You, of course, see where I am going."

The grocer nodded. "The circumstances of his situation, his need to get rid of the stove quickly, placed him in a position where he has little room to bargain?"

"Yes," Thomas answered. "So? Is it ethical, Harry?"

Harold Green frowned. He had never liked his brother-in-law, and now he thought the insurance agent was being crafty. "But," he answered, "this man does not *have* to sell! It is his choice whether to wait for other calls. It is not the fault of the buyer that the seller is in a hurry. It is the right of the buyer to get what he wants at the lowest price possible. That is the rule. That has *always* been the rule. And the reverse of it applies to the seller as well."

"Yes," Thomas said, sipping coffee from the Styrofoam cup. "But suppose that in addition to his hurry to sell, the owner was also of a weak soul. There are, after all, many such people." He smiled. "Suppose he placed no value on the money?"

"Then," Green answered, "your example is academic. Here we are not talking about real life. One man lives by the code, one man does not. Who is there free enough to make a judgment?" He laughed. "Now you see," he told his brother-in-law. "Much more than a few dollars are at stake. If this one buyer is to be condemned, then so are most people in the history of the world. An examination of history provides the only answer to your question. This code will be here tomorrow, long after the ones who do not honor it are not."

They argued fiercely late into the afternoon, the brother-in-law leaning heavily on his readings. When they parted, a little before 5:00 P.M., nothing had been resolved.

Neither was much resolved during the meeting between Green and Nelson Reed. Reached at home by the grocer in the early evening, the leader of the group spoke coldly at first, but consented finally to meet his adversary at a nearby drugstore for coffee and a talk. They met at the lunch counter, shook hands awkwardly, and sat for a few minutes discussing the weather. Then the grocer pulled two gray ledgers from his briefcase. "You have for years come into my place," he told the man. "In my memory I have always treated you well. Now our relationship has come to this." He slid the books along the counter until they touched Nelson Reed's arm.

Reed opened the top book and flipped the thick green pages with his thumb. He did not examine the figures.

"All I know," he said, "is over at your place a can of soup cost me fifty-five cents, and two miles away at your other store for white folks you chargin' thirty-nine cents." He said this with the calm authority of an outraged soul. A quality of condescension tinged with pity crept into his gaze.

The grocer drummed his fingers on the counter top. He twisted his head and looked away, toward shelves containing cosmetics, laxatives, toothpaste. His eyes lingered on a poster of a woman's apple red lips and milk white teeth. The rest of the face was missing.

"Ain't no use to hide," Nelson Reed said, as to a child. "*I* know you wrong, *you* know you wrong, and before I finish, *everybody in this city* g'on know you wrong. God don't *like* ugly." He closed his eyes and gripped the cup of coffee. Then he swung his head suddenly and faced the grocer again. "Man, why you want to *do* people that way?" he asked. "We human, same as you."

"Before *God!*" Green exclaimed, looking squarely into the face of Nelson Reed. "Before God!" he said again. "*I am not an evil man!*" These last words sounded more like a moan as he tightened the muscles in his throat to lower the sound of his voice. He tossed his left shoulder as if adjusting the sleeve of his coat, or as if throwing off some unwanted weight. Then he peered along the counter top. No one was watching. At the end of the counter the waitress was scrubbing the coffee urn. "Look at these figures, please," he said to Reed.

The man did not drop his gaze. His eyes remained fixed on the grocer's face.

"All right," Green said. "Don't look. I'll tell you what is in these books, believe me if you want. I work twelve hours a day, one day off per week, running my business in three stores. I am not a wealthy person. In one place, in the area you call white, I get by barely by smiling lustily at old ladies, stocking gourmet stuff on the chance I will build a reputation as a quality store. The two clerks there cheat me; there is nothing I can do. In this business you must be friendly with everybody. The second place is on the other side of town, in a neighborhood as poor as this one. I get out there seldom. The profits are not worth the gas. I use the loss there as a write-off against some other properties." He paused. "Do you understand write-off?" he asked Nelson Reed.

"Naw," the man said.

Harold Green laughed. "What does it matter?" he said in a tone of voice intended for himself alone. "In this area I will admit I make a profit, but it is not so much as you think. But I do not make a profit here because the people are black. I make a profit because a profit is here to be made. I invest more here in window bars, theft losses, insurance, spoilage; I deserve to make more here than at the other places." He looked, almost imploringly, at the man seated next to him. "You don't accept this as the right of a man in business?"

Reed grunted. "Did the bear shit in the woods?" he said.

Again Green laughed. He gulped his coffee awkwardly, as if eager to go. Yet his motions slowed once he had set his coffee cup down on the blue plastic saucer. "Place yourself in *my* situation," he said, his voice high and tentative. "If *you* were running my store in this neighborhood, what would be *your* position? Say on a profit scale of fifteen to forty percent, at what point in between would you draw the line?"

Nelson Reed thought. He sipped his coffee and seemed to chew the liquid. "Fifteen to forty?" he repeated.

"Yes."

"I'm a churchgoin' man," he said. "Closer to fifteen than to forty."

"How close?"

Nelson Reed thought. "In church you tithe ten percent."

"In restaurants you tip fifteen," the grocer said quickly.

"All right," Reed said. "Over fifteen."

"How much over?"

Nelson Reed thought.

"Twenty, thirty, thirty-five?" Green chanted, leaning closer to Reed.

Still the man thought.

"Forty? Maybe even forty-five or fifty?" the grocer breathed in Reed's ear. "In the supermarkets, you know, they have more subtle ways of accomplishing such feats."

Reed slapped his coffee cup with the back of his right hand. The brown liquid swirled across the counter top, wetting the books. *"Damn this!"* he shouted.

Startled, Green rose from his stool.

Nelson Reed was trembling. "I ain't *you*," he said in a deep baritone. "I ain't the *supermarket* neither. All I is is a poor man that works *too* hard to see his pay slip through his fingers like rainwater. All I know is you done *cheat* me, you done *cheat* everybody in the neighborhood, and we organized now to get some of it *back!*" Then he stood and faced the grocer. "My daddy sharecropped down in Mississippi and bought in the company store. He owed them twenty-three years when he died. I paid off five of them years and then run away to up here. Now, I'm a deacon in the Baptist church. I raised my kids the

way my daddy raise me and don't bother nobody. Now
come to find out, after all my runnin', they done lift that
same company store up out of Mississippi and slip it
down on us here! Well, my daddy was a *fighter,* and if he
hadn't owed all them years he would of raise him some
hell. Me, I'm steady my daddy's child, plus I got seniority
in my union. I'm a free man. Buddy, don't you know *I'm
gonna raise me some hell!"*

Harold Green reached for a paper napkin to sop the
coffee soaking into his books.

Nelson Reed threw a dollar on top of the books and
walked away.

"I *will not* do it!" Harold Green said to his wife that
same evening. They were in the bathroom of their home.
Bending over the face bowl, she was washing her hair
with a towel draped around her neck. The grocer stood
by the door, looking in at her. "I will not bankrupt myself
tomorrow," he said.

"I've been thinking about it, too," Ruth Green said,
shaking her wet hair. "You'll do it, Harry."

"Why should I?" he asked. "You won't leave. You
know it was a bluff. I've waited this long for you to calm
down. Tomorrow is Saturday. This week has been a hard
one. Tonight let's be realistic."

"Of course you'll do it," Ruth Green said. She said it
the way she would say "Have some toast." She said,
"You'll do it because you want to see your children grow
up."

"And for what other reason?" he asked.

She pulled the towel tighter around her neck. "Because
you are at heart a moral man."

He grinned painfully. "If I am, why should I have to prove it to *them?*"

"Not them," Ruth Green said, freezing her movements and looking in the mirror. "Certainly not them. By no means them. They have absolutely nothing to do with this."

"Who, then?" he asked, moving from the door into the room. "Who else should I prove something to?"

His wife was crying. But her entire face was wet. The tears moved secretly down her face.

"Who else?" Harold Green asked.

It was almost 11:00 P.M. and the children were in bed. They had also cried when they came home from school. Ruth Green said, "For yourself, Harry. For the love that lives inside your heart."

All night the grocer thought about this.

Nelson Reed also slept little that Friday night. When he returned home from the drugstore, he reported to his wife as much of the conversation as he could remember. At first he had joked about the exchange between himself and the grocer, but as more details returned to his conscious mind he grew solemn and then bitter. "He ask me to put myself in *his* place," Reed told his wife. "Can you imagine that kind of gumption? I never cheated nobody in my life. All my life I have lived on Bible principles. I am a deacon in the church. I have work all my life for other folks and I don't even own the house I live in." He paced up and down the kitchen, his big arms flapping loosely at his sides. Betty Reed sat at the table, watching. "This here's a low-down, ass-kicking world," he said. "I swear to God it is! All my life I have lived on principle and I ain't got a dime in the bank. Betty," he turned suddenly toward her, "don't you think I'm a fool?"

"Mr. Reed," she said. "Let's go on to bed."

But he would not go to bed. Instead, he took the fifth of bourbon from the cabinet under the sink and poured himself a shot. His wife refused to join him. Reed drained the glass of whiskey, and then another, while he resumed pacing the kitchen floor. He slapped his hands against his sides. "*I* think I'm a fool," he said. "Ain't got a dime in the bank, ain't got a pot to *pee* in or a wall to pitch it over, and that there *cheat* ask me to put myself inside *his* shoes. Hell, I can't even *afford* the kind of shoes he wears." He stopped pacing and looked at his wife.

"Mr. Reed," she whispered, "tomorrow ain't a work day. Let's go to bed."

Nelson Reed laughed, the bitterness in his voice rattling his wife. "The *hell* I will!" he said.

He strode to the yellow telephone on the wall beside the sink and began to dial. The first call was to Lloyd Dukes, a neighbor two blocks away and a lieutenant in the organization. Dukes was not at home. The second call was to McElroy's Bar on the corner of 65th and Carroll, where Stanley Harper, another of the lieutenants, worked as a bartender. It was Harper who spread the word, among those men at the bar, that the organization would picket the grocer's store the following morning. And all through the night, in the bedroom of their house, Betty Reed was awakened by telephone calls coming from Lester Jones, Nat Lucas, Mrs. Tyrone Brown, the widow-woman named Murphy, all coordinating the time when they would march in a group against the store owned by Harold Green. Betty Reed's heart beat loudly beneath the covers as she listened to the bitterness and rage in her

husband's voice. On several occasions, hearing him declare himself a fool, she pressed the pillow against her
eyes and cried.

The grocer opened later than usual this Saturday morning, but still it was early enough to make him one of the
first walkers in the neighborhood. He parked his car one
block from the store and strolled to work. There were no
birds singing. The sky in this area was not blue. It was
smog-smutted and gray, seeming on the verge of a light
rain. The street, as always, was littered with cans, papers,
bits of broken glass. As always the garbage cans over-
flowed. The morning breeze plastered a sheet of newspa-
per playfully around the sides of a rusted garbage can.
For some reason, using his right foot, he loosened the paper and stood watching it slide into the street and down
the block. The movement made him feel good. He
whistled while unlocking the bars shielding the windows
and door of his store. When he had unlocked the main
door he stepped in quickly and threw a switch to the right
of the jamb, before the shrill sound of the alarm could
shatter his mood. Then he switched on the lights. Everything was as it had been the night before. He had already
telephoned his two employees and given them the day off.
He busied himself doing the usual things—hauling milk
and vegetables from the cooler, putting cash in the till—
not thinking about the silence of his wife, or the look in
her eyes, only an hour before when he left home. He had
determined, at some point while driving through the city,
that today it would be business as usual. But he expected
very few customers.

The first customer of the day was Mrs. Nelson Reed.
She came in around 9:30 A.M. and wandered about the

store. He watched her from the checkout counter. She seemed uncertain of what she wanted to buy. She kept glancing at him down the center aisle. His suspicions aroused, he said finally, "Yes, may I help you, Mrs. Reed?" His words caused her to jerk, as if some devious thought had been perceived going through her mind. She reached over quickly and lifted a loaf of whole wheat bread from the rack and walked with it to the counter. She looked at him and smiled. The smile was a broad, shy one, that rare kind of smile one sees on virgin girls when they first confess love to themselves. Betty Reed was a woman of about forty-five. For some reason he could not comprehend, this gesture touched him. When she pulled a dollar from her purse and laid it on the counter, an impulse, from no place he could locate with his mind, seized control of his tongue. "Free," he told Betty Reed. She paused, then pushed the dollar toward him with a firm and determined thrust of her arm. "Free," he heard himself saying strongly, his right palm spread and meeting her thrust with absolute force. She clutched the loaf of bread and walked out of his store.

The next customer, a little girl, arriving well after 10:30 A.M., selected a candy bar from the rack beside the counter. "Free," Green said cheerfully. The little girl left the candy on the counter and ran out of the store.

At 11:15 A.M. a wino came in looking desperate enough to sell his soul. The grocer watched him only for an instant. Then he went to the wine counter and selected a half-gallon of medium-grade red wine. He shoved the jug into the belly of the wino, the man's sour breath bathing his face. "Free," the grocer said. "But you must not drink it in here."

He felt good about the entire world, watching the wino

through the window gulping the wine and looking guiltily
around.

At 11:25 A.M. the pickets arrived.

Two dozen people, men and women, young and old,
crowded the pavement in front of his store. Their signs,
placards, and voices denounced him as a parasite. The
grocer laughed inside himself. He felt lighthearted and
wild, like a man drugged. He rushed to the meat counter
and pulled a long roll of brown wrapping paper from the
rack, tearing it neatly with a quick shift of his body resembling a dance step practiced fervently in his youth. He
laid the paper on the chopping block and with the black-
inked, felt-tipped marker scrawled, in giant letters, the
word FREE. This he took to the window and pasted in
place with many strands of Scotch tape. He was laughing
wildly. "Free!" he shouted from behind the brown paper.
"Free! Free! Free! Free! Free! Free!" He rushed to the
door, pushed his head out, and screamed to the confused
crowd, *"Free!"* Then he ran back to the counter and
stood behind it, like a soldier at attention.

They came in slowly.

Nelson Reed entered first, working his right foot across
the dirty tile as if tracking a squiggling worm. The others
followed: Lloyd Dukes dragging a placard, Mr. and Mrs.
Tyrone Brown, Stanley Harper walking with his fists
clenched, Lester Jones with three of his children, Nat Lucas looking sheepish and detached, a clutch of winos,
several bashful nuns, ironic-smiling teenagers and a few
students. Bringing up the rear was a bearded social scien-
tist holding a tape recorder to his chest. "Free!" the grocer screamed. He threw up his arms in a gesture that
embraced, or dismissed, the entire store. *"All free!"* he
shouted. He was grinning with the grace of a madman.

The winos began grabbing first. They stripped the shelf of wine in a matter of seconds. Then they fled, dropping bottles on the tile in their wake. The others, stepping quickly through this liquid, soon congealed it into a sticky, bloodlike consistency. The young men went for the cigarettes and luncheon meats and beer. One of them had the prescience to grab a sack from the counter, while the others loaded their arms swiftly, hugging cartons and packages of cold cuts like long-lost friends. The students joined them, less for greed than for the thrill of the experience. The two nuns backed toward the door. As for the older people, men and women, they stood at first as if stuck to the wine-smeared floor. Then Stanley Harper, the bartender, shouted, "The man said *free,* y'all heard him." He paused. "Didn't you say *free* now?" he called to the grocer.

"I said free," Harold Green answered, his temples pounding.

A cheer went up. The older people began grabbing, as if the secret lusts of a lifetime had suddenly seized command of their arms and eyes. They grabbed toilet tissue, cold cuts, pickles, sardines, boxes of raisins, boxes of starch, cans of soup, tins of tuna fish and salmon, bottles of spices, cans of boned chicken, slippery cans of olive oil. Here a man, Lester Jones, burdened himself with several heads of lettuce, while his wife, in another aisle, shouted for him to drop those small items and concentrate on the gourmet section. She herself took imported sardines, wheat crackers, bottles of candied pickles, herring, anchovies, imported olives, French wafers, an ancient, half-rusted can of pâté, stocked, by mistake, from the inventory of another store. Others packed their arms with detergents, hams, chocolate-coated cereal, whole chickens

with hanging asses, wedges of bologna and salami like
squashed footballs, chunks of cheeses, yellow and white,
shriveled onions, and green peppers. Mrs. Tyrone Brown
hung a curve of pepperoni around her neck and seemed
to take on instant dignity, much like a person of noble
birth in possession now of a long sought-after gem. Another woman, the widow Murphy, stuffed tomatoes into
her bosom, holding a half-chewed lemon in her mouth.
The more enterprising fought desperately over the three
rusted shopping carts, and the victors wheeled these along
the narrow aisles, sweeping into them bulk items—beer in
six-packs, sacks of sugar, flour, glass bottles of syrup,
toilet cleanser, sugar cookies, prune, apple and tomato
juices—while others endeavored to snatch the carts from
them. There were several fistfights and much cursing. The
grocer, standing behind the counter, hummed and rang
his cash register like a madman.

Nelson Reed, the first into the store, followed the nuns
out, empty-handed.

In less than half an hour the others had stripped the
store and vanished in many directions up and down the
block. But still more people came, those late in hearing
the news. And when they saw the shelves were bare, they
cursed soberly and chased those few stragglers still bearing away goods. Soon only the grocer and the social scien-
tist remained, the latter stationed at the door with his
tape recorder sucking in leftover sounds. Then he too
slipped away up the block.

By 12:10 P.M. the grocer was leaning against the
counter, trying to make his mind slow down. Not a man
given to drink during work hours, he nonetheless took a
swallow from a bottle of wine, a dusty bottle from

beneath the wine shelf, somehow overlooked by the winos. Somewhat recovered, he was preparing to remember what he should do next when he glanced toward a figure at the door. Nelson Reed was standing there, watching him.

"All gone," Harold Green said. "My friend, Mr. Reed, there is no more." Still the man stood in the doorway, peering into the store.

The grocer waved his arms about the empty room. Not a display case had a single item standing. "All gone," he said again, as if addressing a stupid child. "There is nothing left to get. You, my friend, have come back too late for a second load. I am cleaned out."

Nelson Reed stepped into the store and strode toward the counter. He moved through wine-stained flour, lettuce leaves, red, green, and blue labels, bits and pieces of broken glass. He walked toward the counter.

"All day," the grocer laughed, not quite hysterically now, "all day long I have not made a single cent of profit. The entire day was a loss. This store, like the others, is *bleeding* me." He waved his arms about the room in a magnificent gesture of uncaring loss. "Now do you understand?" he said. "Now will you put yourself in my shoes? I have nothing here. Come, now, Mr. Reed, would it not be so bad a thing to walk in my shoes?"

"Mr. Green," Nelson Reed said coldly. "My wife bought a loaf of bread in here this mornin'. She forgot to pay you. I, myself, have come here to pay you your money."

"Oh," the grocer said.

"I think it was brown bread. Don't that cost more than white?"

The two men looked away from each other, but not at anything in the store.

"In my store, yes," Harold Green said. He rang the register with the most casual movement of his finger. The register read fifty-five cents.

Nelson Reed held out a dollar.

"And two cents tax," the grocer said.

The man held out the dollar.

"After all," Harold Green said. "We are all, after all, Mr. Reed, in debt to the government."

He rang the register again. It read fifty-seven cents.

Nelson Reed held out a dollar.

Just Enough
for the City

THE Germans are unlike the Redeemer's Friends. They look sheepish when they come. The Friends seem self-righteous and smug, possibly in possession of great secrets. They are so knowing at their centers they seem arrogant. Although the Germans tend to look humble, if one listens closely he can tell they are pretending. They talk like evangelists, but like most Lutherans they are careful in choosing their words. Catholics do not come out these days. I have not talked with a Mormon for many years. But Jewish families abound in this area. When you see them walking you know it is Saturday. On Thursdays the Muslims come by selling fish.

Whenever I buy a magazine I talk with the young man behind the counter of the shop about his new religion. He has bright wide eyes and a smile with television potential. When he explains, he always begins with "Master says...." Master is an elderly East Indian with a personal myth. This one does not wear a beard. The young man gives me broadsides written about Master by his dis-

ciples. The writing is enthusiastic. Master is always pictured smiling radiantly. I always accept these broadsides,
because pretending interest allows me to linger in the
shop and read magazines I would never buy.

"Look at these headlines," I have said more than once
to the young man. "Has there ever been such a fuzzy
time?" But he never responds to my feelers. He always
seems pleasantly distracted, not unlike a man drugged.
Once, he made me privy to Master's ambition to start
business ventures in Ethiopia, Ceylon, perhaps certain of
the Caribbean Islands. All the disciples, the young man
says, are waiting for the word from Master before making
their moves. I sense he wants me to join them. But I
remember having seen this all before. I do not tell him
this, but I prevent myself from going too often into his
shop.

The Muslims have evolved into good makers of pastry.
More and more their clerks resemble the executives in the
bank across the street from their bakery. I like to go in
there mornings and buy a cheese Danish from the girl behind the counter. She is beautiful. She seems to have inner peace and an unbothered mind. I like the way her
body moves against the inside of her long blue dress. I
want badly to tell her that I like seeing her move every
morning, but whenever we begin to talk she undermines
my mood by proselytizing. "You are not just black," she
discloses to me. "We, of course, knew it all along. But
now the truth can be revealed. You are a descendant of
Mohammed's beloved muezzin, the greatly respected
Bilalia." She smiles at me with such peace in her face.
"Now that you know the truth," she tells me, "you must
submit." At such times I want badly to comment on the

tempo of her body inside the blue dress. But I always content myself with a cheese Danish and going away.

Lately I have been trying for a simple definition of love.

The Germans who come to my house speak with thick accents. But for their accents I would not let them in. I answer their knocking because I worry they are tourists and might otherwise go away feeling slighted.

"Did you come to this country just to knock on doors?" I ask, just to test their command of English. But my speech is too fast for them, or they are too fast for my speech. They do not allow themselves to be eight-balled. The blond young man talks about the prophet for whom they are working. He promises the usual remedies. "Vee haff found our best success amongst der kolored people," he says. "I would not doubt it," I tell him. "Most people have." The fellow does not understand fully. He looks slyly at his companion. An older woman with unabashedly direct gray eyes, she has the steady manner of a nun. "He means," she says in crisply enunciated English, "der kolored people are der first to accept us or reject us." They both watch and wait for me to disclose myself. Backed into a corner, I have no choice but to shift their focus. "Where do you get your money?" I ask them. "Who finances your operation?"

They go away.

At least the Redeemer's Friends are more direct. To them everything not mentioned in the Bible is false religion. Their God is not a mystery: He has already said what He will do. A craftsman building steadily toward the millennium, He will offer no surprises to those who are prepared. His people are sincere about this. I respect them for it. But I feel in the mood to tease. "I have read someplace," I say to the young minister on his second visit, "that your group caters specifically to people who lack the toughness to compete in the real world. I have heard that you consider greed a sin." The black-suited young man turns quickly to a passage in his Bible. He crosses the room and holds the book under my eyes. With a pale white finger he taps a passage printed in red ink. He recites from memory, without pronouncing the words, while I read aloud. "This may be true," I say when I have finished. "I have no personal argument with the consequences of greed. But as a purely pragmatic matter, I have come to an accord with all I once called evil. It seems to me now that evil has its rights, and we have our obligations to it." The young man shudders. "The denial of this, it seems to me," I continue, despite his look of condescension, "is in itself a more subtle form of evil. Virtue, you know, can often be as clumsy as evil is vigilant. Both add to the store of cripples in the world."

We argue about this point. The pale young minister flips to other passages in his Bible, some in red ink and others in black. I am not convinced. He inquires closely into my background. I volunteer little. He speaks woefully about the present state of the world. I say nothing in response. Finally he shows me a picture of creatures living in harmony with each other and nature. A happy man holds a white dove on his finger; two sheep, one black and one white, romp playfully on the green grass; a little girl strokes a lion's mane; from behind puffy white clouds floating over a purple mountaintop, a magnificent yellow sunlight pours down on this idyllic scene. It is an image to be lusted after. "Aha!" I exclaim, perhaps a bit theatrically. "I notice that the feline is a male, and he seems to have a full belly. Obviously his mate has only recently brought him a meal. That is why the artist was able to draw the girl alive and the lion happy."

Like the Germans, this young man leaves my home.

I think love must be the ability to suspend one's intelligence for the sake of something. At the basis of love therefore must live imagination. Instead of thinking always "I am I," to love one must be able to feelingly conjugate the verb to be. *Intuition must be part of the circuitous pathway leading ultimately to love. I wish I could ask someone.*

By not coming in the evening, the Germans miss the most potential converts. During the day, in this neighborhood, only senior citizens are at home. They do not like their communion with television interrupted. They will not open their doors. Besides, most of them drink during the day. It is at night, after the television news, that they are most in despair. Evening is the time they would be most receptive to the message. But the schedule-bound Germans insist on arriving in the late afternoon, just before the early news begins. I am one of the few who will let them in. But despite my hospitality, they arrive ill-prepared to debate the issues. They have a conceptual faith, but anyone with an unobstructed eye can see their message does not flow directly from their souls. "Der simple problem," the nunlike lady tells me, "is dat vee do not luff one anudder." I agree with this. But I insist that they define for me the term. Both the lady and her companion begin thumbing through their Bibles. This irritates me, and before they can begin to recite I say: "A precocious young man, feeling ill at ease in this world, decided to take his own life. But he felt deeply toward his parents, his brothers and sisters, and a girlfriend whom he loved with all his heart. He worried about their grief after his suicide and resolved finally to kill those who loved him most, in order to save them unnecessary anguish after he had acted against himself. Fortified in this resolve, he killed his mother and father, his sisters and brothers, but hesitated before he could deal equally with his sweetheart. He wrestled with himself over this impasse, his parents having been moral people. Finally he decided. He wrote a note explaining why, of all those he loved, he had spared his sweetheart. This done, he cursed the world once more and hung himself. When his actions were discovered, the authorities delivered the note to a professor of moral philosophy who, upon reading it and reflecting, concluded that the young man had indeed been precocious. He pronounced the young man morally right in his actions. Now," I say to the Germans, "what reason for not acting against his sweetheart did the young man leave behind in the note? Tell me without a single look into your Bibles."

The Germans never do come back.

George, the Arab grocer around the corner, flirts with all the ladies in the neighborhood. Most of them are old, and with the inflation his only profits derive from the whiskey and wines he sells them. Well on his way to becoming a white man, George pounces on me whenever I enter the store and vouches expansively for my character to my neighbors. "This is my personal friend," he will say to anyone who seems important. "He is a very good man, very good. I know. I trade with him. My friend, George tells you he is a very good man." I feel good about helping to Americanize George: I believe he could not make the transition without me. I like him. He works twelve hours a day, every day, holidays not excepted. He maintains he is the son of an aristocrat, a former owner of orange groves outside Jaffa. George speaks lovingly of Jaffa oranges; he says they are the sweetest in the world. Whenever I sense he is feeling like an Arab, I ask him about the Koran. "It teaches the only religion in the world for a businessman," George answers, spreading his arm toward the dusty shelves with the authority of a saint. "It teaches you must charge the same price to your own mother you would charge to any other person. No exception, my friend, no exception! If you do not do this, you yourself become a woman, a whore. And it is the right of any man to cheat you. My buddy, a man must not be a whore. I sell to you, I sell to my own mother, same price, buddy, same price." Then he smiles, always craftily, and if it is a slow morning he will launch into politics. If it is indeed a slow morning, I never linger for the full lecture. I buy a doughnut, though it is overpriced, and take away from the store whatever I have learned about the Koran. But I bring away nothing new about love.

This evening I hear they've fired my favorite waitress at the restaurant where I like to take my lunch. The woman passes this intelligence to me when by chance I meet her on the street. She is an elderly woman whose husband died last year. If she was not too busy during lunch hours she would come to my table and trade small talk. She said things like, "Is the meal all right, honey?" I am sure this was her way of compensating for not having youth and a marketable face. Now she reports that the owner of the place, a Greek, has fired her in order to hire a younger woman at a lower salary. The Greek has accused her of not sharing in the side work. "But that's not

the truth," she tells me. "And don't you *know* it, honey? I
did my side work. Mr. G. only said that so he could hire
a younger girl." The worst part, she reports, is that the
Greek has blocked her getting unemployment compensation. This was a vicious tactic, but I understand the
Greek's position: People with knowledge of assaults
against their dignity must be destroyed, or at least sub-
stantially degraded. Otherwise, if they survive whole, fes-
tering sores will surely break out into open wounds. The
stroking of such wounds, in a healing imagination, leads
inevitably to considerations of revenge. I applaud the cun-
ning of Mr. G., even while I sympathize with the plight of
his late employee. "I will," I offer, "testify on your behalf
before any bureaucracy you may have to address. I went
into that restaurant several times a week. I saw you always hard at work; I know you are not lazy. I'm sure
there are other customers willing to do the same. Let Mr.
G. call all of us liars at the same time." The ex-waitress is
elated. "God is on our side," she tells me. "We can't lose.
You tell me, honey, with God on our side how can we
lose?" She opens her purse to write down my name and
number. A prayer book almost slips out of the cloth bag.
"See?" She focuses my attention on the book. "I was on
my way to prayer meeting. God sent you to me." This
distortion of my gesture disturbs and offends me. "God
did no such thing," I reply. "The truth of the matter is I
am constipated and decided to walk around for exercise.
As for the constipation, it was caused, as it always is, by
too much Mexican food. I will accept God as the causal
factor only if you can prove to me that, among His many
miracles, God has also bothered Himself with the progress
of refried beans." But I cannot make her see matters

clearly in this perspective. She insists otherwise. I give up finally, volunteer my name and number, and walk away.

Love must be a going outward from the self from the most secret of safe positions. God is no more than the most secret possible place from which such emanations can be sent.

The Redeemer's Friends do not give up on a soul. They always come back with reinforcements. This time the young minister brings a stout black woman with him. She is not really black: she is the color of cinnamon on a brown hardwood table. She glares accusingly around my living room at the books, papers, and whiskey glasses. In her manner is the earned authority of the South. "I'll tell you this here," she says with much conviction, "and it's just common sense, too. If all these other religions done prove theyselves false, and if the Redeemer done prove His Self to be perfect, wouldn't you feel safer believin' in a theocracy underneath of His rule?" She is a forceful woman. Something in her manner advises one to defer. The ghost-pale young minister leans against an awareness of this. He sits on my sofa with his Bible on his knee, his head lowered reverently. He smiles knowingly while the mammy need in me responds, despite my restraint, to the mammy milk charging her voice. The minister is depending on this. I am shamefully aware. He says, "I did not mention this to you before, but at one time I, too, was in demonology." "What is that?" I ask him. "The worship of *Satan!*" the stout woman says, glaring sternly but protectively at her young companion. "Woe unto you," she chants, "scribes and Pharisees, hypocrites! For ye compass sea and land to make one proselyte, and when he is made, ye make him twofold more the child of hell than yourselves." The young minister lowers his head more and looks penitent. It is obvious his faith is still not as strong as hers. Yet the strength of her faith irritates me. It lacks the edge of doubt. Also, she has brought too strong a sense of reform into a room where, so far as I know, there have been only mundane crimes.

"Mother," I call to her from her chair. "Mother, I need an answer to a question that has troubled me these past months. It seemed an evil man and a good man knelt side by side to pray. The evil man had considerable knowledge of the evil in men's hearts; the good man had considerable knowledge of the good. Both wanted to achieve power. As a strategy toward this end, both petitioned God to change the moral habits of their neighbors. One man asked God to fill men's souls with knowledge of Him so they would better distinguish good from evil. The other asked God to shrink men's souls so they would no longer be concerned with such bothersome refinements. God heard and answered the petitions of both. But because He was in a playful mood, He added calculus to the action of His will. Thereafter, the good man responded only to evil and the evil man responded only to good. This had a profound influence on their respective constituencies. Because the once evil man could now speak only of the good in men, he confused the minds of his followers by introducing doubt. The same was true of the once good man. Unable to bear any longer the lack of certainty, both constituencies banded together and conspired to kill the two men. This was done, and after they were buried, God caused a red rose to sprout on the grave of the once evil man, and a black one to blossom on the grave of the once good man. Both constituencies observed this phenomenon and grew even more confused. And after arguing and fighting among themselves as to the cause, reason prevailed and they elected two of their number, both converts to opposing causes, to petition God for an answer. These two confused men knelt side by side to pray. Not now being in a playful mood, God put the answer into the heart of a single man in the crowd of onlookers, a blind man who could not speak or hear. Now, Mother, without relying on your Bible, tell me, what was the answer given to this unfortunate man, and how did he communicate it to the others?"

Both the young minister and his helper vow to come again when I am in a better mood.

If one is not too strict in his conjugation of the verb to be, *he might wind up with a sense of living in the present. I believe now that love exists at just that point when the first person singular moves into its plural estate: I am, you are, he is, she is,* we are. . . . *The saying of it requires a going out of oneself, of breath as well as confidence. Its image is of expansiveness, a taking roundly into and a putting roundly out of oneself. Or perhaps another word should be used, one invented or one transported from another context: I am, you are, he is, she is,* we be. . . . *Or again, perhaps a beat of silence alone could best bear the weight of it, a silence suggesting the burden of subjectivity: I am, you are, he is, she is, they are* . . .

The restaurant where I now take lunch is run by a Chinese named Lester. He is a short fellow with a frozen smile and precise movements behind the counter. He and his wife Doris work as a team: While he fries on the grill, she services the counter. Doris is lovely, with very high

cheekbones and a small, fleshy mouth. You can tell she
has more imagination than her work can employ because
she sings along with the radio while she works. The radio
station she favors plays only Muzak; she herself supplies
the words. In her memory must be recorded all the phras-
ings and stylistic devices of a thousand popular singers.
Her voice is high, but pleasant and sweet. I compliment
her on it. But Lester seems disturbed by this affirmation
of her beauty from a stranger. He smiles desperately while
frying hamburgers, his round eyes roaming up and down
the counter. He is nervous when he makes a joke. I have
never seen a Chinese insecure about his woman. In defer-
ence to his fear, I begin a conversation with the silver-
haired insurance salesman on the stool next to mine. He is
a patron of the grill and grows expansive with each new-
comer to the luncheon hour. "You want to know why
things are out of focus?" he offers. "I'll *tell* you just why.
The *Big Boys* are mad at us!" When he says this he lowers his sandwich onto his plate and looks reverent.
"People are doing things now that the Big Boys don't like.
Well, they are not going to stand for too much of that.
They'll make you *suffer*."

Lester calls down the counter, "I don't cheat nobody in
here. I charge what I have to and get along with everybody."

The insurance agent smiles, then glares up and down
the counter to see who else is listening. He says, "Anybody with any *sense* knows that the Big Boys won't let
you get away with anything. You want to know what's
happening? It's as simple as that. There's no free lunches
when it comes to the Big Boys." He pauses to smile at
Doris who is humming now. He winks at her. "But they
are not heartless men," he says to Doris as much as to

me. "They have mercy on us. Oh, they'll let us knock each other around a bit. They're playful that way." He winks again at Doris, then at me, finally at Lester standing by the grill. He takes a bite from his sandwich and chews casually. "They'll be a bit rough, but they won't let us go completely to war. And after it's over, in years to come, they might even be a bit more generous, if we play ball. They just want to teach us there ain't *no such thing as a free lunch!*" He smiles benignly around the counter. Everyone is silent, watching him. Lester concentrates on scraping hot grease from his grill. Lester is as intent as a little boy in a sandbox. The insurance salesman wipes his mouth carefully. He drains his glass of water. He tosses a quarter on the counter. Then he salutes those of us sitting near his stool. He says, "Same time tomorrow," and goes out. Everyone is silent for a minute. But Doris begins to hum along with the Muzak and people begin talking again. Wiping the counter, she lights on the smothered tempo and begins to sing like a morning bird. I want to tell her that her voice is beautiful. I want to tell her this insurance salesman knows nothing about love. But I say nothing.

I am refusing these days to bow on my knees and cry holy.

There is a fascinating girl working behind the counter of this bookstore. She is not at all pretty, her body and arms are thin and overlong, but there is something secret about her face. I study it each time I come in here. Each time I leave I am always only on the outskirts of its mystery. The face is a thin, pale, blank, and elusive thing; its eyes do not glow, its lips betray nothing. Outside this bookstore one would never notice her. But inside here, somehow, in the almost silence of listlessly turning pages, the face has a mystery that is alive. I always come back for another look. I prowl the aisles and watch her. I study the face intently while I pretend to read the books. Her own imagination seems to be living elsewhere. Always open on the counter beside her register is a book by Dante. She reads it slowly, her lips sometimes moving, as if translating from another language. About her is an air of peace and privacy that invites interruption. During my first visit to the store, I thought perversely that this was the source of the mystery.

Other people who come in have made the same mistake. They invade her space with noises. They talk at her. She nods and smiles, but never answers back. An on-duty policeman, dashing in to buy discounted paperback murder mysteries, swaggers, and leans his gun-weighted hip against the counter. He talks desperately about the weather, his eyes moving from her face to the busy street outside the plate-glass window. She nods and says nothing. The cop looks worshipful. An elderly woman, easing heavy shopping bags to the floor, inquires reverently into the stock of religious materials. But this is only a ploy. Once answers are forthcoming, she confesses her fear that the earth has become peopled by the alien occupants of flying saucers. She looks at the shopgirl imploringly. A student comes looking for esoteric titles. He stands at attention by the counter and rattles them off. Then he lingers there, volunteering, for some reason, unabashed insights into the sources of his frustrations. The girl listens carefully. She listens to all of them. But she smiles in such a secret way that they cannot be sure she has heard. Most people buy books to pay her for her time. I buy books so

I can stand at the counter and get a closer inspection of her mystery.

This time I am sure her face is the source of all this interest. It is a free face, a fresh face. In it I can see no servitude to the expressions of faces I have seen before. Hers is a smile completely unaware of any predecessor. It derives entirely from within itself. Her mystery, I think, is an awareness of this liberation from the familiar. But not even her smile seems conscious of this. People approach her as they would approach an altar, a mass, a saint. The smile invites them to disclose themselves. From such faces, I think, Catholics must draw their strength. I place my books on the counter and muster the tact needed to ask about her religion. But at this moment a young man leans his head in the door. He balances his body on the doorknob he is holding and lifts one leg out toward the street. He looks approvingly at the girl. He says, "I got ten minutes, baby. Can I rap to you?" The affront is in his manner, not his asking. The girl lowers her head, shuts her eyes, and whispers, "No!" The young man shrugs, straightens, and shuts the door. I put my money on the counter. When the girl opens her eyes again, they are cold, distant, businesslike, and profoundly familiar. Something has retreated into its refuge deep, deep inside her. She now looks withdrawn, drab, and wounded, like so much of everything else in the world. I pay quickly for my books. I want to say, but do not dare to say, that I saw briefly in her face the shadow of a human soul.

I am . . .

I admit to having fallen in love with the Redeemer's Friends. They are steadfast in pursuing matters of the spirit. Unlike the Germans, they are slow to take offense.

The fact that they keep returning confirms my suspicions that I have a soul worth saving. This time the stout black woman brings with her, along with her pale companion, a more mature-seeming minister of their sect. They crowd into my living room, surrounding me. As always, the white ministers defer to the black woman. She sits on the sofa, her Bible balanced on her knee, and smiles triumphantly. "All right, now," she says, "what foolishness have you done thought up *this* time?"

The two ministers watch me warily, like hungry cats.

"Simply this," I answer. "A man who considered himself reasonably sane one day became afflicted by a disturbing clarity of vision. It happened in this way: Turning suddenly at a doorway to address a companion to whom he had just said good-bye, he saw settling into the man's face a hatred of such intensity that his heart trembled. Since he had always considered the companion a friend, he grew confused; and more so because, at the very instant he turned, a look of friendship, one familiar to him, was swiftly reclaiming the features of his erstwhile friend. This incident troubled his mind for many days afterward. But this was only the beginning of his torment. Suspecting now that words were of little importance, he found himself watching gestures and facial expressions, listening to the rhythms of voices and not to the words spoken, for telltale insights into the true nature of reality: the finesse with which a puny-hearted bureaucrat stabbed the buttons of his intercom; the vacant, slack-jawed smile of a man professing high ideals; the way a woman's smile always centered at a certain place on the cusp of her teeth; the tones of voice, used by a cheap businessman, borrowed from rituals of courtship, wedding, lovemaking. These insights, contrasted with the words used on each occasion, made him painfully aware that the world was indeed a terrible place to be. Unable now to believe in any words, he retreated into a room, questioning even the character behind his own name. At first he laughed at the world. Then he nursed great contempt for specific individuals. He looked at television with the sound turned off, watching only the pictures. Soon he began to hate in much more general terms. This hatred filled him with tremendous energy. All his resources became focused on acts of revenge. In his imagination he hurled bullets, knives, custard pies, aged and smelly eggs, at faceless enemies. He paced his room at nights inventing new means of retribution. He . . ."

The stout woman says to the others, "Didn't I *tell* you? Just as *crazy* as they come."

The young minister nods. "I, too, have been in demonology," he says. He looks extremely sad.

But the new minister waves them into silence. There is authority in the gesture and they both defer. "I am waiting for the question," he says to me. He has a round red face and smiles with a pained patience. His manner is that of a man who has developed techniques for handling lunatics.

The recognition in his face irritates me. "The question . . ." I begin.

"The answer," he interrupts, "is an old one. And so is his story. He explodes from the inside of himself and becomes a spot of grease on the floor. Your question is, what should be done with the smoldering spot of grease before it burns whomever comes to ask about his health? Is this the question?"

I answer yes.

The middle-aged minister laughs and rises from the sofa.

The stout black woman says, "Didn't I tell you. Just as *crazy* as they come."

"I, too, was once in demonology," the pale young minister says.

The three of them go away smiling.

I go immediately into the bathroom and look again into the mirror.

For private reasons I do not see these people when I see them on the street. The men have crew-cut, brown-blond hair, listless like the coat of a mongrel alley cat. They have sagging, sun-fearing, death-white skin. Their women are pale and billowy plump, always spreading outward from their bodies as if greedy for more space to claim. Their hair is straw-blond and stringy, like the leavings of winter wheat after a spring thaw. Their little noses sniff the air, as if smelling out enemies. They wear thin and puckered lips seeming always on the verge of meanness. I know their viciousness, yet now they seem pathetically poor and hopeless. I know their details. Yet at other times, in other places, they do not exist for me. But here at the lunch counter of Lester's Grill, while Doris hums and Lester deep-fat fries, I look past the many plates between us down the crowded counter and see them whole. I watch the three of them, a man and two women. The man is chubby, droop-jowled, dingy in a laborer's faded denim pants. His women are outlandish in dresses made of five-and-dime store fabrics. They are gaudy and surreal in contrast with Lester's other clientele. They reek of the grotesque. But when Doris, humming, brings them plates of sizzling hamburgers, limber lettuce, grease-drenched fries, I see them look into their meals as I would look at a beautiful woman. I see them bend their heads and close their eyes, almost in unison, over red and yellow condiment holders, plastic glasses of Coke, the steaming plates. It is such a private, natural gesture in its smoothness of reflex that I, like they, forget we are in a very public place. Something breathes quickly against the cobwebs inside me. But because I fear what I feel is love, I turn my face away.

Tu es . . .

I am becoming sufficient.

A Sense of Story

AT the murder trial, the defendant, Robert L. Charles, after having sat four days in silence while his court-appointed lawyer pleaded for him, rose suddenly from his chair during his counsel's summation and faced the jurors. "It wasn't no accident," he told them in a calm voice. "I had me nine bullets and a no-good gun. Gentlemens, the *onliest* thing I regret is the gun broke before I could pump more than six slugs into the sonofabitch."

Thus ensuring his doom, the defendant sat down.

The entire courtroom was hushed, except for defense counsel's condemnation of his client. The judge quickly ordered the jurors from the room and motioned both counsel, and the court reporter, to approach the bench. The defendant remained seated, ignoring the heated remonstrations of his lawyer. And while the others huddled before the judge—the assistant district attorney, a dapperly dressed student DA, the court stenographer and, reluctantly, the defense attorney—Robert L. Charles remained impassive in his chair. He looked neither ahead nor be-

hind him, neither to his right nor to his left. His eyes were
unfocused. He seemed to have accepted whatever fate he
had assigned himself.

The judge was in a quandary. There was no rule cover-
ing such an outburst. There was no way it could be erased
from the jurors' minds. There was no point in going on
with the trial. The two lawyers and the judge agreed
finally that, since the outburst had occurred during the
defense counsel's summation, the record of prior proceedings should be examined. In this way it could be
determined whether a preponderance of the evidence had
already tipped the scales of justice against the defendant,
making his confession of insignificant weight. This unfortunate decision was to be left with the judge. A thoughtful, painstaking man, he recessed court, dismissed the
jurors, and retired to his chambers with as much of the
transcript of the trial's proceedings as his clerk could supply. He ordered the court stenographer to transcribe the
most recent testimony as rapidly as possible. Then, in his
book-lined, green-carpeted office, the judge read hurriedly
through the record.

It was an open-and-shut case. The defendant, Robert
Lee Charles, was accused of shooting his employer of
thirteen years, Frank Johnson, on the afternoon of June
12, 197–. Though there was no witness to the actual
shooting, a second Johnson employee, a mechanic named
Jed Jones, had rushed into the office after hearing six
shots, and had seen the defendant, Charles, bending over
the body of the deceased man. The smoking gun was still
in his left hand. With his right hand, according to Jones,
Charles was stuffing bullets into the deceased man's
mouth. Charles had not resisted the arresting officers: he
had waited quietly in the room for them to arrive. At the

pretrial hearing he had pleaded nolo contendere and remained silent, leaving it to his court-appointed attorney to plead mitigating circumstances in an effort to convince the jury that manslaughter, with life imprisonment, was all that was due the state. By presenting such evidence, the defense counsel had contrived to prevent Charles from being the first man condemned to death under the state's new, carefully drafted, capital punishment statute. But by his speech in the courtroom, whether inspired by madness or by overconfidence in his lawyer's case, the defendant had doomed himself to death.

The judge leafed through the record of three days before. He scanned part of the testimony by the arresting officer, Lloyd Scion:

MR. LINDENBERRY: Officer Scion, at the time of the arrest, what was the scene when you entered the deceased's office?

MR. SCION: Mr. Johnson was on the floor next to the desk in a pool of blood. The defendant—that man, Robert Charles, seated over there—was sitting on the desk holding a gun. Mr. Jones there was standing by the door, possibly to prevent the defendant's escape.

MR. LINDENBERRY: What did the defendant do when you entered the office?

MR. SCION: Nothing. Well, I mean I had my own gun drawn, so there wasn't nothing much he could do. I ordered him to drop his gun. He did. I put the cuffs on him.

MR. LINDENBERRY: What did he say?

MR. SCION: Nothing. He didn't say anything. He threw the gun on the floor near the body of the deceased. There was no fight in him. I took him on down without a word, without a tussle.

MR. LINDENBERRY: Officer Scion, what was the condition of the deceased's body at the time of the defendant's arrest?

MR. SCION: He had six bullets in him, three in the belly, two in the chest, and one in his right arm. There was also . . .

MR. GRANT: Objection.

COURT: On what ground?

MR. GRANT: Counsel and Officer Scion have already established that Mr. Johnson was dead. My client has not denied that he shot the deceased.

MR. LINDENBERRY: Your Honor, I think that what Officer Scion has to say may be of interest to the jury. I think it should be let in.

MR. GRANT: May my colleague and I approach the bench, Your Honor?

COURT: Proceed . . .

MR. LINDENBERRY: Officer Scion, according to your records, was the defendant drunk at the time of his arrest?

MR. SCION: No sir . . .

MR. GRANT: I have no questions . . .

Here was the testimony of Jed Jones, the employee who had been first in the office after the shooting:

MR. LINDENBERRY: How long have you worked at Rogers' Auto Service?

MR. JONES: Ten years.

MR. LINDENBERRY: Was the defendant an employee there when you were hired?

MR. JONES: Yes, sir.

MR. LINDENBERRY: How long had he been employed there?

MR. JONES: Before me?

MR. LINDENBERRY: Yes.

MR. JONES: Two or three years. Closer to three, I think.

MR. LINDENBERRY: Was he, at the time of your arrival, a difficult fellow?

MR. GRANT: Object.

COURT: Sustained.

MR. LINDENBERRY: Did you get along with Mr. Charles?

MR. JONES: We got along. But we never got to be friends.

MR. LINDENBERRY: Why was that?

MR. GRANT: Objection.

COURT: Does counsel have a line of questioning in mind?

MR. LINDENBERRY: Yes, Your Honor. I hope to establish something about the character of this witness, relating to an ancillary issue involved here.

COURT: Proceed.

MR. LINDENBERRY: Was it Mr. Charles's race that prevented you from becoming friends?

MR. JONES: No. I get along with most everybody. I've drunk beer with several of the other colored . . . black guys that work up at Rogers'. We don't visit each other's homes or stuff like that, but we get along. But Bob was different.

MR. LINDENBERRY: You refer to the defendant, Mr. Robert L. Charles. How, in your opinion, was he different?

MR. JONES: Well, he never joshed around like the others do. It's a mite hard to explain. He was always off in a corner moping or something. And it wasn't just me. Bob didn't have much truck with the other colored fellows there either. It was like there wasn't no funning in him. I know he made them other colored fellows nervous.

MR. LINDENBERRY: How do you know this?

MR. GRANT: Object.

COURT: Sustained.

MR. LINDENBERRY: What recollections do you personally have of the defendant's character?

MR. JONES: Like I say, he was always off in a corner, sulking or something. Bob was a good worker, tops. But even when he was working, it was automatic-like, like his mind was always on something else. I tried once or twice to get friendly with him, but I didn't get very far. So after a while I quit trying. He never said nothing harmful to me personally, but I will say that his manner was cold, businesslike. I would say he was a loner . . .

MR. LINDENBERRY: Would you give us your recollection
of the trouble between the defendant and the deceased
Mr. Frank Johnson?

MR. JONES: I first notice it about eight years ago, two
years after I had come there to Rogers'. This was back
during the time when them foreign cars was flooding the
market. Every shop in town was trying to switch over.
There was few mechanics able to deal with them Jap gas
sippers. Most of our boys was raised on Detroit. But Bob
was one of the few in our shop that could ease right into
the newer models. I think he must of studied them at
home or something. Anyway, he come in the shop one
morning saying he had put together a lube mixture that
was going to add years to the valves and pistons of them
new models. He said the formula was going to grease his
way to a desk job over in the main office. He wouldn't tell
nobody the formula, but I know he talked to Mr. Johnson
in great detail about it.

MR. LINDENBERRY: How do you know this?

MR. JONES: Because about two weeks later old Johnson—Mr. Johnson—told me, "Bobby Lee has gone
crazy. He thinks some bathtub concoction is a miracle
drug. He's sounding like a sarsaparilla drummer singing
down a country road. I can't bother them down to the
main office with this kind of foolishness." I remember he
said that to me just as plain as day.

MR. LINDENBERRY: What else did Mr. Johnson tell you?

MR. JONES: About a month later he told me in the john,
"Bobby Lee has threaten me, Jed. His formula don't
work, he lost it or something, and he thinks I am the
cause."

MR. LINDENBERRY: Would you repeat Mr. Johnson's
words to you so the jurors can hear?

MR. JONES: Mr. Johnson told me that the main office had
rejected Bob's formula, and Bob blamed him for it. He
said, "Jed, Bob has threaten me. His formula don't work,
and he thinks I am the one that soured the main office on
it."

MR. LINDENBERRY: Mr. Jones, in your opinion did the defendant take a hardened attitude toward Mr. Johnson after that?

MR. JONES: Yes, sir. In my opinion, he surely did.

MR. LINDENBERRY: In what ways did you observe this attitude express itself? . . .

MR. GRANT: No questions, Your Honor.

The judge rang for his secretary and ordered coffee and a cottage cheese sandwich. Then he continued poring through the transcript. It was shortly after noon, and there was a judges' conference scheduled for 3:00 P.M. When the secretary brought in his lunch and some additional transcripts, he had reached in his reading the direct examination of Mr. Orion W. Rogers, owner of Rogers' Auto Service and Supply:

MR. LINDENBERRY: Now Mr. Rogers, how would you characterize your late employee, Mr. Frank Johnson?

MR. ROGERS: I would say he had love in his heart for everybody in the world.

MR. LINDENBERRY: How long had the deceased worked for you?

MR. ROGERS: Frank was one of my first employees. He was with me eighteen years ago, when I first started out. He was a very dedicated employee, and one of the few whose insights I trusted in matters of money as well as of morals.

MR. LINDENBERRY: What do you mean by morals, Mr. Rogers?

MR. ROGERS: It was Frank's suggestion, when I opened the shop on Guilford, to add a black or two to the crew there. I must confess that such a thought had never entered my mind. I say this in all candor, as an indication of the level of my social consciousness relative to Frank's. But he prodded and pushed until I agreed to bring a black or two into all three shops.

MR. LINDENBERRY: Would you please look at the defendant. Can you recall whether he is one of the blacks recommended to you by Mr. Johnson?

MR. ROGERS: I can't recall. You understand that a man in my position can't possibly keep such things in mind. But I do recall this man's face. He came up to the main office regularly to deliver invoices, pick up payrolls, a variety of things. He was always civil and soft-spoken. I remember this aspect of his personality distinctly, because he reminded me of my favorite waiter at a resort my wife and I visit frequently on an island off the Carolina coast. As I said, he had those kinds of qualities that made me think of a loyal, gentle person. So you can understand how shocked—outraged, really—I was when this thing happened.

MR. LINDENBERRY: Mr. Rogers, do you recall an incident in which Mr. Johnson spoke to you about the behavior of the defendant? I mean with respect to an automotive lubricant compound supposedly invented by Mr. Charles?

MR. ROGERS: No, sir. I cannot recall such a conversation. But I can assure you that Frank would have been the first to extend his every effort to give its highest recommendation to the company.

MR. LINDENBERRY: Then what, in your opinion, accounted for the development of the animosity on the part of defendant toward Mr. Frank Johnson?

MR. GRANT: Object. Witness is in no position to psychoanalyze the defendant. These judgments are beyond his competence to make.

COURT: Mr. Lindenberry?

MR. LINDENBERRY: Your Honor, I ask you again to consider my position. I assure the court that this is not a fishing expedition. Since I will have no opportunity to examine the defendant, his wife, his children or anyone with an intimate sense of him, I have no choice but to glean testimony shedding light on his possible motives from whatever sources available. Now it strikes me that this witness's insights are valid here, more so in light of the defendant's silence. If this witness, as an employer

with special insights into the nature of typical employer-
employee conflict, is ruled to be not competent to make
such judgments, then why not also strike the testimony of
Mr. Jed Jones? If this witness's testimony on this impor-
ant point cannot come in, I do not see how I can make
the best possible case for the state.

COURT: Mr. Lindenberry, I am still bothered by your
expressed intention to proceed from inferences about the
defendant's personality, based not on direct observation of
the defendant but on an abstraction called "the typical
employee" that exists only in this witness's head. Mr.
Grant, is this the essence of your objection?

MR. GRANT: Yes, Your Honor. And I would add that
anything said by the witness about this particular employee would be doubly immaterial. One, for his lack of
personal knowledge, and, two, because even if his insights
were valid with respect to the typical employee, I submit
that this defendant is not typical. He is in a class by himself. I submit that he is an illiterate Southern black, so-
cialized in an environment of violence, who possesses a
single skill. He is a man who acted out of motives beyond
the competence of this witness, and of most white people,
to know.

COURT: I have taken your point under advisement,
Franklin. It goes against my better judgment, and perhaps
I am wrong, but my intuition tells me there is a sense of
story here. I am going to let the testimony in. I remind
you of our talk at the bench yesterday, and of the responsibility we have to hold this defendant to the same stan-
dard as everyone else. The rules of society are made for
all. His membership in the negro race . . .

The judge paused to fill his pipe and light it. Then he
took a pencil from the green holder on his desk and underlined part of this exchange between himself and
Franklin Grant. He leaned back in his chair, puffing his
pipe and reflecting. Then he looked at his watch and
resumed reading:

MR. LINDENBERRY: Now, Mr. Rogers, I repeat, based on your own experience as an employer, in the typical rub of egos and elbows, what is the most likely source of conflict?

MR. ROGERS: Sometimes you get an employee whose talent does not match his ambition. This is a painful truth, one of which most fair employers have to be aware. The Good Lord did not distribute talents equally, that's in the Bible. But some employees find it hard to accept their lot. They agitate and see offense where none was intended. They blame others, even those with their best interest in mind, for their own personal failings. Such employees—prima donnas, we call them—usually fail to get along. If they have a sense of humor, the situation is bearable. If they do not—well, sometimes the consequences can be tragic.

MR. LINDENBERRY: Would you say that this profile fits the defendant here, Mr. Charles?

MR. GRANT: I object, Your Honor.

COURT: No. Since I've started this I am going to let it in.

MR. LINDENBERRY: In your opinion, Mr. Rogers, does the defendant here fit this profile?

MR. ROGERS: Since this tragic event I've checked our records. I know now that Mr. Charles came to us about thirteen years ago. I don't recall anything personal about him, except that three weeks ago one of my former secretaries called to tell me that he is the same man who, about nine years back, caused a bit of disturbance in my office. She recognized his picture in the papers. She said . . .

MR. GRANT: Hearsay.

COURT: Sustained.

MR. LINDENBERRY: Your Honor, since the time of the incident under exploration here, the secretary, Mrs. Ellen Claus, has been . . .

. . .

MR. ROGERS: . . . demanded to see me without stating the nature of his business. Well, Mrs. Claus, as you might imagine, was protective of my time. He would not state his business, and she therefore could not let him through. That is all I can say about this man . . .

MR. GRANT: I have no questions.

The judge skipped a few pages and then resumed his reading. Here was the testimony of Mr. Otis Pinkett, another employee at Rogers' Auto Service and Supply:

MR. LINDENBERRY: Now, during the incident you speak of, what in your opinion seemed to be the quality of the relationship between the deceased Mr. Johnson and the defendant?

MR. PINKETT: Like I say, I first become uneasy that time I was cleaning up round the office and Bobby Lee come in. This was about five or six years ago, as I recall. Mr. Johnson was at his desk eating his lunch. Bobby Lee walk right up to the desk and say, "Is it time?" And Mr. Johnson look up at him and smile and say, "No. No. Not yet." Then Bobby Lee turn and walk out.

MR. LINDENBERRY: How would you characterize Mr. Johnson's attitude during this exchange?

MR. PINKETT: I told you he smiled. That's all I can recollect to my mind.

MR. LINDENBERRY: And what about the defendant's attitude? How would you characterize that?

MR. PINKETT: He wasn't smiling and he wasn't mad. Truth is, I ain't never seen him look that way before. His face was set and his eyes was almost popping out of his head. But he didn't look mad. He walk like he had a board pressed up against his back. He didn't look at me. He just look down at Mr. Johnson and say, "Is it time?" and Mr. Johnson smile up to him and say, "No. No. Not yet." He said it real soft and easy-like, the way you would talk to a woman. I remember it well, because it like to scare the . . . out of me. I mean to . . .

. . .

MR. LINDENBERRY: And when did defendant communicate this threat to you?

MR. PINKETT: I didn't say . . .

MR. GRANT: Objection.

COURT: Sustained.

MR. LINDENBERRY: When did you hear the defendant remark that he had something against Mr. Johnson?

MR. PINKETT: I never said it was a threat. I myself would not call it a threat. You know how it is when people get mad. They say things they don't mean.

MR. LINDENBERRY: Mr. Pinkett, when did Mr. Charles communicate these words to you?

MR. PINKETT: It was about four years ago. See, I was just kidding around with him about a customer that gived me a hard time. I said something like, "I felt like laying out that so-and-so." Then Bobby Lee look toward the office and say, "I would like to do that very same thing, Otis."

MR. LINDENBERRY: Who was in the office at that time?

MR. PINKETT: Mr. Johnson was in there . . .

• • •

MR. GRANT: I have no further questions, Your Honor.

Testimony of Dr. Walter R. Thorne, resident psychiatrist at the state mental hospital:

MR. LINDENBERRY: Now Dr. Thorne, considering your examination of this defendant's psychological profile, how would you characterize his mental makeup?

DR. THORNE: One must begin by first noting the peculiarities of the area of the subject's earliest socialization, for insights into his emotional background. According to records collected during my investigation, this man spent most of his formative years in the South, in the state of Virginia. As you will recall, during the period of his childhood the South practiced rather crude and often vicious methods of caste segregation. The effects of this on the human personality, especially the concomitant violence, are inestimable. Coupled with this were the traumata of an abrupt move, with a family of three, from an agricultural situation to one that is highly structured, competitive, mobile and impersonal. Such a transition is bound to cause a degree of dislocation. Some of this can be quite serious.

MR. LINDENBERRY: Dr. Thorne, in your opinion, was the defendant stable enough to appreciate the consequences of his act? Would the possible dislocation you describe distort his sense of reality to such an extent that he would not know right from wrong?

DR. THORNE: Not in my opinion. I say this for three specific reasons. First, the move from the South took place while the defendant was still a relatively young man, and I see no evidence that he has not made the necessary adjustment. Second, my examination of his family has convinced me that all of them, especially the oldest boy, show no signs of having been influenced by a maladjusted personality. They are perfectly normal, if one makes allowances for their economic and social status vis-à-vis the broader society. Third, the fact that the defendant never missed a day from work and functioned in the choir of his church demonstrates, for me at least, that he had settled into a structured way of life that was at least comfortable. Considering all this, I am forced to conclude that the defendant was indeed stable when he acted. Why he acted is a conclusion I must leave to you, or at least to these jurors, who are better qualified than I am to apply the law.

MR. LINDENBERRY: Dr. Thorne, in your experience as a psychiatrist, have you had occasion to observe a streak of paranoia in members of the negro race, specifically in negro males?

DR. THORNE: I recall having read some studies on the subject.

MR. LINDENBERRY: Can you summarize what you can remember of those studies?

DR. THORNE: There was one out of Michigan, by a man named Slovik, I believe, noting the frequency with which

negro males instinctively grab their testicles when startled.
Also, an old study out of New York presented data pre-
suming to show that, when confronted by obstacles which
to them appear threatening, negro males tend more frequently than whites to assign blame, not to themselves,
but to whomever happens to be most proximate in positions of authority. This reaction, the study concluded, can
sometimes take on suicidal dimensions. And I recall a
more recent study, done in Florida, purporting to show
that males of that group are more frightened of dogs than
are males of the white group. Well, as you might expect, I
discount a great deal of this. I would say, in my considered judgment, that there is little scientific evidence for
a disproportionate amount of paranoia among males of
the black group than for males of the white group. Of
course, statistics aside, one must always leave room for
chance.

MR. LINDENBERRY: Dr. Thorne, in your opinion, could
this defendant have acted out of a paranoid fear of his
employer, Mr. Johnson?

DR. THORNE: Considering the evidence in this specific
case, I would have to say no.

MR. LINDENBERRY: Your witness, sir.

MR. GRANT: No questions.

The judge sipped the last of his coffee and reflected
over the transcript. It was 1:25 P.M. He was to meet with
his clerk at 2:00 P.M. to prepare for the judges' conference. He cleaned his pipe, then began moving forward
again in his reading. But for some reason he paused. He
turned back a great number of pages he had already
skimmed to a section he had skipped entirely. This was
the cross-examination, and redirect examination, of Otis
Pinkett:

MR. GRANT: Why did you advise the defendant to give up
his job and seek employment elsewhere?

MR. PINKETT: Well, see, I'm like this here. If I see where I ain't wanted in a place, I don't waste my time there. Me, I believes in moving on.

MR. GRANT: Mr. Pinkett, what is your present position at Rogers' Auto Service and Supply?

MR. PINKETT: After Mr. Jones over there, I guess you could call me third in command. I been around a long time, so people usually ask for me when they come in.

MR. GRANT: And to what do you attribute your success?

MR. PINKETT: I guess I know how to deal with the public. There's just a certain way you handle people, certain things you do to get along with the public.

MR. GRANT: Was it the lack of this social grace in Mr. Charles that caused you to advise him to move on?

MR. PINKETT: Well, since you ask, I will have to say yes. Now I don't mean no dirt to nobody, especially Bobby Lee. But it look to me like, being from the South and all, he didn't have no common sense. Me, myself, I felt that I was as good as Mr. Johnson or anybody else. But Bobby Lee, look like he thought he was better than Mr. Johnson. It wasn't like he thought black was better than white. He act like he thought they was something better than black and white, and he already had it in a jug with the stopper in his back pocket. Well, I'm smart enough to know you don't do that around the folks that's paying your salary. That's why I told him I thought it best for him to move along.

MR. GRANT: Could it be, Mr. Pinkett, that you were jealous of the defendant?

MR. PINKETT: No, it wasn't that way at all. I was making more than him at the time, my job was secure, so it wasn't no sweat off my back. I just felt sorry for him.

. . .

MR. GRANT: Mr. Pinkett, can you recall any instance when the deceased disclosed the existence of hostilities toward you because of your color?

MR. PINKETT: No, sir. I have told you that Mr. Johnson have always been kind to me. He liked black people. He

always asked how we was doing, how our families was
doing, whether we needed a credit reference down to a
store.

COURT: Where is this leading, counsel?

MR. GRANT: Your Honor, I hope through this witness to
establish something about the personality of the deceased
that Mr. Pinkett here seems, for some reason, reluctant to
disclose. I hope to establish that the deceased was something less than a model employer.

COURT: Well, this is tedious for me because you seem to
be fishing. But I'll let it go on, if you have no objection,
Paul.

MR. LINDENBERRY: I have no objections so far.

COURT: Proceed . . .

. . .

MR. GRANT: You have testified that the deceased's treatment of you was gracious beyond question.

MR. PINKETT: No nevermind about it. He was a good
man, a prince of a man.

MR. GRANT: Would you say that the defendant shared
your opinion of Mr. Johnson?

MR. LINDENBERRY: Object, Your Honor.

COURT: Sustained.

MR. GRANT: Mr. Pinkett, did the defendant ever express
to you any jealousy of the superior treatment you were re-
ceiving?

MR. LINDENBERRY: Your Honor, I object. Counsel is trying to elicit from the witness speculation about motives immaterial to the issue here. That issue is whether or not
defendant showed sufficient hostility to support the infer-
ence of premeditation. What my colleague seems to be after is speculation. Or is it gossip? . . .

. . .

MR. GRANT: Judge, I accept the ruling. But I feel I must
make my position a matter of record. I remind the court
that the defendant has not contributed in any way to his
defense. His plea of nolo, his refusal to allow his family to

testify on his behalf, and his refusal to even discuss this case with me—these things put me in a very awkward position. Since he has even refused to take the stand in his own defense, I am obliged to defend him as best I can, without any clear sense of his motives having been communicated to me. I was from the beginning reluctant to take this case, but, since I make a point of honoring my assignments, I have tried to do my best. Now, if I am not allowed to introduce what my colleague calls speculation into these proceedings, I do not see how I am to continue ...

• • •

MR. GRANT: Now, Mr. Pinkett, please repeat, as clearly as you can recall, the defendant's words on that occasion.

MR. PINKETT: He said he had given up on life. He said he didn't understand things he thought he understood. We were in the john at the time. I was taking a pee and he was in the stall. I couldn't see his face but I could hear him. He said, "Mr. Johnson has hurt me so bad, Otis, till I don't want to live." He said to me, "There ain't nothing more I want than to get out of life."

MR. GRANT: Did you ever see the defendant argue with or threaten the deceased?

MR. PINKETT: No. I have said before that I seen them together on many occasions, but they never did say nothing much. Only thing I ever heard was this time Bobby Lee and me was in the office on a Friday night picking up our pay. I had got a raise. I don't think Bobby Lee had got one. When Mr. Johnson go to pass the envelope to Bobby Lee, he smile and say, "I'm white."

MR. GRANT: What did the deceased say?

MR. PINKETT: He look at Bobby Lee and say, "I'm white."

MR. GRANT: That was all?

MR. PINKETT: Yeah.

MR. GRANT: Could there conceivably have been a dispute over something, and the deceased was saying, "I'm right"?

MR. PINKETT: That could of been. But it sound to me like he said, "I'm white."

MR. GRANT: How did he look and act when he said that?

MR. PINKETT: He said it in a low voice, and when I look over at him, his face change. It was real funny.

MR. GRANT: What do you mean?

MR. PINKETT: Well, he didn't look mad or nothing. But when I first look, his eyes was all wide and blue and sparkling like he was drunk. But then when I look again, he look sort of sleepy, like he had just woke up and there was something he forgot.

MR. GRANT: Did his look change before or after you heard him say what he said?

MR. PINKETT: It was a little before and a little after.

MR. GRANT: Mr. Pinkett, please be specific.

MR. PINKETT: I don't know, it happened so fast. I don't know if he saw me watching him.

MR. GRANT: Can you remember whether his face changed after he saw you watching him?

MR. PINKETT: I don't know. I can't remember.

MR. GRANT: What color was Mr. Johnson?

MR. PINKETT: Why, he was a white man with light brown hair.

MR. GRANT: And what color is the defendant, Mr. Charles?

MR. PINKETT: As you can see, he is just about as black as the ace of spades.

MR. LINDENBERRY: Your Honor, I must rise to ...

. . .

COURT: I remind you to remember who and where you are, Paul. I was not asleep. Ladies and gentlemen of the jury, at certain points in a trial, especially in a trial as complicated as this one, a judge must weigh ...

. . .

MR. LINDENBERRY: Would you repeat that so the jury can hear?

MR. PINKETT: He lent me that money out of the goodness of his heart. Another time he let me off from work just so

I could go to a ball game. Many a time he put in a kind
word to people downtown so I could get some more
credit. He gave me plenty grace. To me he was a man of
his word. If he told me a chicken spit tobacco juice, I
would never of looked under that chicken's wing for the
snuff box. That's how close Mr. Johnson was to me. He
was a prince, and I can't hold back from saying this much
about him, even if I wanted to help Bobby Lee.

MR. LINDENBERRY: Now, Mr. Pinkett, you have said that
the defendant "went soft." Would you elaborate on this?

MR. GRANT: I object.

COURT: Overruled. I am going to let this in, Franklin.
You had your chance, and now I want to see where this is
going.

MR. LINDENBERRY: Would you elaborate, sir?

MR. PINKETT: What I mean is that Bobby Lee seem to
put himself in positions that was bound to cause friction
between him and Mr. Johnson. I myself notice that he
wouldn't follow orders straight, many a time he took his
own sweet time on a repair job. I think he done that just
to devil Mr. Johnson. Well, something bad was bound to
happen. If you get in people's way too much, they going
to knock you back in your place. I believe that's what
happen to Bobby Lee toward the end there.

MR. GRANT: I have to object strenuously, Your Honor.

COURT: Sustained. Mr. Pinkett, I must warn you to refrain from making value judgments. By that I mean you
are not being asked to assess whether the defendant in
your opinion was a good or bad man, or whether he engineered his own failures. You must tell what you know
that bears on the issue in contention here.

MR. PINKETT: Contention?

COURT: You must tell the truth about Mr. Charles's possible reasons for wanting to kill Mr. Johnson.

MR. PINKETT: But I'm just telling what I know, Your
Honor, sir. I'm not trying to take sides.

COURT: I must remind you, Mr. Pinkett, that you have
been recalled as a prosecution witness. You must refrain,
sir, from voicing opinions not solicited by counsel. You

may not be aware of this, but Mr. Lindenberry is responsible to the rules of evidence, and not to you. You must answer directly the specific questions put to you by him. Do you understand, sir?

MR. PINKETT: Yes, sir, Your Honor.

COURT: Ladies and gentlemen, I feel I must apologize to you for these lengthy excursions. I have attempted to grant leeway to counsel for both sides, because it seemed to me that my own decisions, based solely on the rules of evidence as I know them, would prevent your hearing the cross-light of competing views, which I consider essential to the adversary process. But it seems now that this trial has lost its direction. Still, in my mind, law is an art, and my function here should ideally be no different than that of a literary critic. But, as I have said, I have probably . . .

The intercom on the judge's desk buzzed. It was his clerk, reminding him of the conference in the common room at 3:00 P.M. It was now 2:05 P.M. The judge advised the clerk to buzz him again at 2:30 P.M. Then he rang for his secretary and instructed her to bring in the rest of the transcript as soon as it was typed. This done, he lit his pipe and puffed it almost into flame as he read faster through the thin pile of papers.

He read very fast.

The secretary rapped gently on the door, then entered and placed a note on the desk beside his coffee cup. The judge paused in his reading and glanced at it. The note was from his clerk. It said: "Sir, I must insist that you take time out to be briefed. Garson is up for reelection this year, and his clerk told me he is prepared to shine. It would be bad, considering the circumstances, if he caught the collective eye during this session. There won't be another until February. Call at 2:20 P.M.? Mills."

The judge glanced at his watch. It was already 2:13 P.M. He puffed his pipe and read hurriedly. He read quickly over the testimony of Reverend Lorenzo Blake, the minister of the church attended by the defendant:

MR. GRANT: Sir, what can you tell the court about the character of Mr. Robert L. Charles?

MR. BLAKE: I always took him to be a gentle, God-fearing man. I'm sure there's not a soul in my church that would have a different opinion of him. It hurts me to say this, but what he has done reflects badly on them, and on the black folks of Roanoke.

MR. GRANT: What had Roanoke to do with this?

MR. BLAKE: Most of my congregants come from Roanoke, Robert Charles, too. You'll find that people who come up here usually follow the trails of people from their hometowns who have come before. In every city you find settlements of people from Birmingham, Charleston, Macon, Durham, even the thousands of little towns. The Texans, I believe, go to California, along with those from Arkansas. But we are Virginians. We tend to look out for our own.

MR. GRANT: Considering this bond, did Mr. Charles ever come to you for advice of any sort? Did he ever confide in you about some difficulties he was having?

MR. BLAKE: As I told you before, I can recall no conversation about his job. But I remember one instance about another matter. You see, Robert was very, very concerned about his lack of formal education. He cannot read or write. But he does have a genius for cars, for repairing cars. He repaired cars on weekends at his home. But for some reason he was ashamed of this. He came to me one Sunday and confided that he was losing the respect of his oldest boy, Robert, Jr. It was my understanding that the boy was moving with a fast crowd, was experimenting with drugs, and Robert did not have the time to discipline him.

MR. GRANT: You are saying then, Reverend, that he was a concerned parent?

MR. BLAKE: Yes, sir. He was very concerned. He wanted me to talk with Robert, Jr. He wanted me to help him get the boy involved with boys his own age who had more positive activities. He asked me if I knew any boys who read books.

MR. LINDENBERRY: Your Honor, with all due respect to the Reverend, I must say that this is not getting us anywhere. The jails are full of homicidal maniacs who like to read books.

MR. GRANT: I find intolerable this lapse on the part of my colleague. I must object.

COURT: Paul, I agree with your conclusion, but I must say that I, too, find your sentiment objectionable. Where do you hope to take us, Franklin?

MR. GRANT: I am only trying to show the jurors that the defendant had an interest in his son's education. I want to show that he placed much value on his boy's progress. If I may, I would like to build toward something.

COURT: Well, speed things up a bit.

MR. GRANT: Yes, Your Honor. Mr. Blake, would you call the defendant a devout Christian?

MR. BLAKE: I am not prepared to make that judgment.

MR. GRANT: Well, did he attend church regularly?

MR. BLAKE: Yes.

MR. GRANT: Did he drink?

MR. BLAKE: I can't say.

MR. GRANT: I remind you, Reverend Blake, that you are under oath. I also remind you of your statement in your pretrial deposition. Now I ask you again, sir, did this defendant drink?

MR. BLAKE: Yes, sir.

MR. GRANT: Heavily?

MR. BLAKE: At times, yes. But he was always gentle. Usually, his wife told me, he went to sleep afterwards.

MR. LINDENBERRY: At this point it is really not in my interest to object, but I will. Hearsay. Besides, the best witness is available right in this courtroom.

COURT: Again I ask, Franklin, where is this going? How does the fact of the defendant's drinking help the case you are trying to make? How do his drinking habits detract from his possible motives for killing Mr. Johnson?

MR. GRANT: Your Honor, I remind you again that the defendant and his family have refused to testify on his behalf. I am doing what I can to plead the best possible case for him. I intend to tie things together shortly.

COURT: Well, be brief, Mr. Grant.

MR. GRANT: Reverend Blake, was the defendant known to get drunk at Christmas, Thanksgiving, Easter and on other special occasions? Is that not the custom in the South?

MR. BLAKE: All of us do that, I am sure. But yes, it is a custom.

MR. GRANT: I did not ask your assessment of the habits of mankind. I asked did this defendant have a reputation for getting drunk on special occasions, and does not this habit derive from a widespread custom in the South?

MR. BLAKE: Yes. There is a custom of drinking heavily in the South.

MR. GRANT: And is there not also a tradition of handling guns in the South? Specifically, don't people there sometimes shoot off their guns to celebrate special occasions?

MR. BLAKE: Yes, sir. That is true.

MR. GRANT: Then there are many customs, drinking and handling guns on special occasions among them, that blacks bring up from the South?

MR. BLAKE: I am not aware . . .

. . .

MR. LINDENBERRY: I remind the jury that according to the testimony of Officer Scion, the defendant was not drunk when arrested on the afternoon of June 12, 197–.

. . .

Again the secretary rapped lightly on the door. She entered and placed another note, and the last of the transcript, on the desk beside the judge's coffee cup. This note, also from the clerk, said, "It is 2:25 P.M. I will wait. But you are just hurting yourself. Mills." The judge scribbled "ten minutes" on the back of the note and handed it to his secretary. She walked out on tiptoe. The judge leaned back in his padded chair, stuffed his pipe and lit it. Then he rose from the chair and walked to the window and looked out. Down in the parking lot, against a backdrop of concrete driving ramps, dozens of cars shone in the sunlight like metal, multicolored animals. From this height they looked like toys. He puffed his pipe and looked up. The specially treated glass in the picture window made the sky seem more bright and blue than it really was. The judge straightened his tie. He flicked a spot of ash from the sleeve of his blue coat. Then he went into the bathroom and washed his face and hands. Refreshed, he returned to his desk and began gathering up the transcript. The last few pages he had not read. He skimmed quickly over the summation by Paul Lindenberry, the assistant district attorney. Then he wrote a short note to his secretary, listing things to be done before she went home. He also wrote a note to his clerk, directing how the verdict in this case should be entered: guilty as charged. He put his desk in order, collecting stray papers and laying the bulky transcript of the trial face down on the green mat. He walked toward the door. Then he turned slowly and walked back to the desk. He turned over the last page of the transcript and read the last of defense attorney Franklin Grant's summation:

. . . worth very little to the ideal of justice if you, ladies and gentlemen of the jury, as the conscience of the community, cannot envision in your minds, and find room in your hearts, for an illiterate black. Here is a man, descend-

ed from slaves, who, on the day of his son's graduation
from high school, did the habitual thing for the celebration of such a grand event. He had a drink. We all do it
on the Fourth of July. Why can't he? We shoot off fire-
crackers, cannons, sometimes our mouths. Look at this
man's wife and family out there, look carefully at little
Robert, Jr., and think to yourselves that, but for the grace
of God, this could be your family, this could be your
weeping wife. Or you could be this defendant, made passionate by the fact that his oldest child had achieved
literacy. Here is the picture I want you to see clearly in
your minds, while in that jury room. After attending the
graduation ceremony, this defendant did the usual thing
to celebrate. He had a drink. But linked in his mind with
drinking was that other custom, that other part of the ritual of celebration so honored among blacks in the South.
But he is in the city and feels restrained. So he puts the
gun in his pocket. Then, a man of habit, he goes to work.
There, knowing his boss takes an interest in the families of
his employees, he goes into the office with the news. But
he has had a nip. And in retelling this good news, there
is a lapse of logic in his mind. Perhaps remembering past
friction, but more likely in celebration of the event, the
defendant takes the gun and accidentally . . .

At this point the defendant interrupted.

The judge placed the page neatly, face down, on the
top of the pile.

Elbow Room

"Boone's genius was to recognize
the difficulty as neither material
nor political but one purely moral
and aesthetic."
—"The Discovery of Kentucky"
WILLIAM CARLOS WILLIAMS

NARRATOR *is unmanageable. Demonstrates a disregard for form bordering on the paranoid. Questioned closely, he declares himself the open enemy of conventional narrative categories. When pressed for reasons, narrator became shrill in insistence that "borders," "structures," "frames," "order," and even "form" itself are regarded by him with the highest suspicion. Insists on unevenness as a virtue. Flaunts an almost barbaric disregard for the moral mysteries, or integrities, of traditional narrative modes. This flaw in his discipline is well demonstrated here. In order to save this narration, editor felt compelled to clarify slightly, not to censor but to impose at least the illusion of order. This was an effort toward preserving a certain morality of technique. Editor speaks here of a morality of morality, of that necessary corroboration between unyielding material and the discerning eye of absolute importance in the making of a final draft.*

This is the essence of what he said:

I

Paul Frost was one of thousands of boys who came out of those little Kansas towns back during that time. He was one of the few who did not go back. When he came out it was easy moving forward by not going to the war. But after a while it got harder. Paul was in school up in Chicago when he determined to stand pat and take his blows. He returned home briefly and confronted his family and the members of a selective service committee. These were people who had watched his growing up. They were outraged at his refusal. Watching their outrage and remaining silent made Paul cry inside himself. He went back up to Chicago and did alternate service in a hospital for the insane. He began attending a Quaker meeting. Nights in the hospital, he read heavily in history, literature, and moral philosophy. Soon he began to see that many of the inmates were not insane. This frightened him enough to make him stop talking and begin watching things very closely. He was living, during this time, in a rented room out near Garfield Park. He went out only for work, meals, and to the library for more books. He knew no women and wanted none. Because he lived inside himself, he was soon taken by other people for an idiot. Their assumptions enabled Paul to maintain and nourish a secret self. He held conversations with it nights in his room. His first public speech, after many months of silence, was to a mental defective one evening at the hospital over a checkerboard down in the recreation room. "I don't think you're crazy," he whispered to the man. "So what are you *doing* here?" This patient looked warily at

Paul and then smiled. He had that wistful, wide-eyed
smile of the uncaring doomed. He leaned across the board
and looked directly into Paul Frost's bright brown eyes.
"What are *you* doing here?" he said. This question unset-
tled Paul. The more he thought about it the more nervous
he became. He began walking LaSalle Street during his
free time, picking conversations with total strangers. But
everyone seemed to be in a great hurry. In the second
year of his alternative service, he secured a transfer to another hospital out on the Coast. There, in Oakland, he did
a number of wild things. Activity kept him from thinking
about being crazy and going back to Kansas. His last act
as a madman was to marry, in San Francisco, a black girl
named Virginia Valentine, from a little town called Warren outside Knoxville, Tennessee.

II

Virginia Valentine had come out of Warren some ten
years before, on the crest of that great wave of jailbreak-
ing peasants. To people like her, imprisoned for generations, the outside world seemed absolutely clear in
outline and full of sweet choices. Many could not cope
with freedom and moved about crazily, much like long-
chained pets anticipating the jerks of their leashes. Some
committed suicide. Others, seeking safety, rushed into
other prisons. But a few, like Virginia, rose and ranged
far and wide in flight, like aristocratic eagles seeking high,
free peaks on which to build their nests.

Virginia's quest was an epic of idealism. At nineteen
she joined the Peace Corps and took the poor man's
grand tour of the world. She was gregarious in a rough

and country way. She had a talent for locating quickly the human core in people. And she had great humor. At twenty she was nursing babies in Ceylon. At twenty-one she stood watching people in a market in Jamshedpur, India, learning how to count the castes. Deciding then that Hindus were more "black" than anyone she had ever seen at home, she began calling herself "nigger" in an affirmative and ironic way. She developed a most subtle and delicious sense of humor. In Senegal, among the fishermen, she acquired the habit of eating with her hands. On holiday, in Kenya, she climbed up Kilimanjaro and stood on its summit, her hands on her hips in the country manner, her eyes looking up for more footholds. In the sweaty, spice-smelling markets of Cairo, Port Said, and Damascus she learned to outhaggle conniving traders. Seeing slaves and women still being sold, she developed the healthy habit of browbeating Arabs. There are stories she tells about old man Leakey, about squatting beside him in a Masai compound in north Tanzania, about helping herself to a drink of milk and cow's blood. The old man, she says, was curt, but eager to show his bones. The drink, she says, was not bad. The Masai did not dance. She entered the areas behind the smiles of Arabs, Asians, Africans, Israelis, Indians. In the stories they told she found implanted different ways of looking at the world.

When she returned home, at twenty-two, she was bursting with stories to tell. There were many like her. In Boston, New York, Philadelphia, Chicago, and all parts of California, people gathered in groups and told similar stories. They thought in terms new to them. In conversation they remarked on common points of reference in the four quarters of the world. The peasants among them had become aristocratic without any of the telling affectations.

The aristocrats by birth had developed an easy, common touch. They considered themselves a new tribe.

But then their minds began to shift. In the beginning it was a subtle process. During conversation someone might say a casual "You know?" and there would be a hesitation, slight at first, denying affirmation. Virginia had painful stories to tell about increases in the periods of silence during the reacculturation. People began to feel self-conscious and guilty. If pushed, she will tell about the suicide in her group. People saw less and less of each other. Soon they were nodding on the street. Inevitably, many people in conversation began saying, "I don't understand!" At first this was tentative, then it became a defensive assertion. It took several months before they became black and white. Those who tried to fight grew confused and bitter. This was why Virginia, like many of the more stubborn, abandoned the East and ran off to California. Like a wounded bird fearful of landing with its wings still spread, she went out to the territory in search of some soft, personal space to cushion the impact of her grounding.

III

I went to the territory to renew my supply of stories. There were no new ones in the East at the time I left. Ideas and manners had coalesced into old and cobwebbed conventions. The old stories were still being told, but their tellers seemed to lack confidence in them. Words seemed to have become detached from emotion and no longer flowed on the rhythm of passion. Even the great myths floated apart from their rituals. Cynical salesmen hawked them as folklore. There was no more bite in humor. And language, mother language, was being whored by her best sons to suit the appetites of wealthy patrons. There were no new stories. Great energy was spent describing the technology of fucking. Black folk were back into entertaining with time-tested acts. Maupassant's whores bristled with the muscle of union organizers. The life-affirming peasants of Chekhov and Babel sat wasted and listless on their porches, oblivious to the beats in their own blood. Even Pushkin's firebrands and noble brigands seemed content with the lackluster: mugging old ladies, killing themselves, snatching small change from dollar-and-dime grocers. During this time little men became afflicted with spells of swaggering. Men with greatness in them spoke on the telephone, and in private, as if bouncing safe clichés off the ear of a listener into an expectant and proprietary tape recorder. Everywhere there was this feeling of grotesque sadness, far, far past honest tears.

And the caste curtains were drawn, resegregating all imaginations. In restaurants, on airplanes, even in the homes of usually decent people, there was retrenchment, indifference, and fear. More than a million stories died in the East back during that time: confessions of fear, screams of hatred orchestrated into prayers, love and trust and need evolving, murders, retribution, redemption, honestly expressed rage. If I had approached a stranger and said, "Friend, I need your part of the story in order to complete my sense of self," I would have caused him to shudder, tremble, perhaps denounce me as an assailant. Yet to not do this was to default on my responsibility to narrate fully. There are stories that *must* be told, if only to be around when fresh dimensions are needed. But in the East, during that time, there was no thought of this. A narrator cannot function without new angles of vision. I needed new eyes, regeneration, fresh forms, and went hunting for them out in the territory.

A point of information. What has form to do with caste restrictions?

Everything.

You are saying you want to be white?

A narrator needs as much access to the world as the advocates of that mythology.

You are ashamed then of being black?

Only of not being nimble enough to dodge other people's straitjackets.

Are you not too much obsessed here with integration?

I was cursed with a healthy imagination.

What have caste restrictions to do with imagination?

Everything.

A point of information. What is your idea of personal freedom?

Unrestricted access to new stories forming.

Have you paid strict attention to the forming of this present one?

Once upon a time there was a wedding in San Francisco.

Virginia I valued for her stock of stories. I was suspicious of Paul Frost for claiming first right to these. They were a treasure I felt sure he would exploit. The girl was not at all pretty, and at first I could not see how he could love her. She was a little plump, had small breasts, and habitually wore Levi's and that flat, broad-brimmed type of cap popularized by movie gangsters in the forties. But the more I looked into her costume, the more I recog-

nized it as the disguise of a person trying to deflect attention away from a secret self. When she laughed, it was
loudly, and behind the laugh I heard a hand reaching out
secretly to tug down loose corners of the costume. Even
her affection of a swagger seemed contrived to conceal a
softness of heart. Listening to the rough muscles of her
voice, when she laughed, I sensed they were being flexed
to keep obscure a sensitivity too finely tuned to risk ex-
posure to the world. She employed a complicated kind of
defensive irony. When her voice boomed, "Don't play
with me now, nigger!" it said on the underside of the very
same rhythm, *Don't come too close, I hurt easily.* Or
when the voice said, "Come on in here and meet my fi-
ancé, and if you don't like it you can go to hell!", the
quick, dark eyes, watching closely for reactions, said in
their silent language, *Don't hurt my baby! Don't hurt my
baby!* She spiced her stories with this same delicious
irony. Virginia Valentine was a country raconteur with a
stock of stories flavored by international experience. Telling them, she spoke with her whole presence in very
complicated ways. She was unique. She was a classic kind
of narrator. Virginia Valentine was a magic woman.

Paul Frost seemed attracted to her by this outward display of strength. I am convinced he was by this time too
mature to view her as just exotic. He was the second generation of a Kansas family successful in business matters,
and he must have had keen eyes for value. But because of
this, and perhaps for reasons still unclear to him, his
family and the prairies were now in his past. I think he
felt the need to redeem the family through works of great
art, to release it from the hauntings of those lonely prairie
towns. I know that when I looked I saw dead Indians living in his eyes. But I also saw a wholesome glow in their

directness. They seemed in earnest need of answers to honest questions always on the verge of being asked. This aura of intense interest hung close to his face, like a bright cloud, or like a glistening second coat of skin not yet thick enough to be attached to him. It seemed to inquire of whomever his eyes addressed, "Who am I?" But this was only an outward essence. Whatever else he was eluded my inspection of his face. And as I grew aware of myself in pursuit of its definition, I began to feel embarrassed, and a little perverse. Because the thing that illuminated him, that provided the core of his mystery, might have been simple guilt, or outright lust, or a passion to dominate, or a need to submit to a fearful-seeming object. All such motives enter into the convention of love.

And yet at times, watching Virginia's eyes soften as they moved over his face, I could read in them the recognition of extraordinary spiritual forces, quietly commanded, but so self-assured as to be unafraid of advertising themselves. I am sure he was unaware of his innocence. And perhaps this is why Virginia's eyes pleaded, when he openly approached a soul-crushed stranger, *Don't hurt my baby! Don't hurt my baby!*, even while her voice laughed, teased, or growled. She employed her country wits with the finesse and style of a magic woman. And after I had come to understand them better, I began to see deeper into their bond. She was an eagle with broken wings spread, somewhat awkwardly, over the aristocratic soul of a simple farm boy. Having his soul intact made him a vulnerable human being. But having flown so high herself, and having been severely damaged, she still maintained too much grace, and too complete a sense of the treachery in the world, to allow any roughnesses to touch the naked thing. Paul Frost was

a very lucky innocent. Virginia Valentine was protecting
him to heal herself.

This wedding was a quiet affair in a judge's chambers.
Paul's brother was best man. A tall, strapping fellow, he
had flown out from Kansas to stand beside his brother.
He held the ring with a gentle dignity. Paul's parents did
not attend. They had called many times making the usual
pleas. When these failed they sent a telegram saying BEST.
But Virginia's parents were there from Tennessee. They
were pleasant, country folk who had long begged her to
come home. But when they saw they could not change
her mind, they flew out with country-cured hams, a
homemade cake, and a wedding quilt sewn by Virginia's
grandmother, who was a full-blooded Cherokee living far
back in the Tennessee woods. They also brought a hand-
ful of recipes from well-wishing neighbors. The mother
wore a light blue dress and a white hat. A very dark-
skinned little woman, she sat on the judge's leather chair
looking as solemn as an usher at Sunday church service.
Mr. Daniel Valentine, the father, a large-framed, hand-
some, brown man, smiled nervously when the judge had
finished, and shook hands all around. He had the delicate
facial features of an Indian, with curly black hair and
high cheekbones. Virginia's color was deep reddish brown.
She wore a simple white dress with a red sash. She
smiled often and reassuringly at her brooding mother, as
if to say, "It's all right. I told you so." Paul, in a black
suit and black bow tie, looked as responsible and as sober
as a banquet steward in a plush private club.

At the reception, in a sunny corner of the Golden Gate
Park, Mr. Daniel Valentine offered around cigars. Then
he strolled slowly about the grounds, his hands in his
pockets. It was a warm November afternoon, much warm-

er than his body said it had a right to be. He was out of
his proper environment and was obviously ill at ease. I
walked along with him, smoking my cigar. In his brown
face I saw fear and pride and puzzlement. He felt obliged
to explain to himself how one of the most certain things
in the world had miscarried. He had assumed that color
was the highest bond, and I think he must have felt
ashamed for someone. "We told her many the time to
come home," he said while we walked. He stared at the
late-blooming flowers, the green trees just starting to
brown, the shirtless young men throwing Frisbees. He
said, "I don't pretend to know the world no more, but I
know enough about the lay of the land to have me a
good, long talk with him. I laid it *right on the line,* too.
My baby come from a long line of family, and her mama
and me's proud of that. Right there in the South, there's
plenty white women that have chase me, so I know a little
something about how the world go round. But I ain't nobody's pretty plaything, and my baby ain't neither." He
swelled out his chest and breathed deeply, inspecting
closely the greenness of the grass, the spread of the trees.
I sensed that his body was trying desperately to remember
the coolness of the Tennessee autumn. He was sweating a
little. He said, "Now, I don't give a *damn* about *his*
family. They can go to hell for all of me. But I care a lot
about *mine!* And last night I told him, 'If you *ever* hurt
my baby, if you *ever* make her cry about something that
ain't the fault of her womanly ways, I'm gonna come
looking for you.' I told him I'd wear out a stick on him."
He said this to me as one black man to another, as if he
owed me reassurance. And I had no way of telling him
that his daughter, in her private mind and treasured,
secret self, had long ago moved a world away from that

small living room in which conventional opinion mattered. "That's just what I told him, too," Mr. Daniel Valentine said. Then he averted his eyes, puffed his cigar, and nodded toward where the others stood crowded around a eucalyptus tree. Mrs. Valentine was unpacking the lunch. Paul was laughing like a little boy and swinging Virginia's hand. "But they do make a fine couple, don't they now?" he asked me.

They made a very fine couple. Paul rented an apartment in the Mission district and brought all their possessions under one roof. Virginia's posters, paintings, and sculpture acquired while traveling were unpacked from their boxes and used to decorate the walls and end tables. Paul's many books were stacked neatly in high brown bookcases in the small living room. The few times I saw them after the wedding they seemed very happy. They seemed eager to pick up and mend the broken pieces of fragmented lives. Virginia worked as a clerk for a state agency. Paul worked for a construction company during the day and studied for his degree nights in a community college. Paul worked very hard, with the regularity and order of a determined man. I think the steady rhythms of the prairie were still in him, and he planned ahead with the memory of winter still in mind. But they made special efforts to live in cosmopolitan style. Both of them were learning Spanish from their Chicano neighbors. They chose their friends carefully with an eye on uniqueness and character. They were the most democratic people I have ever seen. They simply allowed people to present themselves, and they had relationships with Chicanos, Asians, French, Brazilians, black and white Americans. But they lived in a place where people were constantly coming and going. And they lived there at a time when a certain structure was settling in. It was not as brutal as it was in the East, but it was calculated to ensure the same results.

During this time Paul's father, back in Kansas, was putting on the pressure. I think the idea of Virginia had finally entered his imagination and he was frightened for the future of his name. He called long-distance periodically, vowing full support for Paul when he finally reconsidered. He seemed to have no doubt this would occur. They argued back and forth by telephone. The father accused the son of beginning to think like a Negro. The father accused the son of being deluded. The son accused the father of being narrow-minded. The son accused the father of being obtuse. Nothing was ever resolved, but the discussions were most rational. The father was simply a good businessman. In his mind he had a sharp impression of the market. I am sure he thought his son had made a bad investment that was bound to be corrected as soon as Virginia's stock declined. There was, after all, no permanent reification of color. From his point of view it was this simple. But from Paul's point of view it was not.

When they invited me to dinner in early December, Virginia said, "This old rascal thinks that one day he'll have to kiss a pickaninny. If I had a cold heart I'd send him one of them minstrel pictures." She laughed when she said this, but there was not the usual irony in her voice. She pushed her hands into the back pockets of her Levi's and leaned her butt against the kitchen stove.

Paul was at the kitchen table drinking wine. He seemed upset and determined. He said, "My father is a very decent man in his own way. He just knows a little part of the world. He's never talked seriously with anybody that's not like him. He doesn't understand black people, and he would have a hard time understanding Ginny." He laughed, his clear eyes flashing. "She's a bundle of contradictions. She breaks all the rules. All of you do."

I sat down at the table and poured myself a glass of the red wine. Virginia was baking a spicy Spanish dish, and the smell of it made me more relaxed than I should have been. After draining the glass I said, "I can understand your father's worry. According to convention, one of you is supposed to die, get crippled for life, or get struck down by a freak flash of lightning while making love on a sunny day."

Paul laughed. He sipped from his glass of wine. "This is real life," he said, "not the movies. And in any case, *I* don't have to worry."

Virginia was stirring a dish of red sauce on the stove. The air was heavy with the smell of pungent spices.

I said to Paul, "The producers in Hollywood are recycling."

Paul laughed again. "This is *real* life," he told me. But he was getting a little drunk. He sipped his wine and said, "In this house we pay close attention to reality. By public definition Ginny is black, but in fact she's a hybrid of African, European, and Indian bloodlines. Out in the world she roughhouses, but here at home she's gentle and sweet. Before anybody else she pretends to be tough, but with me she's a softy. It took me a long time to understand these contradictions, and it'll take my family longer. My father has a very unsubtle, orderly mind. I'm willing to wait. I see my marriage as an investment in the future. When my father has mellowed some, I'll take my wife home. As I said, *I* don't have to worry."

Virginia called from the stove, "That old rascal might at least *speak* to me when he calls."

Paul fingered his wineglass, looking guilty and cornered.

It was not my story, but I could not help intruding upon its materials. It seemed to me to lack perspective. I poured myself another glass of wine and looked across the table at Paul. Above us the naked light bulb reflected eerily in my glass of red wine. I said, "Time out here is different from time in the East. When we say 'Good afternoon' here, in the East people are saying 'Good night.' It's a matter of distance, not of values. Ideas that start in the East move very fast in media, but here the diversity tends to slow them down. Still, a mind needs media to reinforce a sense of self. There are no imaginations pure enough to be self-sustaining."

Paul looked hard at me. He looked irritated. He said, "I don't understand what you're talking about."

I said, "Someone is coming here to claim you. Soon you may surprise even yourself. While there is still time, you must force the reality of your wife into your father's mind and run toward whatever cover it provides."

He really did not understand. I think he still believed he was a free agent. He sat erect at the kitchen table, sipping from his glass of wine. He looked confused, hurt, almost on the edge of anger. I felt bad for having intruded into his story, but there was a point I wanted very much for him to see. I pointed toward a Nigerian ceremonial mask nailed to the wall just over the kitchen door. The white light from the bulb above us glowed on the brown, polished wood of the mask. "Do you think it's beautiful?" I asked.

Paul looked up and inspected the mask. It was an exaggeration of the human face, a celebration in carved wood of the mobile human personality. The eyes were mere slits. Teeth protruded from a broad mouth at unexpected angles. From the forehead of the face, curving upward, were appendages resembling a mountain goat's horns. Paul sipped his wine. He said, "It's very nice. Ginny bought it from a trader in Ibadan. There's a good story behind it."

I said, "But do you think it's beautiful?"

"The story or the mask?" Virginia called from the stove. She laughed with just a hint of self-derision, but the sound contained the image of a curtain being pulled across a private self.

"The mask, of course!" Paul called to her coolly. Then he looked at me with great emotion in his eyes. "It's nice," he said.

I said, "You are a dealer in art. You have extraordinary taste. But your shop is in a small town. You want to sell this mask by convincing your best customer it is beautiful and of interest to the eye. Every other dealer in town says it is ugly. How do you convince the customer and make a sale?"

Paul's eyes widened and flashed. He started to get up, then sat back down. "I don't like *condescension*," he said. "I don't much like being talked down to!" He was angry, but in a controlled way. He started to get up again.

Virginia shouted, *"Dinner!"*

I said to Paul, "You have enlisted in a psychological war."

He looked trapped. He turned to face his wife. But she had her back to him, making great noises while opening the stove. I think she was singing an old Negro hymn. He turned toward me again, a great fear claiming control of his entire face. "Why don't you just *leave!*" he shouted. "Why don't you just *get out!*"

I looked past him and saw Virginia standing by the stove. She was holding a hot red dish with her bare hands. She was trembling like a bird. In her face was the recognition of a profound defeat. She cried, "Go away! Please, go *away!* No matter what you think, this is my husband!"

I left them alone with their dinner. It was not my story. It was not ripe for telling until they had got it under better control.

Analysis of this section is needed. It is too subtle and needs to be more clearly explained.

I tried to enter his mind and failed.

Explain.

I had confronted him with color and he became white.

Unclear. Explain.

There was a public area of personality in which his "I" existed. The nervous nature of this is the basis of what is miscalled arrogance. In reality it was the way his relationship with the world was structured. I attempted to challenge this structure by attacking its assumptions too directly and abruptly. He sensed the intrusion and reacted emotionally to protect his sense of form. He simply shut me out of his world.

Unclear. Explain.

I am I. I am we. You are.

Clarity is essential on this point. Explain.

More than a million small assumptions, reaffirmed year after year, had become as routine as brushing teeth. The totality guarded for him an area of personality he was under no obligation to develop. All necessary development preexisted for him, long before his birth, out there in the world, in the images, actions, power, and status of others. In that undefined "I" existed an ego that embraced the outlines, but only the outlines, of the entire world. This was an unconscious process over which he had little control. It defined his self for him. It was a formal structure that defined his sense of order. It was one geared unconsciously to the avoidance of personal experience challenging that order. I tried to enter this area uninvited and was pushed back. This was his right. A guest does not enter a very private room without knocking carefully. Nor does a blind man continue moving when he hears an unfamiliar sound.

Clarity is essential on this point. Please explain.

I think he understood enough to know that he was on a moral mission.

After Christmas, Virginia contacted me by telephone and said, "No matter what you think, he has a good heart and he's sorry. But you *did* provoke him. One thing I learned from traveling is you accept people the way they are and try to work from there. Africans can be a cruel people. Arabs I never *did* learn to trust. And there's a lot of us *niggers* that ain't so hot. But them raggedy-ass Indians taught me something about patience and faith. They ain't never had nothing, but they *still* going strong. In Calcutta you see crippled beggars out in the street, and people just walk on around them. Now a Westerner would say that's cruel, but them fucking Indians so damn complicated they probably look at that same beggar and see a reincarnated raja that lived in us a thousand years ago, ate too much of them hot spices, and died of gout. *Shit!* He don't *need* nothing else! So they don't worry about how he looks now. But patience is a Christmas-morning thing. You have to accept what's under the tree and keep on believing there's a Santa Claus. Both you *and* that nigger of mine have to learn that. I ain't giving up on *nothing!* I ain't giving up on *shit!* So why don't you heist up your raggedy ass and come with us to Mass on New Year's Eve?"

I have said Virginia Frost was a magic woman.

The cathedral was massive, chilly and dark. Huge arched stained-glass windows reflected the outlines of sacred images in the flickering lights of red and yellow candle flames. Two Episcopal priests, in flowing white albs, stood in the chancel and read invocations from their missals. Little boys in black cassocks paced reverently up and down the aisles, censing from gray-smoking thuribles. Seated on the benches around us were people—young and old and middle-aged, the well dressed and the shabby, the hopeful and the forlorn. Young men with great scraggly beards sat silently with lowered heads. Beside them were young women, pale and hard-faced, looking as beaten and worn as pioneer women after too many years of frontier life. Single girls wore sequined denim jackets over long frocks with ruffled bottoms. Many wore leather boots. Here and there, almost invisible in the crowd, men and men and women and women, segregated by sex, sat holding hands with heads bowed. Virginia was wearing her mug's cap, and it sat rakishly on her strong curly hair. I sat on her right, Paul on her left. We sat close together. The place projected the mood of a sanctuary.

Above us, in the balconies, two choirs in black and white robes sang a mass. Their voices cried like wounded angels bent on calling back to earth a delinquent God. The effort was magnificent. But all around us, people

looked abstracted, beaten, drained of feeling. There was a
desperate concentration on the choir, an effort of such intensity it almost made its own sound. It seemed to be
asking questions of the songs floating down from the
choir. We closed our eyes and said private prayers. It was
nearing midnight, and we heard the faith of Bach insisted
on in the collective voices of the choir. And in response,
breathing in the stillness of the people, one sensed a profound imploring. But then a voice behind us imposed itself on the silence. "Young man," it rasped, "if you're too
dumb to take your hat off in church, get out!" From all
along the two rows came the sounds of stiff necks creak-
ing. "Young man," the voice demanded of Virginia, "did
you hear me? Or are you too *dumb* to know the English
language?" I opened my eyes and turned. Beside me, Virginia was closing her eyes tighter. Beside her, I saw Paul
lift his own head and turn fierce eyes on the old gentleman's face. In his voice was a familiar arrogance from a
source he had just begun to consciously tap. "You old
fart!" he said, his tone disrupting the harmony floating
down from above us. "You old fart!" he said. "This is *my
wife*. If you don't like what she's wearing, *that's tough!*"

The choir lifted their voices, as if bent on erasing the
incident with the strength of their sound. Around us
people coughed softly. Paul put his arm around Virginia's
shoulder. He closed his eyes and whispered in her ear. I
closed my own eyes and tried to lose myself in the music.
But I was made humble and hopeful by that other thing,
and I thought to myself, *This one's a man.*

From January on, Paul began confronting the hidden
dimensions of his history. Something in his mind seemed
to have opened, and he was hungry for information. He

read books hungrily for other points of view, sifting through propaganda for facts. He underlined a great deal, scribbled questions in the margins, asked questions openly. He discarded much of what he read, but what stuck in that private place in his mind made him pensive, and silent, and a little sad. I watched him closely, though I kept my distance. I admired him for his heroic attempt to look back.

But in early February, while he was with Virginia in the parking lot of a supermarket, a carful of children called him nigger. Their dog barked along with the sing-song rhythm. "I just laughed at the little crumbsnatchers," Virginia said.

She said she could not understand why Paul became so upset.

In late February, when he was walking with Virginia in the rain through the Sunset district, two younger children called him nigger.

"What's a nigger?" he asked me on the telephone. "I mean, what does it *really* mean to you?"

I said, "A descendant of Proteus, an expression of the highest form of freedom."

He hung up on me.

I did not call him back. I was convinced he had to earn his own definitions.

In early March Virginia found out she was pregnant.

That same month Paul disclosed that his father, during one of their arguments, had mentioned to him the full name of the black janitor who swept out his office. But the old man was most upset about the baby.

During the months after Christmas I saw very little of them. I had become interested in a man recently paroled after more than fifty years in prison. He had many rich stories to tell. I visited him often in his room at a halfway house, playing chess and listening while he talked. He sang eloquent praises to the luxuries of freedom. He detailed for me the epic nature of the effort that had got him sprung. He was alive with ambition, lust, large appetites. And yet, in his room, he seemed to regulate his movements by the beat of an invisible clock. He would begin walking toward the door, then stop and look puzzled, then return to his chair beside the bed. His window faced the evening sun just where it sank into the ocean, but the window shade was never lifted. He invited me once to have lunch with him, then opened a can of peaches and insisted that we share a single spoon. He invited me to attend a party with him, given in his honor by one of his benefactors. There, he sat on a chair in the corner of the room and smiled broadly only when a curious stranger expressed interest in his recollections. He told the same stories line for line. Late in the evening, I spoke briefly with the hostess. This woman looked me straight in the eye while denouncing prisons with a passionate indignation. Periodically, she swung her empty martini glass in a confident arc to the right of her body. There, as always, stood a servant holding a tray at just the point where, without ever having to look, my hostess knew a perfect arc and a flat surface were supposed to intersect. I saw my own face reflected roundly in the hostess's blue-tinted spectator's sunglasses, and I began to laugh.

The above section is totally unclear. It should be cut.

I would leave it in. It was attempting to suggest the nature of the times.

But here the narrative begins to drift. There is a shift in subject, mood, and focus of narration. Cutting is advised.

Back during that time there was little feeling and no focus.

Narrator has a responsibility to make things clear.

Narrator fails in this respect. There was no clarity.
There was no focus. There was no control. The hands of
a great clock seemed to be spinning wildly, and there was
no longer any great difference between East and West.

This thing affected everyone. There was a feeling of a
great giving up. I sensed a bombed-out place inside me. I
watched people clutch at bottles, pills, the robes of Jesus,
and I began to feel cynical and beaten. Inside myself, and
out there in the world, I heard only sobs and sighs and
moans. There was during this time a great nakedness,
exposed everywhere, and people dared you to look. I
looked. I saw. I saw Virginia Frost losing control of her
stories. As her belly grew, her recollections began to lose
their structure. The richness was still there, but her accounts became more anecdotal than like stories. They
lacked clarity and order. She still knew the names, the accents, the personal quirks of individual Indians, Asians,
Israelis, but more and more they fragmented into pieces
of memory. There was no longer the sense of a personal
epic. She no longer existed inside her own stories. They
began bordering dangerously on the exotic and nostalgic.
At times, telling them, she almost became a performer—
one capable of brilliant flashes of recollection that stunned
briefly, lived, and then were gone. She had inside her an
epic adventure, multinational in scope, but the passion
needed to give it permanent shape was obviously fading.
One part of her was a resigned mother-to-be, but the
other part was becoming a country teller of tall stories
with an international cast.

I have said it was the nature of the times.

Something was also happening to Paul. In his mind, I think, he was trying desperately to unstructure and flesh out his undefined "I." But he seemed unable to locate the enemy and, a novice in thinking from the defensive point of view, had not yet learned the necessary tactics. Still, he seemed to sense there were some secrets to survival that could be learned from books, conversations, experiences with people who lived very close to the realities of life. He cut himself off from the company of most white males. He got a job with a landscaping crew and spent most of his days outdoors. His muscles hardened and his face grew brown. He grew a long black beard. He read the Bible, Sören Kierkegaard, abstract treatises on ethics. He underlined heavily. The beard merged with his intense, unblinking eyes to give him the appearance of a suffering, pain-accepting Christ. During this time he flirted with the clothing styles of the street-corner dandy. Often in conversation he spoke bitterly about the neglect of the poor. He quoted from memory long passages from Isaiah, Jeremiah, the book of Lamentations. He denounced his father as a moral coward. He was self-righteous, struggling, and abysmally alone. But his face still maintained its aura. His large brown eyes still put the same question, though now desperately asked, "Who am I?"

And many times, watching him conceal his aloneness, I wanted to answer, "The abstract white man of mythic dimensions, if being that will make you whole again." But the story was still unfinished, and I did not want to intrude on its structure again. The chaos was his alone, as were the contents he was trying desperately to reclaim from an entrenched and determined form. But to his credit it must be said that, all during this time, I never once heard him say to Virginia, "I don't understand." For the stoic nature of this silence, considering the easy world waiting behind those words, one could not help but love him.

Then, in early June, both sets of parents began making gestures. Virginia's people called up often, proposing treasured family names for the baby. Paul's mother sent money for a bassinet. She hinted, in strictest confidence to Paul, that more than European bloodlines ran in her veins. But the father was still unyielding. His arguments had grown more complex: If he recognized the baby he would have to recognize Virginia's family, and if he ever visited the family they would have to visit him. From this new perspective the objection was grounded in a simple matter of class distinction. His mind lacked subtlety, but one had to admire its sense of order. On his personal initiative, he told his son, he had engineered the hiring of a black employee by his company. Paul told his father this would not do. The mother told Paul the father would think it over, and after he had thought it over Virginia and the baby would be welcome in their home. But Virginia told Paul this would not do either.

They had never seen the problem from her point of view.

Virginia said, "I don't want my baby to be an honorary white."

She said this to me toward midsummer, in the park, during a conversation at the Japanese Tea Garden. Around us under the pavilion sat tourists munching cookies, sipping warm tea, huddled against the coolness of the morning mist. Virginia now wore a maternity smock over her pants, but her mug's cap still rode defiantly atop her curly hair. Her belly protruded with the expanding child.

Her brown cheeks were fleshy and her eyes looked very tired. She said, "I'm black. I've accepted myself as that. But didn't I make some elbow room, though?" She tapped her temple with her forefinger. "I mean up *here!*" Then she laughed bitterly and sipped her tea. "When times get tough, *anybody* can pass for white. Niggers been doing *that* for *centuries,* so it ain't nothing new. But shit, wouldn't it of been something to be a nigger that could relate to white and black and everything else in the world out of a self as big as the world is?" She laughed. Then she said, "That would have been *some* nigger!"

We sipped our tea and watched the mist lifting from the flowers. On the walkways below us the tourists kept taking pictures.

I said, "You were game. You were bold, all right. *You* were some nigger."

She said, "I was *whiter* than white and *blacker* than black. Hell, at least I got to *see* through the fog."

I said, "You were game, all right."

A tourist paused, smiled nervously, and snapped our picture.

Virginia said, "It's so *fucked up!* You get just two choices, and either one leaves you blind as a bat at noon. You want both, just for starters, and then you want everything else in the world. But what you wind up with is one eye and a bunch of memories. But I don't want my baby to be one-eyed and honorary white. At least the black eye can peep round corners."

Inside myself I suddenly felt a coolness as light as the morning mist against my skin. Then I realized that I was acting. I did not care about them and their problems any more. I did not think they had a story worth telling. I looked away from her and said, "Life is tough, all right."

Virginia was turning her teacup. She turned it around and around on the hand-painted tray. She looked out over the garden and said, "But I'm worried about that nigger of mine. I told you he had heart. In his mind he's still working through all that shit. Underneath that soft front he's strong as a mule, and he's stubborn. Right now both his eyes are a little open, but if he ever got his jaws tight he might close one eye and become blacker than I ever thought about being. That's the way it's rigged."

I did not feel I owed them anything more. But because she had once shared with me the richness of her stories, I felt obliged. I looked at the tourists moving clumsily between the hanging red and purple fuchsia. They knocked many of the delicate petals to the ground. The pavilion was completely surrounded by tramping tourists. I looked down at Virginia's belly and said, "Then for the sake of your child don't be black. Be more of a classic kind of nigger."

She laughed then and slapped my back.

I walked with Paul around the city before I returned East. This was in the late summer, several months before the baby was due, and I felt I owed him something. It was on a Sunday. Paul had attended a Quaker meeting that morning and seemed at peace with himself. We walked all afternoon. Along the avenues, on the sidewalk, paralleling the beach, down the broad roads through the park, we strolled aimlessly and in silence. The people we saw seemed resigned, anomic, vaguely haunted by lackluster ghosts. My own eyes seemed drawn to black people. In Golden Gate Park I watched a black man, drunk or high on dope, making ridiculous gestures at a mother wheeling a baby in its carriage. The man seemed intent on parodying a thought already in the young mother's mind. I stopped and pointed and said to Paul, "That's a nigger." On the Panhandle we paused to study an over-dressed black man, standing in a group of casually dressed whites, who smiled with all his teeth exposed. His smile seemed to be saying, even to strangers, "You know everything about me. I know you know I know I have nothing to hide." I nodded toward him and said to Paul, "That's a nigger." Paul looked about more freely. On Lincoln Way, walking back toward the bus stop, he direct-ed my eyes to a passing car with stickers plastered on its bumpers. They boosted various mundane causes, motor lubricants, and the Second Coming of Jesus. In the middle of the back bumper there was a white sticker with great black letters reading, BE PROUD TO BE A NIGGER.

Paul laughed. I think he must have thought it a subtle joke.

But a few blocks from the park I nodded toward a heavily bearded young white man on a sparkling, red ten-speed bike. He was red-faced and unwashed. His black pants and black sweatshirt seemed, even from a distance, infested with dirt and sweat and crawling things. As he pedaled, crusty, dirt-covered toes protruded from sandals made from the rubber casings of tires. He seemed con-scious of himself as the survivor of something. He maneu-vered through the afternoon traffic, against all lights, with a bemused arrogance etched into the creases of his red face. When he was far down the block, I said to Paul, "That one is only passing. He is a bad parody of a part-time nigger."

He did not laugh. He did not understand.

I said, "Imagine two men on this street. One is white and dressed like that. The other is black and seems to be a parading model for a gentleman's tailor. In your mind, or in your father's mind, which of them would seem unnatural?"

Paul stopped walking. He looked very hurt. He said, "Now it's finally out in the open. You think I'm a racist."

I felt very cool and spacious inside myself. I felt free of any obligation to find a new story. I felt free enough to say to Paul, "I think you were born in a lonely place where people value a certain order. I saw a picture on a calendar once of a man posed between the prairie and the sky. He seemed pressured by all that space, as if he were in a crucible. He seemed humbled by the simplistic rhythm of the place. I think that in his mind he must have to be methodical, to think in very simple terms, in order to abide with those rhythms."

But he still thought I was accusing him, or calling him to account. He said, "People *do* grow. You may not think much of *me,* but my children will be great!"

I said, "They will be black and blind or passing for white and self-blinded. Those are the only choices."

Paul walked on ahead of me, very fast.

On Nineteenth Avenue, at the bus stop, he turned to me and said, "Don't bother to come all the way back. Ginny's probably taking a nap." He looked away up the street to where several buses were waiting for the light to change. The fog had come in, it was getting darker, and in the light of the traffic his eyes looked red and tired. I was not standing close enough to him to see his face, but I am sure that by this time his aura had completely disappeared. He looked beaten and drained, like everything else in sight.

We shook hands and I began to walk away, convinced there were no new stories in the world.

Both buses passed me on their way to the corner. But above the squeaks and hissing of their brakes I heard Paul's voice calling, "At *least* I tried! At *least* I'm *fighting!* And I know what a *nigger* is, too. It's what you are when you begin thinking of yourself as a work of art!"

I did not turn to answer, although I heard him clearly. I am certain there was no arrogance at all left in his voice.

Almost two months later, when I called their apartment before leaving for the East, the telephone was disconnected. When I went there to say goodbye they were gone. A Chicano couple, just up from LA, was moving in. They spoke very poor English. When I described the couple I was looking for they shook their heads slowly. Then the husband, a big-bellied man with a handlebar mustache, rummaged in a pile of trash in the hall and pulled out a sign painted on a piece of cardboard. He held it up across his chest. The sign said, WE ARE PARENTS. GO AWAY.

I went back to the East resigned to telling the old stories.

But six months later, while I was trying to wrestle my imagination into the cold heart of a recalcitrant folktale, a letter from a small town in Kansas was forwarded to me by way of San Francisco. It was the announcement of a baby's birth, seven or eight months old. Also enclosed were three color pictures. The first, dated in October, was a mass of pink skin and curly black hair. The second, a more recent snapshot, was of a chubby brown boy, naked on his back, his dark brown eyes staring out at the world. On the back of this picture was printed: "Daniel P. Frost, four months, eight days." The third picture was of Virginia and Paul standing on either side of an elderly couple. Virginia was smiling triumphantly, wearing her mug's cap. The old man looked solemn. The woman, with purple-white hair, was holding the baby. Paul stood a little apart from the others, his arms crossed. His beard was gone and he looked defiant. There was a familiar intensity about his face. On the back of this picture someone had written: "He will be a *classic* kind of nigger."

Clarify the meaning of this comment.

I would find that difficult to do. It was from the beginning not my story. I lack the insight to narrate its complexities. But it may still be told. The mother is, after all, a country raconteur with cosmopolitan experience. The father sees clearly with both eyes. And when I called Kansas they had already left for the backwoods of Tennessee, where the baby has an odd assortment of relatives. I will wait. The mother is a bold woman. The father has a sense of how things should be. But while waiting, I will wager my reputation on the ambition, if not the strength, of the boy's story.

Comment is unclear. Explain. Explain.